Fallen Angels and Demons

Jan McDonald

Raven Crest Books

Copyright © 2015 Jan McDonald

The right of Jan McDonald to be identified as the author of this work has been asserted by her in accordance with the Copyright, Designs and Patents Act 1988

ISBN-13: 978-0-9934439-0-9
ISBN-10: 0-99-344390-7

For Bill

"The Demons have declared war on Mike Travis and it aint going to be pretty, see. You just offed one of their big boys and his bitch and they aint going to let that go easy down there."

Dai Bricks, The Sin Eater.

CHAPTER ONE: FIRST LINKS IN THE CHAIN

When a chain of events, each separated by millennia, link together towards a single outcome, it usually means bad news for someone. Such a chain of events was about to come together and unleash an evil that had no mercy - only revenge - in the core of its being.

And the name on its foul lips was Mike Travis.

Hell was full of demons waiting for the chance to be the one to squash him underfoot. He'd killed one of their A List; not simply exorcised it and sent it back to Hell, but killed it, finito. It seemed he'd got his hands on one of the rare weapons that had that power, and now it posed a threat to all the demons that walked the Earth, unless they took him out. It was another incentive to the highest ranked among them to find a way out of the Pit and make the planet demon-friendly again. After all, they had done such a good job before and they would do again.

But these things don't just happen; sometimes they are orchestrated and we are no longer the masters of our own destiny. The events that spanned time to arrive at this point began almost four millennia ago. Then, link by link, the chain was forged; the chain that would result in Mike Travis becoming the number one most wanted by the demons and turning him into a hunter.

Sodom and Gomorrah – 1900 BC

Archangel Seraquel looked down on the two cities south of the Dead Sea in the Valley of Siddim, which he was about to blast from the face of the earth. His instructions had been clear and direct: destroy them both because of their iniquities. Wipe them from the face of the earth. He

1

raised his hand and focussed his power, ready to smite them; God's mandate indelible in his mind.

But the cry of the newborn came to him, tremulous on the warm breeze. Seraquel paused and began to scan the two cities. Yes, they were wallowing in their sin; yes, they were turning their back on God, their behaviour worse than that of animals; and yes, that tiny cry of the innocent brought the angel's focus into sharp relief.

Then, as he continued to scan the two cities, he saw the old woman tending her crippled grandchild; he heard the tender lullaby of the new mother; he smelled the fragrance of the incense carrying aloft the prayer of the young man who had stayed true to his God. These were just a few of the innocents who would perish along with the sinful.

He lowered his arm and turned away. He knew that others would come to do what he could not, and he knew his disobedience would incur censure, but his burgeoning free will took precedence over the consequences, and he walked away.

Strike One.

Egypt – 1446 BC

On the banks of the Nile at the time of the festival of Osiris, Archangel Seraquel was troubled. The hot Egyptian air was carried on a soft breeze, laden with the scent of frankincense and myrrh. It came from the delta as he watched the labourers driving their oxen in the fields, their brows beaded with sweat from the endless toil, many of them Hebrew slaves. He turned towards Pharaoh's palace and looked at the contrast; slaves they were still, but their lives were infinitely better. Better food, better clothes and surroundings. Then his gaze fell on Pharaoh himself, seated on his throne, his heart hardened against freeing the Hebrew slaves. Nine plagues they had all endured and still he wouldn't budge; nine plagues that had taken the innocent along with the stubborn. Now, he was there to deliver the tenth plague. Again, Seraquel's instructions could not have been clearer. His heart was heavy, because this final assault on Rameses would claim an innocent life in every household, from the throne of the king to the lowliest of the labourer's in the fields. He was to smite every firstborn throughout the land.

This he could not do. This he would not do. Once again he would disobey.

There were others on the payroll that would gladly take his place, but *he* could not raise his hand to smite the multitude of innocents, who were after all just pawns in the Game of Gods.

He sensed the presence of another angel behind him; one that was climbing the celestial ladder, one who would have no problem with the given task, one who would become Azrael the Angel of Death.

Apparently from nowhere, a lesser, Egyptian demon rushed at Azrael. Seraquel was swift and instinctive in protecting a brother angel, despite his feelings about him. With a blast of electric blue light, the demon was ashes.

He didn't glance back at Azrael as he left, his task abandoned.

Strike Two.

Jerusalem – 950 BC

The construction of Solomon's Temple was well under way but there was a problem. The demons were mostly quiet and in their own realms, except for one.

Solomon stood watching the workers, his eyes focussed on a young boy who had become his favourite. He frowned.

Despite giving the boy double wages and double food rations, he looked drained and was getting thinner by the day. He beckoned to him.

"Shimel, I have given double wages and food to you and yet you are so thin. Why is that? What is it that ails you, child?"

"My Lord King, I am plagued by a demon. Each night

he takes half my wages and half my food, and then he sucks on my finger and all of my strength leaves me and nightly I become thinner."

Solomon was troubled and prayed for help in gaining authority over the demon, and so it was that Seraquel was sent to deliver a magic ring to the king; a ring that would give him power over the demon.

As he stood within the Temple, the ring in his hand, Seraquel knew a bad idea when he saw one. He knew that Solomon wouldn't rest until he had control over *all* the demons. And that meant only one thing. They would be released into the world, and one day Solomon would lose control over them.

Archangel Michael appeared beside him. "This was your last chance Seraquel. And still your disobedience knows no bounds. Give me the ring."

"Stop and think, Michael. If Solomon has the ring, *this* ring, in mortal hands! He will lose control one day, he is *human*, and the world will be plagued by the demons. God loves this king and wants to help him, especially if it means the building of his Temple, but it's a bad idea."

"I'm sure He will be delighted to hear that you said His idea was a bad one. In the meantime, give me the ring."

"No." Seraquel knew he was out-gunned by Michael in every way, but he knew he could play no part in the release of the demons upon the world.

"Fair enough, you leave me no choice. I am to escort you to the fifth heaven where you will stay until such time as you sort out your problem with authority. I'm guessing you'll be there for a very long time. And now I'll take the ring."

In a flash of electric blue light the ring was in Michael's hand and Seraquel faced an eternity in the void of nothingness that was the fifth level of Heaven, a place where disobedient and subversive angels were sent to cool their heels before they fell or were cast out.

Strike three.

The ring did indeed give Solomon power over the demon that plagued his favourite, but he didn't let it rest there. Seraquel's fears were made manifest. Solomon challenged and took control of many demons and set them to building his Temple until, after many years, his wisdom weakened, he took countless wives and became obsessed with gathering the enormous wealth for which he later became famed. His obsession shifted and he became enamoured of a Shunamite woman who he wanted by his side and in his bed, but she held him to ransom, to turn away from his God and worship hers, begging him to make a sacrifice to her God.

And so it began.

Gradually, Solomon lost his grip on his kingdom; and his power, and just before the last remnants of his sanity left him, he wrote down his story of the demons in *The Testament of Solomon*.

And what became of the ring?

An eternity passed in which Seraquel remained unrepentant for his disobedience, and it was there that his future rejection of unreasoned authority was born. His fate was sealed.

Angels are astonishing creatures; powerful, weird and wonderful, sometimes surprising, sometimes funny, sometimes cranky; but one archangel in particular rubbed Seraquel up the wrong way: Metatron. Self-appointed Chancellor of Heaven and occasional Voice of God, Metatron was a sycophant of the highest order in Seraquel's opinion, and when he showed up with an ultimatum - toe the line, make apologies, and shape up, or .... - Seraquel chose the 'or' option.

Metatron appeared to revel in the finer points of 'or'.

"You will be cast out; sent down to the earth as a human. No angelic powers, no magic, no special gifts, no angel name, no lifeboat ... oh, and no wings. There you will continue to serve in a way that will teach you obedience, and you *will* learn obedience Seraquel, because if you do

5

not, you are on your own. Much has changed on the earth since last you cast your eyes down there. I can assure you, it is no place for angels."

Seraquel was resigned. "Do what you came to do, Metatron. Spare me the homily and get on with it."

Metatron pulled a face, as if his next words would stick in his throat. "I have to tell you that there is a path to redemption for you. There is one down there that will be on a dark path in the service of light, you must help him. You will know him when you meet him. Now, if there is nothing else ... I need your wings."

Seraquel's screams of agony resounded throughout the celestial Heaven as his wings were ripped from his back, sending shards of light in a symphony of exquisite pain into his brain and throughout his falling body.

CHAPTER TWO: SECOND LINK

Meadow Vein, Cwmpergwm Coal Mine, Gwent 1915

It had been twenty-five years since the explosion in the adjacent colliery had reaped the lives of one hundred and seventy-six miners, creating an indelible stain of grief on the entire Welsh valley. But coal mining was all there was here, it identified them, and everyone struggled to make their living down in the extremes of temperature, damp and dark, hacking at the rock to bring out the coal that barely satisfied the ravening hunger of the industrialisation of the country.

The Meadow Vein was the richest seam of coal in the entire eastern reaches of the South Wales Coalfield and the miners counted themselves fortunate to have a stall at the coal face. But the earlier disaster was ever at the forefront of their minds, stories recounted from father to son, never to be forgotten.

Ivor Jenkins was the nearest they had to a safety man back then and, at the beginning of his shift down Cwmpergwm, he ventured to the end of the heading to check for firedamp, the gas that would claim the lives of anyone in the vicinity. The pit owners had been determined to blast further under the mountain to gain access to the rich vein of coal and the tunnel had descended to a depth previously unknown, despite unease from the miners about venturing into an area so close to the explosion.

The heading was silent apart from the regular tramp, tramp of his boots echoing in the tunnel, accompanied by the rhythmic drip, drip, of water from the rock above his head and the occasional skittering announcing the

7

departure of a few resident rats. The atmosphere was heavy but the blue flame in his lamp showed him it had nothing to do with any gas.

He paused, listening to his own heartbeat and the insidious creaking of the roof timbers. It was hot in the tunnel and perspiration dripped down his neck, running in rivulets down his spine, but there was no way he was taking off his jacket. Not down there. He wasn't exposing any more skin than necessary.

Bloody fools, fired by greed, the pit owners only cared about the bottom line. He had a bad feeling about the extension but they wouldn't listen to him. After all, he was just one of the poor bastards that delivered the black stuff and at a time of mass unemployment there would always be another to take his place.

He shivered, despite the heat.

The sound came from just ahead; a scratching sound. And the sound of someone breathing.

But that couldn't be; he was the only one down there.

The sound came closer and he peered into the gloom, feeling the urgent need to relieve himself against the tunnel wall. And then it stopped.

His lamp went out, plunging him into utter blackness. And through the blackness the red eyes stared at him, just before their owner grabbed Ivor, ripping his thick jacket open, swiftly followed by his chest, before he could utter a single cry. It dragged his bloodied body after it back into the depths, to the small hole that had appeared in the floor of the heading; the hole which appeared bottomless and led only into Hell itself.

When they came looking for Ivor, they found only his lamp and nothing else except for the small hole in the floor at the side of the tunnel that hadn't been there the night before.

The hole was boarded up and tests were carried out to determine the strength of the floor and three miners were sent to knock out fresh stalls at the coalface.

Idris Roberts was thirteen the day before his first shift with his Da, Aldwen, and the other two at the coal face. No one knew what happened to them, because when they didn't come back at the end of their shift, all they found was Idris, wild-eyed with a madness that left him incoherent. All they could make out from his babble was the word 'eyes'. When they got him to the surface, his hair was white, and they returned him to his mother with his mind gone to a place where there was no retrieving it.

Idris's brother, Evan, reluctantly took over his Da's stall at the coal face, his mind full of the few words that Idris ever spoke; 'eyes' and 'ysbryd du' – black ghost . Idris only seemed to want to communicate with Evan, maybe because he was the only other family member left down the pit. It was to Evan that Idris rambled on about how there was a noise like a wild wind coming from beneath his feet and the coal dust began to swirl around like a whirlwind until it gradually took the shape of a hideous black demon with burning red eyes; a hideous black demon which had reached out and pulled their Da, and the other two miners, down into the bottomless darkness that had opened up below their feet.

Evan did his best to try not to think about Idris's tales of the terror as he hacked away at the black seam of coal, but he was forever looking over his shoulder at the slightest sound. Every creak of the timbers sent icy fingers crawling down his spine and broke beads of sweat on his brow that had little to do with exertion of swinging the pick or the fear of a roof-fall. Every tiny gust of wind from the ventilation shafts made him fight back the nausea that was never far away when he was at the coal face.

His dram was over full and he struggled to keep the huge lumps of coal from slipping onto the floor where they would break up into smaller pieces that held less value. Every lump counted towards his pay check, so he bent to pick a particularly large lump when an icy gust made the temperature drop so fast and hard, he could see his breath. He turned around slowly, no longer able to see his breath, because he wasn't breathing.

A low moaning sound accompanied a swirling vortex of black dust as the demon began to take shape. The eyes, the red eyes, stared back at him. There was a scream that echoed around the stall and into the main tunnel, and it took him a second to realise that the scream was from his own lips. It was the last information processed by his terrified brain, as the demon pulled him lifeless and bloodied, down into the cavern below the main tunnel.

One by one the miners disappeared; and, one by one, the others refused to enter that particular offshoot of the Meadow Vein, no matter how many threats came from the owners; the miners knew that they could always trudge further over the mountain to the next pit along the valley. Memories of the earlier disaster combined with fear of the new disappearances, the seam became known as the Demon's Hole, and with no-one willing to risk his life or soul to work it, the owners had no choice but erect the huge iron door that closed off the working.

Whatever was down there would stay down there. Alone.

CHAPTER THREE: AFTER THE FUNERAL

Brookstone, Monmouthshire – Present Day

Mike Travis sat in his study, drinking and thinking - mostly drinking. His thoughts were tangled up in what had happened that day.

He had walked through the sitting-room to his study after Dai Bricks' funeral. The cold and damp of the day had made its way into his bones and his leg had begun to throb painfully. He went straight to the old sideboard in front of the huge window that looked out onto the garden and the woods, picked up the whisky bottle, and poured a hefty measure.

Without turning around he'd said, "I wondered how long it would take you."

There had been a faint creak of leather from behind him that came from the armchair opposite his desk. He turned to face Dai, who was still trying to settle into his new form. Adjusting to being a spirit wasn't easy. He'd looked the same to Mike, paler perhaps, but still Dai.

"Didn't think I'd leave you to it, did you boy? Work still to do isn't. It's the edges see. The thing with edges is they have two sides, look. And I'm thinking that having me on the other side, so to speak, will only be an advantage." He'd put his ghost hand to his cap and Mike had grinned as he appeared to push it to the back of his head. "Thought I'd better come sooner rather than later, isn't, on account of the consequences. 'Cos there are consequences, but then I think you know that. And I got to thinking you could do with all the help you can get."

Mike had nodded at him, "I told you at the start of all this that things were different. I'm different. You said I was no longer an investigator but a warrior; I think I know what you meant now."

He'd put an involuntary hand on the black marks on his chest - marks left by a demon's claws, where there was no feeling underneath; his skin was numb, as it would always be.

"Ben says I'm marked," he continued. "Demon fodder. So I guess I have to get them before they get me, right? Does that make me some kind of hunter?"

Dai had shaken his head. "No, boy. They'll come looking for you, isn't. You need to learn everything you can about them. Ben will help you; he's all ready for it. Don't underestimate him, look. There's a lot more to Benjamin Lovecraft than you know; a hell of a lot more, but you'll soon find that out for yourself. Arm yourself with knowledge and prepare yourself for what's coming, because what's coming is big. And you need to take care of those two darlings of yours, Mike. Get them out of the way, somewhere safe, at least for a while. The Demons have declared war on Mike Travis and it aint going to be pretty, see. You just offed one of their big boys and his bitch and they aint going to let that go easy down there. Been sent back to point you in the right direction, isn't. You didn't come back last time for no reason, Mike. And I guess this is the reason. They've just been easing you in gentle like."

"They?" he'd queried.

Dai had sighed. "You know well who I'm talking about. Think of them as The Boss and the Board of Directors."

Mike's thoughts petered out and he picked up the phone on his desk and dialled. It was answered quickly by his friend Benjamin Lovecraft.

"Ben, it's Mike. We need to talk."

Mike could picture the man at the other end, built like a bear with a ready smile that could light up the darkest reaches of Hell. He'd be wearing his collarless white shirt under a black leather waistcoat, a bandana on his head and huge black boots on his feet. Ben had 'biker' written all over him. He thought of his old friend's words; *'You need to learn everything you can about them. Ben will help you; he's all ready for it. Don't underestimate him, look. There's a lot more to Benjamin Lovecraft than you know; a hell of a lot more, but you'll soon find that out for yourself. Arm yourself with knowledge and prepare yourself for what's coming, because what's coming is big.'*

His mental image of Ben made him smile, which creased his face and distorted the long scar down his left cheek; a relic of the helicopter crash in Afghanistan that had left him maimed and flat-lining – until a miracle had happened and the medics had resuscitated him, bringing him back from death with a gift; the gift of being able to see ghosts. It was this gift that had led him into a new life, the life of a paranormal investigator, and now his life was about to change again in ways that were impossible to imagine. He had encountered and killed a high-ranking demon and, according to Dai, the message from 'the other side' was that the demons were coming for him, big time. Well, if *'they'* thought he was going to sit and wait for the demons to come knocking on his door, *'they'* were wrong. He'd hunt them down, every one he could. He'd get them before they had chance to get him. That was the way it was going to be.

Ben had always been an enigma to Mike. Almost a recluse, he'd been a Catholic priest and exorcist until corruption in the Vatican had caused him to leave the Church. He had then trained as a psychiatrist, another profession that he had subsequently turned his back on. Now- Ben was a recluse who custom-built motorbikes to scrape a living in an old shepherd's cottage on the outskirts of the Monmouthshire village of Skenfrith, and he had tagged the word 'freelance' to the title 'exorcist'.

Mike knew what it was like to have his life reshaped by things outside his control and it was perhaps this mutual experience that had led him to trust Ben, who on one occasion early in their friendship, had saved his life during an investigation. Now, with Dai's words still ringing in his head, Mike was again reaching out to him for help. And again, it seemed as if his life was on the line.

Ben's voice boomed from the telephone, "I'm here Mike. Yes. We do need to talk. Or rather you need to listen. I take it you've had a visit from a mutual friend?"

Mike fell silent for a moment, and then, "Yeah. How did you know?"

Ben's booming laugh came down the phone, "Hell, I'd have been surprised if you hadn't. So he told you what the demon marks on your chest meant, eh? I did warn you, Mike. And I guess he told you to come to me for 'lessons', right?"

Mike was relieved that he didn't have to explain, but a little discomforted that Ben was already four steps ahead of him.

"Yep. He also said I shouldn't underestimate you; that there was more to you than I knew. Care to explain?"

"Not right now, Mike. But I will, when the time is right. But you need to know something before we get into this: being marked by demons isn't something to take lightly. It means you're a target and demons are vindictive bastards; they don't forget easily. There are two things you can do; run or fight. Personally, I recommend the first option. What are you going to do, Mike? Run or fight?"

"What do *you* think?"

"I *think* we need to get started. And I think we need to do something to try and neutralise those marks."

Mike replaced the telephone and resisted pouring another drink; he'd had a large scotch and now intended to drive. He sat back in his chair and let his thoughts roam to the dream he'd had the night before. At the time he'd thought it was because of Dai's impending funeral. Now, he wasn't sure.

The demon had been in his face, hissing and spitting all the filth of the Pit.

"You will pay, Mike Travis. You will pay dearly. But we won't kill you straight away. No. We'll take everyone you love first. Then your own death will be slow. Very slow, and very painful."

CHAPTER FOUR: THE SHADOW DEMON

Hell is no place for angels.

With one exception, that is: Archangel - the Angel of Death – Azrael, has the ability to track human souls into Hell, where the plight and the screams of the damned weigh heavily on him. Believing that some of these souls are worthy of redemption, he alone of all the angels, has the power to sneak into Hell and search for a likely candidate; a demon worthy of another shot.

Azrael, in human form, was huge. He was well over six feet tall, with piercing eyes and weathered skin, his middle-eastern origins apparent in his features. He had been watching one of the minor demons for many years and believed that somewhere deep within the darkest shadows of the lost soul was the faintest glimmer of light; a faint glimmer that he believed could eventually re-ignite if given the chance. He decided to take a risk.

In Hell, the fires are the only light in the perpetual darkness. The souls of the damned constantly search for escape, but there is little hope; except for when a door is opened from our side. The vigilant among the demons watch for such an opportunity, and these are the times when they are free to walk among us. The door may be opened by the evil, the naive, or the downright foolish.

The demons don't care which.

And so it was, that a vigilant demon was about to breach the bounds of Hell on the same day that Azrael would liberate Bazaliel, his chosen one.

Despite his low rank, Bazaliel had been one of the leaders of the rebellion in heaven alongside Lucifer; an action which resulted in the fall of two hundred angels into the fiery pits of Hell. It was there that Bazaliel had become known as the Shadow Demon. Azrael had kept him under careful scrutiny and come to the conclusion that Bazaliel would be of more use on earth than in the Pit; and there was a distant, very distant, memory of one act of kindness from this most ruthless of fallen angels that had become a demon. He just needed the right candidate to work with. And Azrael needed to be able to control the Shadow Demon. Everything would depend on if he could broker the deal or not. From his memory of Bazaliel, he was a tough mother not averse to treachery, and that also raised the question – if he brought him out, could he really trust him?

He would need control before any bargain was struck, which would mean possession of the demon's seal. And that was going to be expensive. Still, he lived in hope. Azrael was nothing if not optimistic, and he knew that in any world you got what you paid for. His bargaining chips were not used lightly but he had an idea.

Bazaliel was confined in the darkest region of Hell, which suited him in a perverse way, living as a shadow as he did, true to his name. The temperature dropped rapidly the further from the fires that Azrael wandered, careful to remain in the shadows; after all, that was where he was most likely to come across Bazaliel who was a part of them.

Clawed hands reached out to grab him as he passed, but were quickly withdrawn, as the touch of the angel burned and seared the flesh of the grasping demons. A rustle and a hiss in a moving shadow made him halt.

"Bazaliel, show yourself. Come from the shadow, demon!"

There was movement among the layers of darkness. Azrael spun around and threw out his hand. The streak of electric blue light seared the shaded eyes through the grey gloom that surrounded the demon who was himself, shadow.

16

"Sssssssssssssss. What do you want, Angel? You have no busssinesss here!"

"On the contrary, I think we may have business - if you want to get out of here, that is."

"Ha! Azrael. I might have known it. You have nothing I'm interested in. I'm doing just fine here; I'm in command of my own legion and answer only to Morning Star."

Azrael's laugh was brittle and abrupt. "Yes, I can see how well you're doing; creeping around the darkness wearing only shadow for cover. You're doing great! Congratulations." He turned away.

"Still the same Azrael. Come to make a deal have you? Well, take it somewhere else. Not interested."

Azrael shrugged in the shadows. "I get it. You already made it clear. Know anyone else that would be interested in coming back up top?"

He was aware of several demons slithering closer; he could smell them a mile off. Bazaliel was also aware of the encroachment on his territory. His shadow grew in height until it filled the entire cavern in which they stood, his hands tipped with filthy claws threatened them, and his icy breath hissed at them before spitting out the spell that sent them reeling back into the shadows.

He returned to his previous size and peered out of the ragged grey shadow into Azrael's darkened eyes. Azrael caught the look and took advantage of it. Bazaliel was curious.

"Good trick. Pity it's an illusion. Well, I'm here now, so I may as well try and sell the deal. That's if you've got the time. Oh ... I forgot ... you've got eternity."

"Azrael, you're a bastard."

"Thanks. I try."

"So, what's the deal you're dying to spill your guts over?"

"It's simple. A ticket up top in exchange for some help. The humans are really struggling up there; wars, religious and otherwise; half of them are starving, and there are more of you lot up there sticking their oar in than I care to count."

"My fucking heart bleeds. That it? You want me to help that worthless lot? Don't know what He was thinking when He made them. Knew they'd be trouble all along with that 'free will' filth. So, what's your angle? What's in it for you? It's not like the mighty Azrael to do it for nothing."

"Well, if you're going to be like that, I'll leave. I just thought you'd be ready to leave this stinking hole by now. Oh, and in case you're wondering, no repentance is needed. He's not listening anyway. Call this a project of my own."

Bazaliel narrowed his eyes. "Project?"

"No more until I get something from you."

The Shadow Demon sneered. "That's more like the Azrael I knew."

"So ... am I wasting my time here? Because there are others that will jump at the chance of a clean slate."

"Okay then, why me and what's it going to cost?"

"The price of your ticket out of here is your seal."

"You *have* to be joking!"

"Do you see me laughing? We can't have you running loose up there now, can we? Your seal will make sure you stay where you're put."

"And that would be where?"

"I haven't decided yet. But when I do, you have to know you'll be bound. No demon magic, no interference, just being a good boy."

"You're talking about possession?" His shadow-face brightened.

"Yes, in some ways; possession with permission, and without control. So do we have a deal? Your seal for your freedom?"

"Some freedom!"

"I take it the answer's no, then. Okay, have a nice rest-of-eternity." He turned to leave and calculated how many steps he would take before Bazaliel called him back. He guessed at thirteen; he took ten.

"Bastard!"

Azrael smiled to himself before turning around.

"This is a one-time-only invitation to the prom. So, are we dancing or what? No seal, no deal."

"What do I get for it?"

"Release from this shit hole on parole. Fine print to follow."

"Full pardon, no parole. No fine print. And I get to keep access to my seal."

"Conditional discharge is the best I can do. And we'll talk about the fine print. And your seal is one of the conditions."

"How do I know you won't shaft me? My seal is my protection."

"You don't know. It's called trust. Something you may be unfamiliar with, but I suggest you get with the programme. Deal's about to go south. Give me your answer, or I walk."

CHAPTER FIVE : THE DEMON'S HOLE

Meadow Vein, Cwmpergwm Pit, – Present Day

Avarice is one of the emotions that make demons happy; because when in the grip of it, humans get sloppy.

Bailey Shaw tapped the plans of the lower level of Cwmpergwm Pit that were laid out on his desk, pinning Bevan Hughes with his dark eyes.

"The Meadow Vein - that's where the mother-load is. We both know that seam is one of the biggest ever seen and I mean to have it out of there. I don't give a damn about your superstitious bullshit. I want the men down there, even if it takes double the money. I didn't put everything I own into buying this mine only to hack about with a few tons here and there."

Bevan shook his head and took a wary step backwards. "And I'm telling you there's not enough money to pay an experienced miner to go down that part of the Meadow Vein. It's not sealed off with a foot thick iron door for no reason. You know what they call it."

"Pff! Yeah, I know. The Demon's Hole, right? Didn't have you miners pegged as a bunch of fairies. Get out of here, and get me a crew willing to be men and go down to the level. If you can't get experienced miners, then get inexperienced ones. But get them. Understood? Or do I need a more co-operative manager?"

Bevan's misery was written all over his face and he was aware of the perverse pleasure that Shaw took in seeing it. Son-of-a-bitch.

He took a deep breath, if he was sacked, well, what the hell? There was no way this arrogant bastard was going to get away with ridiculing the valley's miners.

21

"Listen, *Mr* Shaw, let me tell you about Welsh miners. In the past they hewed the coal face together; they walked miles together over the mountain through hail, rain and snow in thin clothing to get to the pit; they drank together and they went to chapel together. And when they were too old or frail to wield the pick, their sons took it from their hand, and their sons after them, and their sons after that. There was nothing except the pit.

"Nothing's lost; nothing's forgotten. The children learned the songs and legends at their father's knee and they watched their grandfathers cough the black phlegm from their lungs, and still there was nothing but the pit, except their pride. And that was the last thing to be taken from the men of this valley.

"So, when they say they won't go down the Demon's Hole, I say they have good reason. And if you ask me if I believe there is anything down there, I say it's the entrance to Hell itself. So excuse me if I fail to recruit the experienced miners who know this pit; and, yes, you'll probably settle for young, arrogant and inexperienced men that have nothing but the dole and their own bravado. But remember this: I have warned you to stay out of that part of the Meadow Vein. Now, if you'll excuse me, I have men to employ."

Since the pit had closed back in the eighties, the valley had drifted into a dark shadow of unemployment and a lack of identity. For centuries, since the beginning of the Industrial Revolution, the Welsh valleys had resounded with the proud songs of the miners and iron-workers, despite the hardships and risk. But there had been a drastic decline in markets for the black jewels they mined, what with the closure of the local steel works and everyone banging on about carbon footprints and doomsday scenarios. The hypocrisy was that they were still importing thousands of tons of the black stuff from China, for both the domestic and industrial markets at a fraction of the cost - but now, under the rule of supply and demand, the cost had rocketed.

So when Bailey Shaw bought Cwmpergwm Pit and announced the re-opening there was no shortage of ex-miners ready to go down to the face again. Except for that one part of the Meadow Vein.

Bevan had been met with scorn to downright hostility. No-one was prepared to go down the Demon's Hole, none of the experienced miners that was, no matter how big an increase in the pay. So it was left to the young ones, the inexperienced ones, the ones that laughed at the idea of a Demon's Hole, to venture down there. After all, the equipment was advanced now, and the work, whilst still dirty and confined was easier due to the new mining technology. And with all the health and safety regulations the risks were less than their fathers and grandfathers had taken.

Training over, the new crew set off down towards the heading, ready to take down the iron door which, for a century, had closed off the darkness of the Demon's Hole; the door that was made of iron, because demons are vulnerable to iron.

Bevan was uneasy and had travelled to pit bottom with the crew, ready to oversee the removal of the door. Rob Jenkins, the new foreman and safety man, had sensed his unease and had mocked him during the journey down in the cage, continuing as they walked along towards the heading.

"What's up, Bevan? 'Fraid the demon'll get yer? Should've stayed up top and let the real men go down. Take more'n a demon to scare us, eh boys?"

Laughter and jeering was his answer, so encouraged, he went on.

"Don't worry, Bevan mun, we'll protect you. Just promise you won't piss yerself if the demon comes out of his hole."

Bevan was white. "Shut up, you young idiot. You have no idea, have you?"

23

"Oh, we know the old ghost stories told in The Colliers over a few pints back in the day. Demons, eh? Bunch of tossers afraid of a few shadows, is 'all. We'll show 'em, right boys?"

Bevan shivered. The old iron door loomed in front of them as the lights overhead began to flicker. Rob Jenkins seized the moment and lurched toward Bevan, screaming at full lung capacity. Bevan felt his bladder empty as he fell back against the damp wall of the tunnel.

Rob's scream turned to callous laughter. "Told yer he'd piss himself!" he said.

The others laughed half-heartedly it seemed, because suddenly, in the flickering lights of the damp tunnel, those tales that still survived in the bar of The Colliers, didn't seem so far-fetched.

All the safety-checks complete, the crew set to work in taking down the door. Bolts that were rusted shut had to be eased away or cut through with the acetylene cutter, and hydraulic equipment set in place to lower the door into a position where it could be removed without causing any obstruction. Bailey Shaw wanted to waste no unnecessary time in getting the first of the black gold out of the mine.

As the door moved off its hinges there was a rush of foul air from the other side. Gas testers detected no methane or other explosive gases, so the men removed their respirators, gagging at the stench.

If there's one thing that demons are good at, it's waiting for the opportunity to break through into this world. They have patience, they have cunning and, above all, they have the ability to take on the appearance of anything or anyone that they want to, either by possession or illusion.

The demon Malgron was both cunning and patient but, above all, he was lucky. He had been close by the Demon's Hole when he had heard the machinery working on the iron door. He knew that Astaroth's killer lived in this region of our world and that this was the nearest portal

24

and so he visited on a daily basis, waiting, watching and listening. His patience had paid off.

But Malgron wasn't a demon that would change his appearance by illusion; he enjoyed the pain inflicted by possession, and revelled in the power of control over a human being.

The door came down and lay across the hydraulic trolley on the rail that led back to pit bottom. Bevan had long since fled back that way, humiliated and in shock after Rob's cruel taunt. Malgron stayed in the shadows, watching and assessing. Selecting.

From the depths of the darkness, his eyes fell on Rob Jenkins, a tall, hard man in his early twenties, who revelled in his nickname of Big Rob. The man had a cruel twist to his mouth and a cold light in his eyes, his face set in an unpleasant sneer. Malgron smiled to himself. This one had 'thug' written all over him and would be easy to possess. He would do for the time being; until he could find a more powerful host.

CHAPTER SIX: WEIGHT ON HIS SHOULDERS

Mike took the hot tea upstairs, his thoughts running riot in his already-aching head. Beth wasn't asleep, although her eyes were closed and he could see the traces of fresh tears on her cheek. How could he inflict further distress on her? And, worse, put her very life in peril. And what of Adain, their five-year-old daughter? They had already had to send her to stay with her godmother in Cornwall to keep her out of harm's way. But what of his responsibilities in other directions? And wouldn't they be in danger if he did nothing? He was damned if he did something and damned if he didn't, unless he took control of it. It was too bloody much, and he needed to offload to Ben and Jack.

Jack Carter had been his best friend and confidante since basic training in the Royal Air Force, quickly becoming more like a brother. Afterwards they had followed each other from posting to posting, ending in the disaster in Afghanistan that had taken Mike's life, only for him to be brought back by the infinite skill of the medics, both at Camp Bastion and back in the UK; and it was Jack who had held his sanity together as he discovered his new 'gift' of seeing and communicating with ghosts - although lately, Mike had begun to see the gift as more of a curse.

More than anyone, Jack would understand his terrible dilemma. He hoped he would be home.

He put the tea down on the nightstand and leaned over to kiss Beth. She opened her eyes and gave him a wan smile. His heartache spiked. He wanted nothing further to do with his work in investigating the paranormal. There was no way he wanted to risk anything more hurting her. But he knew in the dark reaches of his soul, there was no way he could walk away from what was coming.

Beth read him in an instant, knowing his every nuance and expression. "What? What is it?" she whispered.

He tried to muster his characteristic grin that emphasised his deep scar along his cheekbone and failed miserably.

"Nothing," he lied. "But I need to go over and see Ben. There's some stuff left running round in my head that I need to sort out. And not the sort of stuff that Beckett can deal with. It's nothing for you to worry about. I'll try not to be long." He kissed her on the forehead.

"You know what, Travis? You're a rotten liar."

He laughed then; there was nothing he could keep from her. Except this. It was one thing investigating hauntings, and helping the dead to find rest; that was a good thing, right? But lately he had encountered entities from the darkest parts of Hell and in doing so had endangered them all. Now he had to find a way to deal with it and protect them at the same time.

"Time to re-evaluate things, baby. I need Ben and Jack as sounding-boards that's all."

She nodded her understanding and he turned to leave. He was half-way to the door when she said in a quiet voice, "Mike, be careful."

"Of course, wife! I'll be back before you know it."

"Take as long as it you need, Mike. It's important."

"Am I that transparent?" he asked.

"Yes. To me you are. Go get your head straight over whatever it is that's making those lines around your eyes. If anyone can help you, it's Ben. I wish it was me, but Ben is the one to help you, I know that. Go and see him. And whatever the outcome of it all, you should know I'm behind you all the way. Some burdens are just too important to cast away." She had read him well.

During the nine mile drive to Skenfrith, the weight on Mike's shoulder's seemed to increase a thousand-fold. He knew that whatever decision he came to now, would impact on them all for the rest of their lives. Before he knew it, he was driving through Skenfrith village and out the other side to Ben's cottage; converted from an old shepherd's hut in the centre of a small wood it was the ideal home for a reclusive spirit. Ben had lived there with his Rottweiler, Fred, for several years, effectively shutting out the world except for custom-building the most amazing motorbikes to make a living. Now, Jack had moved in with him; theirs was a complicated and celibate relationship born from the soul, and Mike was simply happy to see his friend happy. And that was it: simple.

Mike parked his car in the small pull-in from the road, at the edge of the copse which hid Ben's cottage; the last hundred yards was on foot through the small wood. Jack's car was conspicuous in its absence. He wasn't home. Mike wasn't sure if he was glad or not.

Ben's door opened at his approach; he'd obviously been watching for Mike. Fred bounded out, tongue lolling in a joyous welcome to a friend. Mike patted him absentmindedly, and went inside.

Everything in Ben's cottage on the ground floor was in one room. An old iron range that burned just about everything, dominated one end along with a stone fireplace, either side of which were comfortable leather armchairs and a matching sofa; Jack's compromise to country life. Central to the room was a huge pine table. The other end housed bookshelves that were usually filled with ancient tomes and esoteric volumes of all descriptions; now there were piles of them all over the table. Ben was already at the range tending to the steaming kettle.

"Grab a comfy chair, Mike. We'll have tea first then we'll get down to work. If that's what you want to do, of course."

Mike gave a half-hearted laugh, "Does everyone know what's going on in my head?"

"Mike, if these things weren't crashing your mind, I'd

29

be worried."

"Where's Jack?"

Ben was rolling a cigarette, seemingly with a great deal of concentration. "On his way; he should be here very soon. He's worried about you, Mike. We both are. Which is why I'm going to teach you everything I know. Including how to fight. You fight like a girl; did anyone ever tell you that?"''

Dai's words, *'There's a lot more to Benjamin Lovecraft than you know; a hell of a lot more, but you'll soon find that out for yourself,'* echoed in Mike's head. He stared at his friend, seeking answers that only Ben could give, but Ben was intent on rolling his cigarette and wouldn't give Mike his eyes. Eventually, he looked at him.

"Dai's been to see you, then. I expect he told you some, but not the whole, of it."

Mike tried to penetrate Ben's gaze but failed. "I thought I knew you. Just who are you, Ben?"

Ben sat in the chair facing Mike, lit his cigarette, inhaled the smoke and blew it out in a long breath. "You're asking the wrong question, Mike.

CHAPTER SEVEN: AN ACCIDENT

Ben glanced at the old clock on the wall for the hundredth time. It wasn't like Jack to be this late and not call. He gave another glance at the telephone; a concession to Jack's need for technology. He was uneasy and Mike was picking up the vibe.

As if in answer to their mutual unease and by popular demand, the telephone rang, startling them both. Ben grabbed it in his enormous fist.

"Hello. Ben Lovecraft speaking."

"Mr Lovecraft, this is Monmouthshire Police. We have this as a contact number for Jack Carter, with you named as his next-of-kin, is that correct?"

Ben's blood turned to ice and he felt the vessels in his face drain. Mike's eyes didn't miss a fraction of a second of what was going on. He stood abruptly, knocking his half-drunk coffee all over the table.

Ben's normally booming voice was lowered. "Yes. What's happened?"

"I'm afraid Mr Carter has been involved in a road accident. He is currently being treated at Neville Hall Hospital, in Abergavenny. Are you a relative, sir?"

"I'm his partner, I'll be right there. What kind of accident?"

"I'm afraid I don't have the details, sir. I'm sorry to be the bearer of bad news. I hope your partner is okay."

Ben listened to the sound of a hang-up and the look in his eyes was enough for Mike. He was already at the door, car keys in hand.

"Is he alive?" was all he could say.

Ben nodded, "Yes. I don't know any more than he is in Neville Hall. Some kind of accident, the police said."

Their roles had been immediately reversed and now Mike was the one in control. "C'mon. I'll call Beth on the way."

Images of his dream on the previous night flashed onto Mike's mental screen. He felt sick. If anything happened to Jack because of him … well, there would be hell to pay … literally. And if this was because of him then he had to get Beth and Adain to safety.

And he had to tell Ben everything.

He dialled his home number as he climbed into his old Volvo. A glance at his watch told him Beth would probably be asleep, but he let the phone ring anyway. Eventually, she answered it with a sleepy voice.

"Mike?"

"Yep, honey, it's me. Look … I … Beth, Jack's been in an accident, he's in Neville Hall. Ben and I are on the way over there right now."

"Oh, God. I'll meet you there, love."

"*No!* Stay there! I'll call you when I know anything. Please, Beth, promise me you'll stay there … and lock the doors and windows."

Her silence was enough to tell Mike he'd scared her. Ben was watchful, his eyes never leaving Mike's.

Beth's voice was quiet and he detected a slight tremor. "All right. Ring me, Mike, as soon as you know anything."

Mike threw the car into gear and skidded out of the pull-in at the front of Ben's cottage, flinging gravel every which way.

He daren't look at Ben but he could sense his expression and the atmosphere in the car was taut to snapping point.

"So, are you going to tell me?" Ben asked.

Mike sighed. He'd believed the dream was a result of his own anxiety playing out a scene of terrible possibilities that would never come to pass. He cursed himself, he should have known better; should have listened. Now it looked as if Jack was the first to pay for his negligence and conceit; because conceit it was that he had chosen to believe that the demon of his dream was nothing more than an illusion born of fear; a fear that he had decided he could conquer by ignoring it.

"I had a dream last night," he said. "Well, more of a nightmare really. God, Ben, I was stupid to ignore it! I thought it was nothing more than a nightmare. Jesus! How could I have done that? This is my fault!" He paused and Ben didn't interrupt the silence. He knew what was coming.

Mike drew himself together. "Last night I dreamed a demon was talking to me. Well, threatening really. He … he had a human form … he said that I was marked, that the demons were coming for me and there was *nowhere* to hide; they would always find me by my mark. Like some fucking GPS for demons! In my dream I told him, 'bring it on'. He laughed at me. Said they weren't going to kill me – yet. Not until they had killed or hurt everyone I loved first. Then, maybe, if I was suffering enough, then maybe they'd kill me. Ben, I'm sorry. If I'd honestly thought it was real, I would have told you."

"I know. Mike, this is nothing new. Jack and I both knew what was coming and so did you. This is the way demons work; causing as much suffering as they can, taking pleasure in the pain they inflict. The more pain they can dish out the better they like it. Jack and I talked about it. Bloody hell, Mike, *we* talked about it."

"Well, it's gone far enough. I'm out of my league here, Ben. You know it. Putting a few ghosts to rest, that's one thing, but *this*? I should have seen it coming, I should have walked away."

Ben's expression was distant. "You can still walk away."

Mike took his eyes from the road and stared at his friend, almost in disbelief. "I think it's too late for that, now, don't you? Jack …"

"We don't know that Jack's accident was anything

more than that."

Mike's harsh laugh jarred the atmosphere. "You tell yourself that if you like. But we both know, don't we. *Don't we?*"

CHAPTER EIGHT: MORE TO BEN LOVECRAFT

Further conversation escaped them and they drove the remainder of the journey to Abergavenny in a loaded silence.

Ben was first out of the car and heading for the Emergency Department door, his normally calm exterior nowhere. Mike switched off the engine, took several deep breaths, and followed him in.

Jack was already in surgery, the receptionist informed them, and would then be transferred to the Critical Care Unit. She had no further information, other than that Jack had been involved in a serious car crash and there were no other parties involved. They should make their way to the unit and someone there would perhaps be able to give them a further update. Her kind expression and painted smile did little to encourage them.

Mike felt sick and his head pounded with the incessant voice of self- blame. He could hardly look Ben in the face. If anything happened to Jack because of him!

Ben headed back towards the exit instead of following the receptionist's directions, already fumbling in his ancient tobacco pouch. Outside, he leaned against the wall and rolled a cigarette. Mike dismissed the irony of the fact that he was doing so whilst leaning against a notice that informed everyone that smoking was not permitted anywhere on the hospital site. A passing security guard politely asked him to put out the cigarette, but Ben's expression sent him rapidly in the opposite direction.

The cigarette smoked, Ben turned to Mike. "This isn't just your fight, now. Just so you know. And no, I don't blame you. I blame myself. But blame isn't going to help

35

Jack now, so let's go and find out what happened."

He turned abruptly on his heels and flung open the door, heading towards the Critical Care Unit.

An attractive nurse, trim and business-like in navy scrubs, was solicitous and herded them into an adjacent waiting room. After satisfying herself that Ben and Mike were, indeed, Jack's nearest and dearest, she was more forthcoming.

"I'm Anna Jenkins, the nurse in charge of the unit. Mr Carter ... Jack ... has suffered severe head trauma and internal bleeding. He's out of theatre now and we have him here; the doctor is with him at the moment and he'll come and talk to you as soon as we know Jack is stable." She hesitated, assessing them for their ability to hear bad news. "You should be aware that Jack is in a very critical condition. The injuries he has received are very serious. He is in a coma and so he's attached to equipment that is breathing for him; you should be prepared for that. For now that's all we know; I'm sorry. Dr Griffiths will be with you as soon as he can, but I'm sure you'll understand if you have to wait a while, we're doing everything we can. In the meantime, please help yourself to the tea and coffee machine in the corner." She nodded towards a table with an automatic drinks machine. She hesitated again, "Can you tell us if Jack had any reason to black out while he was driving? Any history of anything like that?"

Ben and Mike both looked surprised, and it was Ben who reacted first.

"No. Absolutely not. Why?"

She smiled, trying to reassure them, but that ship had sailed. "It's just that a policeman was here asking the same question. A witness to the accident, the man who was driving behind Jack, said that for no apparent reason Jack suddenly swerved and drove off the edge of the mountain road from Blaenavon. The police may have more information about the accident if you care to contact them. Now, I must get back to Jack." She put a warm hand on

Ben's arm and left them.

Ben was rigid, his face ashen, and Mike was fighting the nausea that threatened to turn into full-blown vomiting. He sat down heavily onto the chair behind him.

"Christ almighty, what the hell happened?" he muttered. "Jack is the best driver I know. Still think it was an accident?"

Ben was breathing heavily and his ashen face was suddenly suffused with red rage, enough to alarm Mike, who stood up abruptly and put a hand out to steady his friend. Ben shrugged it away with a rough gesture.

"I should have been able to protect him! I couldn't! I ..."

"Ben, stop! What the hell are you talking about? How could you have possibly protected him from this? You're not making sense. We've been through this; if anyone is to blame, it's probably me. And as you've already said, this isn't helping Jack. Please ... sit down."

Ben's usually booming voice came out as a strangled whisper, as if all his strength had left his enormous frame. "You don't know! You have no idea!"

"Then tell me," Mike said quietly.

Ben's volcano of rage was building and Mike knew it was about to erupt. He swallowed hard and took a step back, throwing a nervous glance towards the door. The last thing they needed was to be thrown out of the hospital.

The bubbling lava of fury found its escape, but thankfully it was in action and not in a roar of rage that would bring staff and security guards running. The muscles in Ben's cheeks worked furiously as he clamped his jaws together and inhaled deeply and noisily.

"You asked me who I was? And I said you were asking the wrong question. Well, look! See for yourself!"

His massive fists grabbed the edges of his leather waistcoat and shirt and yanked them apart with a ferocity that sent buttons skittering across the floor, as he pulled both garments roughly away from his body and threw them onto the floor after the buttons. He turned around, his back to Mike, and his voice boomed out one word.

"*Look!*"

Mike stared, aghast at what he was seeing, not really understanding the information his eyes were receiving. Ben's chest was heaving but he stayed silent. Mike continued to stare.

Down each side of the entire length of Ben's spine ran huge, livid, ragged scars inches wide and just as deep. Synapses in Mike's brain sparked and joined together as his mind filtered and rejected incoming information and passing thoughts. Then one thought kept repeating itself despite the impossibility of it.

"Ben?"

It had been several years since Seraquel's fall from heaven, his fall from grace, and in that time he had dedicated himself to God in whatever capacity he could find, desperate for redemption, but finding only disappointment. He had none of his angelic powers, none of his connection to heaven; he was human in every sense of the word. And he had given himself a human name – Benjamin Lovecraft.

CHAPTER NINE: FALLEN ANGEL

For years he had waited to find the one that Metatron had hinted at - his passport to redemption, but with every year that passed he found himself understanding humanity more and more, ever at odds with blind authority, until the day came that he understood himself. He walked away, as he was his habit, from a succession of vocations that brought him nothing but frustration, and found contentment of sorts whilst he waited for 'the one'. But he knew that when the time came, it wouldn't be for his own redemption but for the redemption of the one. And he was okay with that. It sat well with him.

And so he waited and learned and trained, remembering his angelic knowledge but none of his previous powers, ready for the time when he would have need of his skills and pass them on to the one. His acquired knowledge and understanding of the evil lose in this world and the tools to fight it as a human being, combined with his knowledge of how Heaven and Hell worked, set him apart and he knew it would be soon that the one would appear.

And he had appeared in the form of Mike Travis.

Mike tried to let the image of the ragged scars on Ben's back settle in his mind. It wouldn't.

"You need to explain it to me, Ben."

Ben's rage was spent and now, suddenly, his huge presence seemed diminished. "Don't worry, Mike. I'm everything you think I am, or have been. It's just that I was something else before all that. ... what do you know about the Book of Enoch?"

Mike frowned and leaned forward, unwilling to allow himself to relax. "Not much. I've never read it - but as I understand it, it's about angels and fallen angels; those that were cast out of heaven by God. Never really paid it any mind, other than as a fanciful ancient text. Why?"

Ben held his gaze.

"Why, Ben? What are you trying to say?" Ben's expression didn't change. "Ben? ... No...you're not trying to tell me ... not trying to say you're ... an angel?" He gave a hesitant laugh, the idea was preposterous. And then his tone changed to deadly serious. "I don't believe you! Not for a minute. What the hell ...?"

Ben's voice was still quiet, almost as if he didn't want to hear his own truth. "Not *trying* to tell you anything, no. And luckily for me, Hell didn't come into it. There's a lot of lore about us, the fallen ones - fallen angels - becoming demons. It's not always true, though some of us did turn to darkness. Well, not every time. It is true that some of us rebelled or just plain disobeyed. I fell into the latter category, no pun intended. I disobeyed, more than once, and for that I was punished."

Mike was on his feet, pacing and staring at Ben.

"You can either leave now, Mike, and this conversation never happened, or you can let me tell you the truth. If you choose to stay, that's what you will get: the truth, the whole truth and nothing but the truth, as they say. I'll give you a minute or so to think about it. But that's what you want, isn't it; to learn the truth and decide on how to act on it? I am telling you the truth, Mike. The question is - can you handle it?"

Whatever Mike had expected, this wasn't it. As if his head wasn't full enough of reeling thoughts, this was the kicker. Something in Ben's voice, along with all the past trust he had built up, told Mike he was sincere. Now he had to decide if he wanted to know the rest.

"Okay, so you're an angel. Tell me everything."

"*Was*. Was an angel. Now, I'm as human as you. A fallen angel, yes, Mike, though not one of the original fallen ones; the ones that either became demons or fathers of the Nephilim, after mating with human women. I didn't rebel like they did, causing the war in heaven. But as I said, I did disobey. I was the angel that was originally sent to destroy two cities that were entrenched in wickedness and evil. I just couldn't do it. I couldn't wantonly take the lives of the few innocent ones, so ... I didn't. I did what I have often done, I walked away."

"You're talking about Sodom and Gomorrah? Bloody hell, Ben, how old are you, for God's sake? Sorry ... I didn't mean ..."

"It's okay, Mike. As an angel I was ageless. As I am now - a human trying to redeem myself - I'm as you see me. Mike, there are as many layers to Heaven as there are to Hell. I was also sent to Egypt and to Jerusalem, and again failed to carry out my instructions because, in my mind, it was wrong. As a punishment I was sent to a level that, for all intents and purposes, is a holding level. On remand, so to speak; to contemplate my disobedience, I suppose. But then I was given a second chance. I was given the chance to incarnate as a human and work my way back up to redeem myself and return. I haven't done too well so far. But then, I met you."

Mike's hands were in his hair, feeling as if he was trapped in a dream that made no sense, a dream he couldn't wake from. He had no words; many questions, but no words to formulate them. And in the forefront of it all was Jack. He was suddenly glad of this distraction, however hard it was to get his head around.

Eventually he was able to string a few thoughts together. "So, you're telling me you're a fallen angel, working his way back to the good books? Is that it? And what does that have to do with me? Why didn't you just stay a priest? Surely that would have earned you some brownie points?"

"I tried, Mike. I just couldn't take the corruption in high places. But then it's not the high places I came down to help. I knew as soon as I met you, that you were heading for dark places; places that you would need help to get out of."

Mike remembered how Ben had first helped him by exorcising the demon in Victoria Little's cottage. How he had instinctively trusted him. His instincts were holding strong, even if his mind was in turmoil.

"So why me? Why do you put such significance in our meeting? What are you to me?"

"Right now, I'm your friend. Soon I'll be your teacher, so listen up."

A sudden and chilling thought took hold of him. "And Jack? What about Jack? What is he to you?" His fear that Jack had been nothing but a pawn in Ben's plan was intolerable.

Ben's face lit with warmth that hid nothing. "Everything," he said. "I hadn't bargained on Jack. But I promise you, Mike, he's everything to me. I will never hurt him."

Something else flitted across Mike's jumbled brain. "So that's why you're celibate. "

Ben smiled and nodded. "Yes, Mike. You know that's the condition of our relationship, and you know that Jack is okay with that."

"Well, at least something makes sense," Mike said, all too abruptly. He suddenly remembered Dai's words on the subject, *'but they're not always all sweetness and light and white fluffy feathers. Piss one off and you'll know it, isn'it.'* Was he the only one not to know the reality? He sighed.

"Dai said something to the effect that all angels aren't nicey-nicey. That some were just plain badass."

Ben laughed. "Oh yeah. Some of us can be real bastards."

"How many of you are there? Down here, I mean?"

Ben shrugged, "Many. Not all are fallen angels, some volunteer. Some, like me, are here as part of a redemption programme, if you like."

Mike's characteristic humour, laced with sarcasm, re-appeared as if to ease his aching head.

"So, why don't you just smite the bad guys? You can do that right? Smiting ... that's the right word isn't it? Angels 'smite' the evil bastards."

Ben failed to see the funny side. "I don't have any power down here, Mike. I'm in a human body, I told you; I'm as human as you are. The only abilities I have are the ones I've worked for and earned the hard way. And smiting, as you put it, was never my strong suit. It's what landed me in this mess to start with. Though, that's one lesson I've learned! So, if we can continue?"

Mike became suddenly serious. "Does Jack know?"

"Yes. Apart from the fact I have hidden nothing from Jack, these scars on my back are kinda hard to explain away, and Jack's not stupid."

"He didn't say anything to me."

"Why would he? I specifically asked him not to."

Mike frowned. Despite the fact he had promised Ben not to say anything to him, it was the first time that Jack had kept anything from him.

Mention of Jack brought Mike's thoughts crashing back to the present situation and the stark reality of it, brought back into focus by the opening of the waiting-room door.

A taut-faced, white-coated, doctor entered. He looked weary and the dark stubble on his chin demonstrated the length of his shift and just how long ago he had the opportunity to shave. His expression was grave as he extended his hand.

CHAPTER TEN: TALKING BLACKMAIL

His face was set as he took Ben's huge fist in his hand and guided him to a chair and sat opposite him. "I'm Dr Griffiths," he said, "I'm looking after Jack. He's your partner I understand?"

Ben nodded. "What's the score, Doc?"

There was a moment's hesitation, and then the doctor met Ben's eyes, open and honest. "It's not good. He's had serious trauma to his head. He's been in surgery and Mr Wilson, our neuro-surgeon, has repaired a bad bleed, but we're worried about the amount of swelling. Jack is in a coma right now, and he's attached to equipment that is breathing for him. We've done what we can to relieve the pressure on his brain, but I'm afraid it's up to him now. There are other internal injuries that are critical also."

Mike swallowed the rising bile, and for a moment his eyes lost focus as they threatened to fill with tears. He shook himself out of it and strode over to Ben. The gesture wasn't unnoticed by Dr Griffiths, who smiled at Mike. "Are you a relative of Jack's?"

Mike shook his head. "He's like my brother; but, sadly, not by blood. Brothers in arms, I suppose you'd say. He's my best friend and has been for years."

Dr Griffiths nodded his understanding and returned his gaze to Ben. "You must understand that at this moment I can't say one way or the other whether he's going to come out of this. And we won't know if there is any permanent brain damage until he wakes up."

Both Ben and Mike heard the unspoken 'if he wakes up'.

The doctor allowed them time to process the information, and then he stood up. "I'll be getting back to

Jack now. You can sit with him later and talk to him if you like; we think it helps coma patients although there is no real evidence either way. If there is anything you want to ask, Sister Jenkins has all the information you need and I'll be more than happy to chat again when we know more." He hesitated again. "These things are unpredictable, I'm afraid, but it would be wrong of me not to warn you how serious Jack's injuries are. It's not very comfortable here, I'm afraid, but you're welcome to stay as long as you like."

He gave a brief smile and a nod as he left.

Mike realised that he hadn't in fact been breathing and exhaled long and loud. Ben's expression remained still and dark and he didn't move.

They fell into a black silence: Mike processing: Ben assessing any options. He couldn't see any. They glanced at each other occasionally but there were no words that could bring either of them any comfort, and so they remained silent.

Time ticked by, marked by the clock on the wall telling them that two hours had passed since the doctor had given them the stark reality of Jack's condition.

Both of them jumped as Mike's phone rang. He answered it quickly, cursing himself for not keeping Beth updated as he saw his home number on the screen. She would be worried sick.

"Beth, I'm sorry, love. I should have called you ages ago. The truth is, well, the truth is love, the news isn't good. Jack is fighting for his life."

The heavy silence at the other end told him that she was struggling to hold back tears and not wanting him to know that. He heard her sharp intake of breath. "I want to be with you and Ben," she said. "Please, Mike, let me come over there."

He hesitated briefly, and then thoughts tumbled through his head, thoughts of demon threats. He wanted her there with him more than anything, but he wanted her to stay safe even more. "I can't explain right now, Beth.

But I want you to stay there. Have you locked all the doors and windows, like I told you?"

"You're scaring me, Mike. What's going on? Does it have to do with what happened when Dai was killed?" Her voice made her sound small and vulnerable.

"I think maybe it does," he answered, his voice low and measured. "Maybe not, but I want you to take no chances. And I want you where I know you're safe. Tell me you'll stay there."

It was several seconds before she replied, but he was reassured by the acceptance in her tone. "Okay, Mike. But please call me when you know anything. I'm staying up until I hear from you. Love you."

"Love you too. I'll call as soon as there is any news."

Mike put his phone back in his pocket at the same time as the door opened again. Both he and Ben stood up immediately, eyes fixed on the doorway, anxiety and dread written on both of their faces, expressions that were a familiar sight in such a setting.

It was no doctor in scrubs or a white coat that appeared, but a familiar figure that brought a sigh escaping from Mike's lips. D.I. Gareth Jones strode into the room, overtired, over-weight, his hand outstretched, reaching for Mike, concern etching his rounded features. Their recent encounter in the haunted village of Aberth, and their new friendship, was lost in Gareth's firm grip that could almost match Ben's. He clapped his free hand on Mike's shoulder.

"I saw Jack's name on the incident report. Came over because I guessed you'd be here." He transferred his attention and grip to Ben. "Hi, Ben. I'm sorry, both of you. How is he?"

Ben swallowed hard, and Mike took the lead as they resumed their seats and Gareth sat opposite them, leaning forwards, elbows on his knees, cradling his plump chin.

"Not good, mate," Mike answered him. "In a nutshell, he's fighting in there, just to survive. He's hanging in there, in a coma right now. That's all we know."

Gareth nodded, appearing to want to say something but not quite sure how to go about it. Eventually, he stood up and walked across to the window overlooking the car park.

"Mike, don't take this the wrong way, but ... was Jack okay? Mentally, I mean?" He held up a hand to stem the angry tide from both Mike and Ben. "Was he depressed, is what I mean?"

Ben's anger was immediately apparent but he managed to swallow it under his curiosity.

Mike met his eyes. "Why do you ask?"

"Because there are several witness reports on the accident. It almost seems ... almost seems as if it wasn't an accident."

Both were on their feet now, and both speaking together.

Ben's voice overpowered Mike's by several decibels. "You'd better explain," he boomed.

"Okay, but both of you need to calm down and listen to me." He stared at Mike, his meaning clear. *'Sit down and calm down and hopefully the big feller will follow suit'*. Mike did as he was silently bid. It worked; Ben sat down with a heavy thump that threatened the integrity of the chair.

"Okay. From the witness reports, and there were three of them, there was no reason for Jack to swerve the way he did. There was nothing in the road, no wandering sheep, nothing. He was driving at a reasonable speed and his car didn't appear to be out of control. On the contrary, it appeared more like a deliberate action. They all said the same thing. It looked as though he deliberately drove over the edge of the mountain road. One minute he was driving slowly as befits that road, and the next he put his foot down and, in what seemed to be in a very controlled way, turned the car straight over the edge. Look, there will be an investigation, and I've managed to 'persuade' the Super to let me handle this one. You know, before Aberth I would have said this was nothing other than a suicide attempt, failing any evidence of mechanical failure. His car is in the police garage as we speak. But knowing what happened recently, I'm wondering if there isn't something else behind it?"

Mike heaved a heavy sigh. "Well, you aren't the only one. It seems that by killing Astaroth, one of the high-ups in Hell, I've pissed off more than a few demons who have threatened to make it their business to make me pay dearly. Beginning with making my family and friends suffer. So, yeah, we're wondering the same thing."

Gareth let out a long, low whistle. "I can't believe I'm even listening to this, but then I remember Aberth. Jeez, when it comes to the weird and the scary-weird, you know how to cut it. You're sure, I suppose? That demons are out for your hide, I mean? I'm half afraid to ask you this but; who told you? "

Mike glanced at Ben. "Dai," he said in a ragged voice.

"Dai. You mean the Dai that ... died?"

Mike nodded.

Gareth Jones shook his head and sighed. "Of course he did. Well, I know one thing for sure. Not one damn word of this can go in my report. I only just managed to hold on to my job, let alone my rank, after the last fiasco."

Despite himself, Mike grinned. "Yeah, how did that go, by the way?"

Gareth grinned back at him. "Funny you should ask that. I wrote my report exactly how it was and the Superintendent was beside himself with rage, and he made it clear that all I had left to do was clear out my desk. Then I 'came across' something that he probably wouldn't want made public. I thought it was my duty to tell him about it." The grin turned into a hearty laugh as the memory came back to him. "He buried my report in some dark corner of the archives, went whiter than any ghost you've ever seen, though on reflection they're more a greeny-grey colour aren't they? And he told me in so many words that the less he saw of me the better, in fact I got the impression that, on balance, he would be glad if he never saw me again. The next day I found myself with a new office in the basement, and a new brief tackling cold cases and anything else that will keep me out of the way. In his words, I will get the cases that are a waste of a half-decent copper's time. In other words, he buried me along with my report. It suits me, because now I can look into all the cases that have been previously 'unexplained', without his lordship breathing down my neck. When I asked him about clear-up rates, he just went a shade of purple and slammed out of the room."

Mike grinned again. "Nice one. I take it we're actually talking blackmail here?"

Gareth raised an eyebrow. "That's a bit harsh, Mike. I prefer to call it leverage at worst, persuasion at best. I discovered recently that playing by the book gets you squat, so yeah, I crossed the line. Do I regret it? Hell, no."

The grin faded from Mike's face as the reality of their situation came to the fore. "Well, there's only one person who knows what really happened tonight, and he's not talking right now."

CHAPTER ELEVEN: A DEAL

In Hell, Azrael turned to walk away again.

"Wait!" Bazaliel was going to agree to the terms and he knew it; he could work on regaining his seal later. "You drive a hard bargain Azrael, you always did. Just tell me one thing. Why me?"

"Because I know your secret. Yes, you are a demon, you have become that way during your time in Hell. But I remember you before that. Before you turned against the rest of us and stood at the side of Lucifer."

"Morning Star," Bazaliel snarled. "His name is Morning Star."

"You call him what you like, but we both know who we are speaking of. You chose the wrong side, admit it. Not all the fallen ones came here; only those whose soul was darkest, whose soul was easy to turn. But I remember one act of kindness from you, millennia ago now, but that one spark of light may still be alive in the shadows within you. You are a demon, Bazaliel, it's what you are now, and that won't change, not for perhaps another hundred years or so. But you don't have to spend that time lurking in the shadows, taking what you can to survive, doing things that damn your soul further into darkness just to stay alive. You may think you control a legion, but a legion of what? The lowest-ranking demons who are barely sentient. I'm leaving now, unless you give me your seal."

Bazaliel swore long and hard but grabbed at his ragged, filthy robe with gnarled fingers that ended in thick black talons, baring his equally filthy chest.

"One thing I always detested about you, Azrael, is your holier-than-thou attitude; you're nothing but a smug bastard with a God complex."

51

Azrael smiled; he knew he'd won. "Yes, but I'm the smug bastard with a God complex that is giving you a ticket out of here, and the smug bastard with a God complex that now holds your seal."

As he spoke, Azrael placed his hand over Bazaliel's chest and began chanting a spell in Enochian, the ancient language of the angels, the words of which translated approximately as 'Demon Seal, reveal yourself to me'.

Bazaliel gave a cry of agony as his seal appeared beneath Azrael's hand and, with a searing of flesh, burned itself into Azrael's palm leaving only a bruise in the centre of the demon's chest.

"Thank you. So, now you will come with me; I will give you safe passage from this Hell and seek your future. It is appropriate at this point for you to say 'thank you', by the way."

"Fuck you."

"Close enough. Now, shall we?"

The dark, squalid, farthest reaches of Hell were suddenly illuminated in an electric blue light as Azrael claimed his prize, leaving the pungent odour of ozone in their wake.

The light blinded Bazaliel and he screamed in pain as he tried to shield his eyes, swearing creatively. Azrael ignored him; searching, scanning, evaluating, until he found what he was looking for. It was a risk, a big risk, but if it worked out it could solve several problems in one hit – if, it worked out. But could he take that risk? If it failed it could also mean a disaster that would have a ripple effect of far-reaching consequences. He looked at Bazaliel, appraising him, and decided that the risk was worth taking.

His palm burned with Bazaliel's seal and he knew that if he didn't pass it on within the next few hours it would fade and return to its original bearer. He wasn't about to let that happen and so he set his plan into action, towards the point of no return.

"I have found a host for you, Bazaliel. Listen to me

carefully. This is not possession; this is something more. You will not be in control, you will not be able to assert your personality or your will, and you will not be able to leave of your own accord. You will not communicate directly with your host, you will not show yourself to your host in any way shape or form, and you will not, above all, not do, say or think anything that will cause harm to your host. Is all that clear?"

Bazaliel made a snorting noise. "Forgive me, Azrael, just precisely what can I do? Because what I'm hearing is I might as well be languishing in some cell and, quite frankly, you're not selling this to me. Maybe you should give me back my seal and I'll find my own way back to the Shadows, where at least I had a life."

Azrael smiled, a smile that unnerved Bazaliel because it was the smile of a poker player that was about to reveal his hand and take the pot. "Oh, I'm sorry, didn't I say? It was a one-way ticket. There's no way back."

CHAPTER TWELVE: DOWN THE MINE

The huge iron door to the Meadow Vein had come down with a crash that reverberated throughout the mine, bringing coal dust and other detritus from around the old beams down into the faces of Rob Jenkins and the others, accompanied by an unsettling creaking from the overhead timber supports. Oddly enough, the bravado of minutes earlier had largely disappeared and the mood had become serious.

Rob Jenkins had taken the job of foreman and safety man with alacrity, the thought of being in charge far outweighed any risk, in his book. He'd been offered the position because Bailey Shaw saw in him the kind of man that would keep the other workers in line in his own way.

Rob and his deputy were about to tread where no miner had gone for a hundred years. The air and the integrity of the timbers needed to be checked before they could install the electricity cables for the lighting. Had there been a fall since the last boots had echoed through the tunnels? Was there any flooding?

Where was the other guy? Rob knew he should wait but he wanted to get this over with.

His training had been brief but thorough and, despite his previous bluster, he knew lives were at stake, including his own, and so his mood became sombre as he decided to ignore the first rule of safety and wait no longer for his deputy and carry out the first tentative checks.

There was a constant sound of trickling water, as he shone his light against the glistening walls. The running water was draining off somewhere because, apart from the ground being wet underfoot, there was no actual flooding. Overhead timbers were still creaking and the occasional fall of dust served to unsettle him. A sudden skittering noise told him the resident rats had been disturbed and were taking cover. He gave an involuntary shiver and wondered if leaving the life on benefits to take a very lucrative job was worth it after all. Bailey Shaw was paying way over the odds for the two-year contract, but the first creeping doubt flitted through his mind.

It was cut short by a sound coming from his right; he shone his light towards it. He'd be glad when the electricians had installed new lighting, which they couldn't do until he'd completed his safety checks. Chicken and egg.

The light flickered momentarily and for one awful second he thought it was going to go out. He felt his bladder tighten. So much for being the big guy. The light steadied itself and he played it over the wall and down onto the floor where a distinct sound of scratching was coming from underneath an area that had been boarded. He frowned and tentatively put his boot in the centre of the planking. The scratching stopped.

Rats, he thought. Goddamn, fuckin' rats! He stamped his foot down hard to repel the creatures underneath but, instead of the sound of them scattering, his boot went straight through the rotting wood. A century of damp had done its work well.

"Shit!" He stepped away from the gaping hole and shone his light onto it; there was nothing but a black void. He took another step back as the words 'Demon's Hole' registered somewhere in the recesses of his none-too-sharp brain.

"Bollocks to that," he said to no one. His voice came back to him in a quiet echo. He shouted it then, "Bollocks!" It echoed around him, bringing a grin to his surly mouth.

The hole would have to be made safe before anyone else ventured down there; number one on his report. He stepped back towards the hole and shone his light into it.

A sudden movement just to the right of the beam made him start. He was going to take great delight in bringing his boot hard into contact with the goddamn rats!

The sound of something like a far off wind blowing came from the hole. He frowned again, making his already unpleasant face look cruel. A sudden gust of air spiralled upwards just in front of his face.

"What the ...?"

The upwards movement of air seemed to have picked up the surrounding coal dust, as the black particles swirled in front of him like a small whirlwind. Rob took an involuntary step backwards and tripped over one of the rotten boards that had previously covered the hole. He landed flat on his back, the air knocked out of him in one long groan.

The swirling black dust appeared to be moving. Moving towards him. He had no breath left in him to cry out as the coal dust began to take shape; the shape of a man, but a man of immense proportions, casting shadows on the tunnel wall, grotesque and clawing, the fingers ending in cruel talons.

And it was hurtling towards him, covering him completely. Once again, the words 'Demon's Hole' came to the forefront of his mind and, this time, he didn't dismiss it with profanity. This time he knew those stories in the bar of The Colliers weren't just old miner's tales. There had been something down there and now it was coming for him.

It was his last conscious thought before Malgron entered him, possessing him, making a home in him until he was ready to move on.

The demon settled quickly into Rob's body, adjusting himself into the new form, familiarising himself with its natural movements, testing out the vocal chords and, above all, assimilating and obliterating all that had once been Rob Jenkins.

"Rob! You stupid bastard, you should have waited for

me!" The voice of 'Pete' Peterson, Rob's deputy, echoed in the tunnel. "For Christ's sake, man! What are you thinking?"

Malgron turned around slowly, appraised the approaching man and decided he wasn't any improvement on his present 'body'.

"You're late," he snarled. "I'll make sure your pay is docked. In future you'd better shape up, there are other boys back there that will appreciate the extra pay." He strode on down the tunnel, noting no roof falls or further incursion of running water. It was damp everywhere and there were thick spider-webs hanging from the overhead timbers that were wafting in the inrush of air, but there was no reason why the electricians couldn't get in there and get the lighting up and running.

His deputy cast him a puzzled look. "You okay, Rob?"

Malgron spun around. "What d'you mean?" he demanded.

"Just ... nothing, sorry." But the wary expression on his face remained.

Malgron was swift to act. The fingernails that had belonged to Rob Jenkins turned to sharp talons, as he showed his true-self to Peterson seconds before he sliced open his throat. He grabbed the slumping body and dragged it towards the gaping hole, where he paused momentarily before tossing it down into Hell, and then bent down and washed the blood from his hands as he returned once more to Rob Jenkins' form.

At pit bottom, the rest of the crew and the electricians waited for Rob's return. Bevan Hughes had rejoined then, over his humiliation and ready for the safety report. As Rob, emerged from The Meadow Vein into the comparative bright lights of pit bottom, Bevan looked past him, concern etching his already pale features.

"Where's Peterson?" he asked.

Rob Jenkins shrugged. "Didn't show at my end," he snarled. "Can't be doin' with a deputy that aint up to the job, Hughes. Get me someone else." He pushed roughly past Bevan, leaving him peering into the blackness of tunnel.

CHAPTER THIRTEEN: MISSING

Malgron squatted inside Rob Jenkins like a malignancy. He pushed past the crew at pit bottom and entered the cage to take him back to the surface. He'd spent long enough in Hell, and this place reminded of it too closely. Dark, cold, damp and home to unspeakable misery.

He slammed the gate of the cage shut and hit the button that started the old lift mechanism.

"Wait! Jenkins, wait!" Bevan Hughes was yelling at him from the other side of the gate. He ignored Bevan and allowed the juddering mechanism to take him topside. Bevan would find the pool of blood soon enough, but no body would ever be found. There would be nothing to pin on him, and, in any case, he intended to be out of this body and into another before that could happen. He would pull the plug on Rob Jenkins as he left, for good measure. That way there would be no minor irritations as he sought out his prey. He knew the name of the one who had slaughtered his brother, Astaroth: Mike Travis. And he also knew that some minor demon had found a ride in one of Travis's friends after a bungled attempt on his life. That could be useful in the future. Bazaliel was no match for Malgron - way out of his league — but, leverage was leverage, it just depended how hard you leaned on it.

As the lift ascended out of Bevan's sight, he swore with uncharacteristic flare. Everything was going wrong, as he knew it would. Now Peterson was missing, and someone had to go and look for him. He was the manager; it was his responsibility.

He turned to anxious faces. There were a couple of miners at the rear of the group muttering something about 'not worth it' and 'buggered if I'm going any further'.

61

Bevan wished he could join them. Instead, he drew himself up to his full five feet eight inches and took a deep breath.

"Okay, men. It seems we have a safety issue. If you'd call the lift back and return to the surface, I'll join you after I've conducted a search of the tunnel. I'd be grateful if you didn't jump to any conclusions or start unnecessary rumours. There will be an explanation and Peterson will be found, safe." He could hear the hollowness of his words and his own lack of conviction.

The men turned to the lift and watched as the mechanism stopped. Rob Jenkins had reached the surface and they were free to recall the lift to pit bottom again. Not before time for a few of them. Bevan knew in his heart that he wouldn't see them again. The job centre was going to be their next port of call.

He gathered his safety gear and switched the lamp on his hard hat on and turned towards the tunnel.

"Hang on, Bevan. I'm coming with you."

Bevan looked back to see Idris Roberts pulling his donkey jacket tighter around him and walking towards him and the tunnel.

He shook his head. "No need, Idris, man. I've got it."

Idris Roberts was the image of his grandfather Evan, the brother of Idris's namesake that had witnessed his father being taken into hell in the Demon's Hole so many years before. He was in his fifties now and had gone down the pit soon after his sixteenth birthday. He was the only experienced miner that Bevan had been able to recruit, but he had his own reasons. As a child he had listened from behind closed doors as his grandfather, Evan, had told how 'Daft Idris', as he had become known, had witnessed what had happened back then in the Demon's Hole.

When the opportunity had come his way, he determined to put the family ghost to rest.

"I'm coming with you, Bevan, man. Lead on."

Bevan nodded. He knew he wasn't about to win the argument and anyway, he was more than glad of another human soul to accompany him into the Demon's Hole. He silently cursed Bailey Shaw and his insatiable greed.

His mind was full of tumbling thoughts, primarily along the lines of quitting once he returned to the surface. Let Shaw go down there himself if he dare, or get another sap to take his place.

The tunnel branched off into the Meadow Vein and the atmosphere chilled as they trod further down, their safety boots echoing throughout the heading. Timbers creaked overhead and the trickle of water running down the walls chilled them to the bone. They slowed their pace but moved on, Bevan calling out Peterson's name - more to drown out the sound of the water than anything. Deep inside, he knew there would be no answering call.

Without warning, Bevan's boot slipped on something wet and sticky underfoot, and he went down like a sack of the coal they were hewing from the rock-face. He put out a hand to try and stop from falling but only succeeded in grazing against the damp wall.

As he hit the floor, the coppery tang of Peterson's blood assailed his nostrils. He closed his eyes and said a silent prayer. He'd known it, but hadn't wanted to believe it. Peterson was long gone.

Idris Roberts swore loudly in Welsh. Cussing in Welsh always sounded more effective somehow. "Cachu Sanctaidd, Bevan! *Holy shit, Bevan!*"

He reached down to haul the mine manager to his feet and froze as his lamp illuminated the dark, wet patch that was Peterson's blood. He ground his teeth together and hauled Bevan up in a single motion. Then without another word, he turned on his heel and walked back down the tunnel towards pit bottom, his life-long curiosity satisfied. Evan had told the truth, all those years ago.

He hit the button that set the lift-cage in motion and waited for Bevan to catch him up. Yanking the cage open and stepping inside, Idris turned to him and said in a quiet, measured tone, "That iron door needs putting back up. If

Shaw refuses, I'll kill him myself."

At the head of the shaft, the fan was working noisily to send cold air to pit bottom and, beyond the cage a group of men were waiting for news of Peterson. Bevan simply shook his head and pushed through them. He had to call the police.

"Go home, boys. Shift's over for today." He thought about heading for Bailey Shaw's office then reconsidered; he'd leave that to Idris Roberts. He had a phone call to make. He slammed open the door of his office, but instead of reaching for the telephone, he grabbed his coat and headed for the exit. He pushed hard on the door, but something was stopping it from opening; it felt like a heavy sack was leaning against it. He heaved on it again; someone's head would roll when he found out who was responsible.

Eventually the door opened enough for him to squeeze through it. Only to trip over Rob Jenkins, who was lying there, eyes and mouth wide open, heaving his dying breath.

It was too much for Bevan and he slumped against the door, eyes fixed on Rob Jenkins helpless stare.

Malgron had moved on.

Bailey Shaw was furious. The new crew of miners had returned to the surface without even having ventured into the Meadow Vein. Someone's head was going to roll; probably Bevan Hughes. He'd heard enough of their crap about the Demon's Hole and now they were saying that 'Pete' Peterson was missing. Skiving, more like! Well he wasn't going to have any of it. They were going down there to do a full shift or they could walk. And Bevan Hughes could walk with them.

He slammed his office door with such venom the glass in the window cracked.

The last person to have seen Bevan reported seeing him hurrying away from the pit head. Shaw was incandescent with rage. Enough was enough; his profits were dwindling in front of his eyes. No one was getting paid that day. He threw open the exit door and almost fell over Rob Jenkins' body. Bevan Hughes was standing over him.

"What the hell ...?" Shaw demanded. "Is he ...?"

Bevan nodded.

"Christ Almighty, I can do without this! Anyone else know?"

Bevan shook his head, words still seemingly beyond him.

Shaw snarled at him. "Get him out of here. I don't care where. Just get rid of it."

Bevan's eyes glazed over as the air around them began swirling around, collecting the coal dust from Rob Jenkins body, swirling it around until it took shape; a shape that rushed forwards and enveloped Bailey Shaw.

CHAPTER FOURTEEN: DEAL BREAKER

Conversation in the Critical Care waiting room had become stilted as Mike and Ben descended into dark thought. Gareth sat back and allowed them their silence and their space but, as well as being their friend - albeit a new one - he also had a job to do. His new-found 'leverage' over his Superintendent would obviously have its limits, but his request to handle Jack's accident investigation had met with little resistance. As far as the Super was concerned, it was an attempted suicide. From the word go, Gareth had felt uneasy, especially coming so soon after his recent encounter with Mike and his 'business'. He'd learned, early on, to listen to his 'copper's intuition'. A hunch it may have been, but he was even more convinced now that it had been no suicide attempt, nor accident.

Mike had resumed his pacing and Ben had his head in his hands, when the waiting room door opened and Dr Griffiths re-entered. He had a harrowed look on his face that made Mike's heart sink; this wasn't going to be good news.

He indicated that they should sit, but none of them did.

"I'll not beat about the bush," he said. "Since we last spoke Jack has had a heart attack, which has left him in a bad way. We've done all we can, and are still waiting and hoping that the swelling in his head will reduce. So far, it hasn't. I think you should go and see him."

The implication of the last statement left Ben and Mike cold. Gareth had heard similar before and knew exactly what the doctor was saying. It was time to say their goodbyes.

Dr Griffiths put a hand on Ben's arm. "I'm sorry. I wish I could be more positive, but Jack's condition has deteriorated. You should know that before I take you to him." He turned to Gareth, "Just two at a time."

Mike felt sick and seriously thought about heading for the toilet, but he fought down the rising stomach acid and followed Ben to Jack's bedside.

Jack looked small and vulnerable, his head swathed in bandages, the tube of the respirator taped to the side of his mouth and bruises covering his swollen face. Mike allowed himself the thought that Jack would hate that; he was a handsome bastard and he not only knew it, he enjoyed it. Well, bruises would heal if he pulled through. It was, apparently, a big 'if'.

Machines were beeping with a regular rhythm, a reassuring rhythm that said Jack's heart was beating, and his chest rose and fell in time with the respirator that was breathing for him.

Ben had Jack's hand firmly clasped in his own huge fist, his face was a canvas of dark shadows and there was a muscle twitching in his cheek. He didn't speak and Mike knew it was because he couldn't trust his voice not to crack, so he laid his hand on Jack's shoulder and did the talking.

"Hey, Jack. What the hell? Beth's mad as hell at you, mate; you're in for a roasting when you get out of here, worrying us all like this. Jesus, Jack, what happened? I know you can't answer me, but if you can hear me, you need to know we're here and we're going nowhere until you open your eyes and spit that thing out of your mouth. I hear the canteen is crap and the coffee's like sludge, so don't keep us here too long, eh?"

Ben still didn't speak, his face had darkened and there was a black glint in his eye that Mike hadn't seen before. It told its own story. Someone, or something, was going to pay, and that was okay in Mike's book.

A small breeze moved the bedside curtain, inducing it

to float outwards. Mike turned and gave a small sigh. "I wondered if you'd come," he said to Dai, who now stood at the foot of the bed, deep concern lining his face as he pushed his spectral cap to the back of his head. Ben didn't appear to hear Mike, deep as he was in a different kind of communication with Jack, so Mike tilted his head to indicate to Dai to move back outside. He gripped Ben's arm, "I need a minute," he said.

Ben nodded but didn't take his gaze away from Jack.

In the corridor outside Mike turned quickly to Dai. "What the hell's happening, Dai? Do you know?"

Dai's image shifted and shimmered as he tried to anchor himself in the material world. His distress was obvious and he shook his head. "Not really, except it has all the hallmarks of a demon attack. Jack's too good a driver to go over the edge of that mountain road, see. And it has that smell to it."

"This is my fault," Mike said miserably.

"That's right - take it on yourself, boy. That's going to help Jack a whole lot, isn'it?"

Mike thought he was about to say more, but the door to the ward opened and Ben loomed in the opening. Mike held his breath, waiting for the words he didn't want to hear, but they didn't come.

"They need to adjust something or other; we have to wait back in the room again. Someone will come when we can go back in. Who were you talking to?"

Mike met his gaze head on. "Dai", he said.

Ben nodded. "Thought so. Or else you'd finally taken a trip to Looneyland. Can't say I'd blame you." He strode past Mike into the waiting room and sat down heavily into a chair. "You okay, old feller?" he addressed Dai although, unlike Mike, he couldn't routinely see him or hear his reply. Gareth looked around to see who Ben was addressing, and shrugged his shoulder.

Dai continued, "All I know is this, see. There's something else comin' but I don't know what. But what I do I know is this: I'm hanging around long as I can, look. I can tell you Jack's spirit is still in his body, holding on for dear life. He's fighting, Mike. Don't give up hope yet."

Mike turned to Ben, "He said he's fine, and not to give up hope."

"You think that's what I've done?" Ben boomed. "Never."

The door opened again, admitting a tall man wearing navy scrubs.; his name badge identified him as Charge Nurse Jason Ryan as he approached Mike and Ben without hesitation.

"I don't have long, so you should listen to me. Your friend is going to die and I can save him."

Ben was on his feet, a snarl on his lips, his fists balled at his side as he lurched towards the man. And Mike knew why.

Ben's face was filled with fury. "You stinking piece of shit, Demon!"

The nurse put up a hand and sent out a blast of dark energy that stopped even Ben in his tracks. Mike felt a sharp pain in his chest and the demon mark began to bleed. Ben nodded at the dark red stain that was slowly spreading across Mike's shirt.

"Looks like you've got a warning system in place. The mark that bastard Astaroth gave you; it's going to bleed in the presence of a demon. Scumbags. We really need to do something about that. I can't stop this happening when you're in close quarters with a demon, but this may help to quiet it; confuse its signal, so to speak."

Ben took what appeared to be a tiny, silver compact from his pocket and flipped open the lid. Inside were some communion wafers spotted with consecrated wine, alongside a tiny vial of oil.

"My old pyx," he said. "Holy oil, Mike. Here." He smeared the oil over the marks on Mike's chest.

The demon's anger erupted. *"Listen to me!"* he screamed. "Listen to me, if you want your friend to live."

70

He looked at Mike and nodded towards Ben, "Control him, or I leave and Jack Carter dies!"

Despite his wish to allow Ben free rein, Mike sensed a grain of sense in the demon's words. He put a restraining hand on Ben's arm. Gareth had his phone out ready to call for back-up, Mike shook his head. The spectre of Dai had shimmered and faded, temporarily overpowered by the energy blast from the demon.

Despite the warning, Ben began to recite the rite of exorcism from the Roman Ritual. "Et mittam te, spiritus immunde, omnis satanica potestas hostis omnis légio inferni turpibus sociis in nomine Dei ... I cast you out, unclean spirit, along with every satanic power of the enemy, every spectre from hell, and your foul companions; in the name of God ..."

Ryan's hand shot out, controlled by the demon, pointing at Ben. "Hey! Shut your mouth! This body is the body of a senior nurse on this unit and I'll blast it to hell if you don't shut your fucking mouth and listen to me!"

Ben began again. "Et mittam te, spiritus immunde ... I cast you out, unclean spirit ..."

Mike tightened his grip on Ben's arm as blood began to pour from Jason Ryan's eyes. "Ben! Wait. For God's sake, wait. There's a decent man in there with that thing and it goddamn means it! It will kill him."

Ben stopped the exorcism and balled his fists again. "You have one minute, scumbag. Then you're going straight back to hell where you belong!"

The demon inside Jason Ryan spoke again. "I can save you the heartbreak of flicking that life-support switch, because that's what it's going to come to. He's about dead, but I can save him."

CHAPTER FIFTEEN: BOUND BY HIS SEAL

Ben's rage boiled over again. "How about you save yourself, you fucking slime-ball and fuck off back ... I demand your name!"

"My name is Bazaliel. You think I want to be here? I used to be on the side of the angels until I ... made an error of judgement. I've been in the pit for millennia and I have been released in order to save your friend, not out of the goodness of my heart - because as you know, demons don't have one - but because this is the way I can save myself. It's a one off deal. A deal that's got a time limit if I'm not mistaken."

It was too much for Ben and he launched himself at the nurse. Mike caught his arm and Gareth was galvanised into movement; it took both of them to pull him away. Mike was in Ben's face, nose-to-nose his own anger and frustration finding an outlet.

"Ben, we're friends, but, I warn you, I'll find the strength from somewhere to take you down if you don't listen. I hear you, it's a goddamn demon! But it's a goddamn demon that's offering to save Jack's life. And I want to hear it out!"

Ben shook them off with one rough movement and his eyes flashed with rage but, he backed away. Mike turned to Bazaliel.

"Speak quickly: how can you save Jack?"

For an instant, Bazaliel hesitated. Something was setting off bells and whistles in his head. Then it was clear: this other guy was Mike Travis – one of Hell's Most Wanted; top of Malgron's hit list. But the instructions had been clear, take alive and deliver to Malgron. This could

73

prove useful when he was ready to leave this host. This was his way out to freedom. Ben's expression was murderous and brought him back to the immediate problem. But he would keep close to Mike and wait for his opportunity. It would come. He changed his tone, with even more reason to occupy this host.

"I need a host body to stay here, and he needs someone like me to hold the damage together and heal his body; and I can. It's beyond human help, believe me."

Ben was on his feet again. "Possession? Are you fucking joking? ... omnis satanica potestas ... every satanic power..."

"Ben! Wait! Do I have this right? He's a fallen angel, turned into a demon? Think about what you told me earlier. Think about it!"

Bazaliel continued to bargain. "Look, the deal is that when he's back in the land of the living, if he wants me out and let his body die, that's up to him, and I have to leave. You need more? Azrael has my seal and he's going to pass it on to Jack Carter to ensure my obedience. Is that enough?"

Mike was confused and looked at Ben, silently asking for an explanation.

Ben obliged through gritted teeth. "A demon is bound by his seal. If Azrael has it and means to turn it over to Jack, then Jack will have control over the demon and, it will be Jack's soul, Jack's spirit, Jack's personality. But possession is possession; that filthy piece of scum will have set up home in Jack no matter how he dresses it up. And we can't trust it." He looked away from Mike and called out.

"Azrael! Show yourself. If you have Bazaliel's seal, then show it to me. I demand you appear before I send your minion back into the Pit! Azrael!"

Mike wasn't sure what to expect, but there was a moment when Jason Ryan's face went blank and his features appeared to contort before returning to their original handsome lines. But when he spoke, it was with Azrael's cultured, middle-eastern voice.

"I see you remember me, Seraquel."

"The name is Benjamin Lovecraft. And yes, I remember you. I remember how you sneak around hell seeking souls to redeem. You should leave them to rot, like you left me to rot. Not in hell, I grant you, but it was no better. And for whose benefit do you seek their redemption? Answer me that. Is it for them, or is it for you? And, I don't get it; since when do demons ask permission to possess a host? In my memory they take what they want. What's changed?"

"Such bitterness, Sera ... Benjamin Lovecraft. Here, here is Bazaliel's seal."

Jason Ryan extended his hand, palm upwards, the centre of which was raised and livid red in the form of the demonic seal of Bazaliel.

"It is ready to pass over to Jack Carter for his control over the demon, but to do so it must remain intact. But, as he has already said: once he is able to decide for himself, if he chooses death over the demon, then Bazaliel must leave. The seal will ensure his obedience. You must make the decision for him and you must decide soon; his life force is slowly ebbing away."

In that instant, Mike became aware of Dai's presence again. He turned to him, his face a portrait of anguish.

There was no preamble from Dai. "From what I can tell, look, Azrael is one of the good guys; a bit of a lone wolf by all accounts, but essentially trustworthy. Mike, you need to know that Jack's spirit is already travelling towards the other side, see. His body's knackered, boy. Can this demon fix it? Hell if I know. It has to be your call; yours and Ben's. But if you decide to let him go, I'll take care of him."

Mike felt as if he'd swallowed a grapefruit whole, as his emotions got the better of him and lodged in his throat. He could see that Ben was also in torment, so he tried to be rational, but failed, his love for his friend sending reason into oblivion.

"Ben, I say yes. There's nothing to lose if Jack has the final say and has control over the demon. The alternative ... is too hard to think about. I say, we allow it."

Jason Ryan spoke again, this time with the voice of the demon. "Tic toc, time's running out. Going once ..."

"Shut your mouth, demon!" Ben yelled. His face showed his mental torture as his thoughts and emotions vied for precedence. His instinct was to exorcise the demon, Bazaliel, but his heart told him to save Jack; he needed to think and think quickly. What would Jack do? What would Jack want?

"Going twice ..."

"Ben, please ..." Mike pleaded. "It's going to be too late!"

"Going for the last time ..."

"All right! All right. Do it. But I warn you, I will send you back to hell as soon as look at you if, for one moment, I think you're harming Jack in any way, or refuse to leave him if that is what he wants. Know this; I can send you to hell in a heartbeat."

For a millisecond, Jason Ryan's expression was one of utter confusion, and then he appeared to pull himself together as if from a momentary blackout as his consciousness was returned to him intact.

He cleared his throat. "You can go back to Jack, now. Thanks for your patience; there are some things that we need to do in there that can sometimes cause distress to family members. I'll take you back in." He indicated the door.

Ben and Mike stared at each other and cast a glance back at Gareth who just managed to look totally bemused by the events of the past few minutes. He shrugged helplessly.

Inside the Critical Care Unit, curtains were drawn around Jack's bed. Jason Ryan nodded to another nurse who was busy making her patient comfortable. She gave Mike and Ben a weak smile, knowing that they were about to have to make a difficult decision.

"Thanks, I'll take over from here," Jason Ryan told her. She nodded to him without speaking and left. Ryan leaned over and placed his palm on Jack's upper left arm, directly over his biceps. There was a fleeting smell of burning flesh but Jack didn't move a muscle and there was no change in the rhythmic beeping of the monitor as the seal was burned like a brand onto his arm. Ryan then leaned in further and appeared to whisper something Jack's ear.

He stood upright and said, in the voice of Azrael, "It is done. He now has the seal of Bazaliel."

Further conversation was halted as the curtains around the bed parted and Dr Griffiths stepped up to the bed. His face was grave and they could both see that this was a part of his job that he would never get used to.

"Can we talk? Away from the bed will probably be best." He didn't wait for a reply but turned and walked slowly back out to the now familiar waiting room. Once inside, he looked meaningfully at Gareth and said to Ben, "Perhaps it will be better if this was private?"

Ben shook his head. "You can say anything in front of D.I. Jones."

Recognition washed over the doctor's face; he knew he had seen the policeman before, usually waiting to take a statement from patients that were never going to be able to make one. This was going to be the case in this instance, he feared. He turned back to Ben and Mike.

"I'm sorry, but the results of my recent tests show that Jack has no brain activity. He isn't going to recover, I'm afraid. There are machines that will deliver oxygen to him and another to pump it around his body, but Jack, himself, is gone. I'd like you to take some time to think about things and then perhaps we can discuss what would be the right thing to do. For Jack." He put his hand on Ben's arm and turned to the door as if to leave.

Before he could take a step, his pager sounded its alert and the waiting room door burst open. Jason Ryan came into the room at a run.

"Doc, come quickly; Jack Carter is awake and freaking out."

CHAPTER SIXTEEN: PRIMUS

October brought full dark onto the Blaenavon Mountain at around five-thirty in the afternoon, but the narrow and precipitous mountain road over to Abergavenny seemed to have been cloaked in a deeper, weightier dark than usual.

It had settled over Jack's car like a heavy pall, mesmerising him as it seeped inside through the air-vents.

He sat further upright in his seat and slowed down his speed. He was an excellent and careful driver with a healthy respect for the deep ravine on the left-hand side of the road that seemed to disappear into the darkness, despite the full beam of his headlights. The road had also descended into a creepy silence; even the throaty sound of his engine was muffled by the darkness.

He considered pulling over, but, with the edges of the road invisible, he dared only to bring the car to a crawl as he leaned forwards and peered into the dark looking for a pull-in on the opposite side of the road. He couldn't see a thing.

He looked into his rear-view mirror that reflected only darkness back into the car. In reality, it was the normal dark of an October afternoon outside and, unseen by Jack, there were two cars following behind; both drivers slowing down and backing off, puzzled by the strange behaviour of the driver in front of them.

The demon at the heart of the unnatural darkness was of low rank and already loose in our world; a messenger, whose message was for Mike Travis – It begins. Jack was the first pawn in the hate campaign in Hell that wouldn't end until Mike had suffered beyond endurance, and then, and only then, would they kill him; his payment for killing Astaroth in the cursed village of Aberth.

Jack put his foot on the brake and brought the speed of the car down almost to a stop. The drivers of the cars behind backed off even further, unsure of the hazard that was causing the problem ahead.

Jack was becoming disorientated; the silence around him was suddenly broken by a distant voice. He couldn't make out the words at first, and then realised that they were Latin. He frowned and leaned forwards, trying to peer through the black pall that had now engulfed his car. He brought it to a halt and turned the key to switch off the engine. It wouldn't turn.

He unfastened his seat belt and pulled on the door handle. The door wouldn't open. He felt panic begin its flight up from his chest into his throat, but his military training conquered it and his breathing returned to normal. He tried the key in the ignition again; it still didn't move. His brain began to analyse the situation, searching for rational, mechanical explanations.

Rational thoughts were obliterated in a heartbeat as the throaty engine began to roar and the pedals began to move on their own volition. The steering wheel turned. He grabbed it, but no amount of struggle could hold it. He felt the wheels beneath him turn towards the edge of the precipice.

"Really? *Fucking really?* What the hell ...?"

In the fleeting moment before his car veered to the left and shot over the edge into the blackness of the sheer drop down into the valley below, he heard one word; a Latin word. 'Primus'. *The First.*

He heard the impact in a far-off corner of his brain. The screeching of twisted metal, the grinding of metal against rock. He felt the impact of his head against the windscreen and had a single thought; the memory of unclipping his seatbelt as he had tried to get out of the car. *Idiot!*

It was his last conscious thought. But not his last unconscious thought.

It was dark and it was cold and there was a sudden deafening silence. He opened his eyes and found himself face-down on the interior roof of the car. He took a moment to try and orient himself to his situation.

Firstly, and most importantly, he was alive. Secondly, he wasn't in any pain. Surprise. He began to test his limbs. He could move them all. Relief. He turned over.

Understanding came slowly. His first thought was that someone else was in the car with him. But that wasn't possible. His next thought sent him reeling. He was looking down on his own body, barely recognisable under the blood. His consciousness had left his body and was hovering near the roof of the car.

He was surprisingly calm, turning over possibilities in his unconscious mind. He needed to get back in his body; that was the thought that was taking precedent. He tried to lower himself back, hoping that contact with his broken body would be enough. The sensation of floating responded to his will and his consciousness appeared to lower itself, but back into his body it wouldn't go.

Frustration took over and he mentally punched the side of the car.

In a fraction of a second he found himself outside of the car and looking upwards to the edge of the road. Lights were stationery at the roadside and there were frantic voices breaking into the silence. Seconds later, sirens and blue lights pierced the darkness.

"Hey! I'm down here! I need help!"

No voices called back to him. "I need to get up there," he thought. And suddenly, he was there at the side of the road. His unconscious mind grinned. This was easier than he thought it would be. Now he had to let someone know he was alive.

He looked around. There was an ambulance, two police cars and a fire-engine and crew. He moved in closer.

"Doubt if anyone survived that," one of the paramedics was saying.

A fireman answered him, "Only one way to find out. But it's going to take time. We need to make sure it's safe to winch someone down there. We're waiting for floodlighting.

Policemen were setting up cones and putting accident procedures into place. Another was writing something in a small notebook, whilst talking to two men. Jack listened in.

"I backed off way back there," one of the men said, pointing behind him. "Don't know what his problem was, but there was nothing in the road. He slowed down, and then stopped, then for no apparent reason the crazy bastard put his foot down and drove right over the edge. I'm still bloody shaking! Drink or drugs, I expect. Son-of-a-bitch could have taken someone else out with him."

"*No! It wasn't like that!*" Jack yelled. No one heard him. "*Bollocks!*"

Another set of blue lights approached; another crew bringing floodlighting.

The emergency teams went into a well-rehearsed routine and in minutes the entire valley floor was bathed in halogen lights. Jack looked down at his mangled car. "Shit! My car! I loved that car. No fixing that." His surroundings began to shimmer as if the entire scene was a dream. He felt himself falling; falling back down to the valley floor, through the roof of the wreck of his car and back into his body. Into oblivion.

CHAPTER SEVENTEEN: A DIFFERENT VIEW

People were in a flurry of activity around him; there was an air of urgency that permeated everything. Then, suddenly, there was a halo of excruciatingly bright lights over him. The sound of metal instruments against metal and an antiseptic smell said 'operating theatre'.

A monitor beeped in alarmingly slow rhythm, and there was a dull but persistent ache in his head. There was a sudden buzzing sound that seemed familiar and yet out of place. His unconscious mind searched its archives.

When it found the answer, the shock evicted him out of his body again and he was looking down on a surgeon with an electric saw in his hand. He knew exactly what that meant without sifting through old files in his head, and he wanted no part of it. Desperate to leave the scene he concentrated on the door to the operating theatre and almost immediately found himself in a brightly lit corridor.

He had quickly become aware that his consciousness responded to his will. He needed to concentrate on where he wanted to go and his out-of-body consciousness followed. It was a relief to be away from what was happening behind the closed doors behind him. The problem was, he didn't really know where he wanted to go.

And then he became aware of a familiar presence; two, in fact. And he knew that Ben and Mike were close by. His conscious mind was analytical and precise, his unconscious mind was not so, and he found himself wandering the corridor seeking out the two most important souls in his life as it hung by a thread.

More by accident than design, he heard Mike's voice coming from a room to his right. He concentrated and

83

found himself inside the waiting room of the Critical Care Unit. He unconsciously nodded in acceptance of the surroundings; they seemed appropriate given his circumstances.

He was suddenly aware of tension between Ben and Mike; they had been arguing.

"Hey, you two! What the hell?" his mind said.

Neither Mike nor Ben acknowledged him. He'd thought that Mike, at least, would have been aware of his presence. Maybe that was a good thing because it meant that he wasn't a ghost – yet.

With a sudden movement that took Jack by surprise, Mike lunged at Ben and grabbed his shirt, bringing him nose-to-nose with the huge bear of man that was Benjamin Lovecraft.

"Ben, we're friends, but I warn you, I'll find the strength from somewhere to take you down if you don't listen. I hear you, it's a fucking demon! But it's a fucking demon that's offering to save Jack's life. And I want to hear it out! I know it's wrong on almost every level, but it's *Jack!*"

D.I. Gareth Jones was there too, a goddamn reunion! He had hold of Ben too. What was happening?

Ben shook them off him with one rough movement, his eyes flashed with rage but he backed away. Mike turned to a moving shadow behind him.

"Speak quickly: how can you save Jack?"

The shadow seemed to solidify into the form of a tall, dark, male nurse in navy scrubs. Jack frowned, totally disorientated now.

"I need a host body to stay here, and he needs someone like me to hold the damage together and heal his body. It's beyond human help, believe me."

What the hell was going on? What were they talking about? Fucking demons? *Come on guys, there's a bigger picture here. I'm dying back there!* he yelled.

Darkness descended over him again and he knew

instinctively that he was back in his bloodied and beaten body. Damn. He wanted to reach out to Mike and Ben; but it had been beyond the capabilities of his out-of-body consciousness.

The darkness turned to oblivion once more.

When he was next aware of anything, his surroundings were alien and most definitely not a hospital. A familiar figure was approaching him: an older man with a cap on the back of his head. He smiled as Dai Bricks came right up to him.

Dai was smiling back at him. "Hi, Jack."

Jack shivered involuntarily. "Dai. I suppose this means I'm dead, then."

Dai shook his head. "No, boy. Not yet. Just in between, isn't it. Right now, it's up to you. Won't stay that way for long, mind, and then it'll not be your decision to make. You can come with me if you want to, or you can stay and fight. Up to you."

Jack frowned. "I saw Ben and Mike. *They* were fighting for Christ's sake!"

"Aye. Letting their emotions get in the way, see. But there's an issue going on down there. There's a way to save you and that's what they're arguing about, isn't it."

"No, that wasn't it. They were going on about demons. I'm down there about to snuff it and they're arguing about some fucking demon!"

Dai nodded. "Aye, that'll be it."

"What do you mean?"

Dai appeared to shimmer and then he was gone.

He felt himself falling again, falling back into his body. He was aware of an immediate crushing pain in the centre of his chest and alarms going off all around him, and then his consciousness was thrown from his body again in an instant.

Ben was shouting in Latin. "... omnis satanica potestas ... *every satanic power...*"

Mike grabbed his arm. "Ben! Wait! Do I have this

right? He's a fallen angel, turned into a demon? Think about what you told me earlier. Think about it!"

Jack was aware then of another presence, something dark, something not of this world, and realisation washed over him that this was the demon that Ben and Mike were arguing over.

He turned to Ben. *"Exorcise the bastard! Get it away from me!"* But Ben didn't hear him.

The demon had been bargaining with them and now it continued to do so. "Look, the deal is that when he's back in the land of the living, if he wants me out and let his body die, that's up to him, and I have to leave. You need more? Azrael has my seal and he's going to pass it on to Jack Carter to ensure my obedience. Is that enough?"

Mike was confused and looked at Ben, silently asking for an explanation.

Ben obliged through gritted teeth. "A demon is bound by his seal. If Azrael has it and means to turn it over to Jack, then Jack will have control over the demon and, it will be Jack's soul, Jack's spirit, Jack's personality. But possession is possession, that filthy piece of scum will have set up home in Jack no matter how he dresses it up. And we can't trust it."

It was no use; Jack couldn't make Ben nor Mike hear him. But Azrael heard him.

"Jack Carter, I'm Azrael, the Angel of Death." The archangel stood before him, enormous and commanding in his presence.

Jack seemed resigned. "Come for me, have you?"

"No. I have brought a solution to your problem."

"If your idea of a solution to my problem is possession by a fucking demon, you can piss off back where you came from. Thank you."

If archangels with an attitude problem could smile, Azrael would have smiled. But instead he flickered with impatience. It made Jack just a little nervous. He took a mental step away.

"I had thought you more sensible than this," Azrael said. "You will hear me out, Jack Carter." He went on to explain why he had chosen Bazaliel and why he had chosen Jack as his host. Jack fell quiet, thinking.

Azrael watched him in silence for several minutes and then he said, "I see you have a good heart, and beneath your playboy exterior you are willing to be compassionate and, above all, you want to do what you can to help save your friend, Mike Travis, from the clutches of the foulest among the demons. I see your thoughts, Jack Carter. You realise that you can do this not just to save yourself, but to save Bazaliel. He will ask you himself and, even though your friends down there have agreed to this on your behalf, as they had to for it to happen, they are not aware that the final decision has to be yours and yours alone. But this is also a test for you, Jack Carter; you will not remember this conversation when you wake up and you will not remember anything about the demon Bazaliel; you have to make the decision consciously.

Darkness again. And then a searing pain in his arm accompanied by the smell of burning flesh. He was aware of someone leaning over him, whispering in his ear.

He listened. And then he said, "Yes."

CHAPTER EIGHTEEN: SECUNDO

Dr Griffiths looked confused; an unsettling expression in a physician. He was out of the door, close on Jason Ryan's heels, without a glance back at any of them.

Ben made to follow but Mike grabbed his arm. "They'll tell us when we can see him. He's awake! That's got to be good news. Look, Ben, we can deal with the other problem later. We've got Jack back. He's got control of the demon inside him, and for now that's got to be enough. I know you want to send Bazaliel back to hell, and so do I. The thought of a demon in Jack sticks in the gullet, but think of the old saying: it's better to have your enemy inside your tent spitting out, than outside your tent spitting in. We could use this against them if we think about it. And, don't forget, when Jack is well enough to decide for himself, he may send the bastard packing himself. But for now – he's alive."

A nod was the only reply as he sat down in silence. Mike had never seen him like this and it worried him; Ben appeared to be a powder-keg ready to blow, the timing was uncertain, but sooner or later he was going to detonate and, for sure, there was going to be fall-out.

"I need to call Beth," he said. "She'll be worried sick. At least now I can give her some news - carefully edited, of course."

He dialled their home number only to hear their voicemail message. He frowned fleetingly; perhaps Beth was on the phone to Martha, their retired headmistress friend. Martha, their dear friend living in Cornwall, was currently looking after Adain, Mike and Beth's daughter; her own precious godchild. She also had a huge fondness for Jack and would want to know of his plight. That would be it; she was talking to Martha. Or maybe she was trying to call him? Or maybe she had inadvertently turned on their answer phone. Or maybe ...

Further conjecture and rising anxiety was stemmed by the entrance of the good doctor again. He looked uncomfortable as he spread his hands out.

"I don't know what to say, other than I'm sorry for having caused you unnecessary pain here. I don't understand it. Jack was gone. His brain scan and his EEG both said the same - no brain activity; we were keeping his body alive artificially. And now ... now he's awake and was extremely agitated and calling for you. I don't know if you believe in miracles, but if you do I'd say one just happened here. As I said, he's asking - no, he's demanding - to see you and I'm happy for you to have a minute, *one* minute, with him. But I have given him a sedative, he needs rest now. Come with me."

Ben and Mike followed in silence, as relieved and thankful as they were anxious; their misgivings were running rampant, unsure of what they were about to see. Would Jack know what had happened? Would he know who he owed his life to? And if he did, what was his reaction going to be?

None of that was apparent when they reached his bedside, however. The respirator had been disconnected, and whilst Jack looked beaten to hell and still critically ill, his deathly pallor seemed to have disappeared. He looked asleep, but as they approached he opened his eyes and tried to speak. The sedative was doing its job effectively and swiftly, and Jack was struggling to string words together.

"Don't," Ben said in a quiet but gruff tone, "Don't try and talk Jack. You're OK. You're going to be OK." He had his hand on Jack's shoulder and his emotions were threatening to overtake his calm exterior.

Jack nodded and turned to Mike. "It took control of the car. It ..."

Mike tried to silence him; there would be time later for explanations. "Hush, Jack. It can wait."

Jack shook his head, too quickly, and his monitor upped the pace of its beeping in time with Jack's racing heartbeat. It attracted the attention of Jason Ryan who was at the bedside immediately.

"I'm afraid you'll have to leave now. We can't have him upset. Perhaps you'll take some time out for yourselves and come back later; now that you've seen he's back with us."

They turned to comply, but Jack caught hold of Mike's arm, weak as he was, to restrain him. "Mike ... listen to me," he whispered.

Mike bent low for Jack to use what was left of his rapidly disappearing consciousness before the drug took full effect. He managed just one word. "Primus."

Mike paled. His grasp of Latin was practically non-existent but he understood that one. Primus – the first. He squeezed Jack's hand, but Jack was already in the arms of a deep, drug-induced sleep.

In the corridor, Mike dialled home again. Again he heard his own voice asking for the caller to leave a message.

"Beth, it's me. Call me, love. There's good news."

Ben had been watching him closely ever since Jack had whispered the one word in Mike's ear. The great bear of a man, emotionally reduced to the brink of tears, took a huge breath and now stood to his full height and bulk.

"Well?"

"He said just one word. Primus. We both know what that means, don't we. It's the start of their campaign against me. I've got to get home, Ben. I've got to get Beth and Adain somewhere safe. You need to stay here with Jack. You need to watch out for him and I need to make sure Beth is safe; she's not answering the phone. Jesus Christ, what have I brought down on you all?"

For the first time since he took the call from the police

notifying him of Jack's 'accident', Ben was now in command of himself and once more Mike's mentor and newly-appointed, teacher.

"First of all," he said, "You have to stop panicking. That's mother's milk to a demon. It's what they want. You have to stay calm and rational. Yes, you need to get them to safety, and you need to do it quickly but calmly. They've got you in their sights Mike, but know this: you have brought nothing down on us. We were all there in Aberth. We were all a part of this and I for one have been for many years. So no heroics; treat this like a military operation, because that's what this is. Their army against ours; yes, they outnumber us, but one thing you'll learn about demons is that the majority of them are extremely stupid. And, we have the advantage."

"And what would that be?" Mike asked, with a note of bitterness just on the edge of his voice.

"Me, for one. You for another."

Despite himself Mike allowed a grin to spread across his face. "I'll call you when I get home," he said.

Well aware of the nature of the road home, he nonetheless floored the accelerator, confident that could handle the speeding car but making sure he still had control. After all, this was the way that they had got to Jack. His second thoughts reminded him that such an attack was unlikely as they hadn't finished making him suffer yet. It was the second thoughts that made him press harder still on the accelerator; he had to get home to Beth quickly.

Beth had lost count of how many times she had dialled Mike's number only to hear his voicemail message. *Hospital,* she thought; *he must have had to turn it off. But if he doesn't call me soon, I'm going over there.* Then, *Idiot! I can call the hospital, I can ask them to let me speak to him. He's bound to be close by.*

She found the number and asked to be put through to the Critical Care Unit, and after a delay of several minutes, a man's voice, abrupt and obviously distracted answered her.

"Charge Nurse Jason Ryan speaking, how can I help you?"

She instantly felt ashamed of bothering them and more than a little silly. "I'm so sorry to trouble you. My husband is a friend of Jack Carter, I know you can't give information over the phone but could I please trouble you to ask him to call me. I'm so worried about Jack; he's a very dear friend."

Jason Ryan's tone was a little warmer. "Of course. I'm sorry I can't give you information, but I'll ask your husband to call you." The line went dead.

Fifteen minutes went by as she paced their living room, staring at the phone constantly as if glaring at it would make it ring. When it did, it startled her. She grabbed it.

"Mike?"

"Hello, Beth. This is Ben, I'm afraid you've missed Mike, he's on his way home to you." He paused a moment. "Beth, are you all right?"

"Yes, of course! I'm so worried that's all. How's Jack?"

"Well, he's pretty messed up, but it looks as though he's going to pull through it. He had a hell of a car accident, Beth. Mike will fill you in when he gets home."

"Oh, hold on, Ben, he's here now; he must have forgotten his key. Hold on a minute ...." She put the phone onto the coffee table and ran to open the door to him, needing his hug, needing his presence.

Ben heard the phone go down onto the table and his blood ran cold.

"Beth!" he shouted into the phone, "Beth wait! He's only left ten minutes ago! It's not Mike! Beth, for Christ's sake! Beeeth!"

The next thing he heard almost brought him to his knees.

"Secundo." The second.

Ben's voice was strangled as the full implication hit

him. "Beth."

CHAPTER NINETEEN: TANK

Ben's thought processes were cascading at a torrent. He had no means of transport since Mike had left him to watch over Jack, knowing that once Mike had settled Beth somewhere safe, he would be back.

If he called a taxi he still wouldn't be able to catch Mike, who had a ten minute start and an anxiety level that was just passing through the hole in the ozone layer. He knew he'd be driving like a bat out of hell: especially as Beth hadn't answered his calls.

That thought made Ben pause; Beth had just phoned from home, so why hadn't she answered Mike's calls? He didn't dare dwell on that, but at least she had been all right up to the point where she had put down the phone to go and greet Mike - or what she believed to be Mike. Maybe the problem had been with Mike's phone and not Beth's? He dialled Mike's number and listened to the message on his voicemail.

That confirmed his suspicion. There was no way under the circumstances that Mike would have turned his phone off. He needed to get to Mike in a hurry and he knew of only one way.

Making a living as he did, building customised motorbikes, it was inevitable that he would be an accepted member of the biker fraternity's inner circle, and he knew who to call: Tank Evans.

Most bikers have nicknames with a story behind them. Tank was no exception; his name originating from the oversized petrol tank on the bike that Ben had made for him, custom-painted as a death's head. His huge build, even bigger than Ben, had also contributed. Ben knew he could call on Tank any hour of the day or night; whether the biker was stoned or not was another matter. He lived in Abergavenny, only minutes from the hospital, so Ben dialled his number, crossing everything, and hoping Tank was home and reasonably straight.

Eventually Tank answered the phone, his voice somewhat distant. He'd obviously been smoking something exotic but he was coherent and obviously delighted to hear Ben's voice.

"So, Wizard, what can a humble biker do for the genius that creates such awesome rides, man?"

Ben smiled at the use of the name 'Wizard' that certain members of the fraternity had attached to him. He didn't kid himself that it was all about the rides he built either; most of the bikers had been in his cottage and some time or other and been in awe at the occult nature of some of the books on Ben's shelves.

"I need a lift, Tank. An emergency, you know, a full-throttle job."

"I'm the very man. Where are you?"

"Nevill Hall."

"Bummer, man. You injured, Wizard?"

"No time to explain, Tank. Can you come and get me?"

"Kicking her alive as we speak, man." The phone went dead.

Ben gave a brief thought as to Tank's fitness to ride the bike, but let it go as more important matters returned to the front of his mind. He returned to Jack's bedside and stood for a moment looking down at him, watching the steady rise and fall of his chest, looking for any sign of distress; there was none. He knew Jack would tell him to get the hell out of there and go to Mike, but even so, he felt a pang of guilt at the thought of leaving him.

He went to the nurse's station, to Jason Ryan, who was busy with a complex drug chart in front of him.

"How long do you think he'll be out like that for?" Ben asked him.

"He's fairly heavily sedated; he'll probably be out cold

for several hours at least. His body has been severely traumatised, and quite honestly, none of us can explain why he's still here. It's a miracle."

Ben wished they would stop using that word, and it brought his anger back to the surface. Miracle it wasn't, and he wondered savagely what the medical team would think of demonic possession. He nodded to the Charge Nurse.

"I need to take care of something. If he wakes before then, please tell him I had to leave and I'll be back as soon as I can."

Jason Ryan smiled at the huge man in front of him, noting the heavy, dark shadows around his eyes. "Of course, though I have been looking at Jack's drug chart and Dr Griffiths has prescribed some heavy duty sedation for the next twenty-four hours. I think I can guarantee he'll be sleeping well into tomorrow. This can be hard on the families of our patients; there's nothing you can do for him here, so why not go and try to get some rest, eh?"

"Thanks," was all Ben could manage by way of response.

Outside the main door of the hospital it had started to rain and the sky was as dark as his mood. He pulled his thick leather jacket tighter around him and yanked up the zip, before pouring his concentration into rolling a cigarette. Seconds later, a deep, throaty roar announced the arrival of his lift.

Tank Evans dismounted his beast of a bike and strode up to Ben, clapping his gloved hand across Ben's back.

"Your rescue awaits, man."

"Thank you Tank. I need to get to the other side of Monmouth pronto."

Tank grinned, unfastened his helmet and handed it to Ben.

"Hell with the lift, man. Take her; I know she's in good hands. Bring her back when you can." He squinted heavily at Ben. "Some heavy shit going down, man?"

Ben smiled back, "Yeah, you could say. I appreciate this."

"No sweat, man."

Tank stood staring after Ben as he straddled the monster bike, fastened the helmet, slammed down the visor, raised his hand, opened the throttle fully and roared off.

The road to Brookstone Cottage was eaten up mile after mile in record time, as Ben pushed the bike to its limit, taking corners with hardly any margin and opening the bike up fully immediately afterwards. Mike had fifteen minutes head start on him, but the bike was making up time, being able to overtake slower vehicles on the narrow road and Ben breaking every speed limit.

He pulled the bike to a halt outside Mike and Beth's cottage, switched off the engine and kicked the stand into place. His heart was full of dread as he took off the helmet and looked at the quiet cottage; the too-quiet cottage. Mike's car was parked in its usual position and as Ben passed it, he put his hand on the bonnet. Still hot. Mike could hardly have been home more than a moment or so. The front door stood wide open and Ben strode inside.

"Mike?"

There was no reply. He pushed open the door to the sitting room. Mike was standing like a statue, frozen in time, staring at a piece of paper. Ben walked over to him and put a hand on his arm, ready for a violent reaction.

"Mike?"

"Raaaaaaaaaaaaaaaaaaaaaagh!" The scream of rage and torment that came from Mike held the violence of an earthquake, making Ben recoil in shock despite the fact that he had expected it. Mike span around and thrust the paper at him. One word of Latin was scrawled centrally, *Captum.*

"Does it mean what I think it means?" Mike snarled through gritted teeth.

Ben lowered his voice, "It means 'Taken."

Mike turned away and steadied himself against the arm of the sofa. Words wouldn't come and Ben simply watched as Mike fought for control, and lost. His arm flew out and swiped the lamp from the table at the side of the sofa, and then, his fury unspent, he overturned the sofa too. Eventually, full of white rage, he turned and thundered, "I swear on my life, that if any harm comes to her, there won't be a demon safe this side of Hell, and then I'm going in there after the rest of them."

"I'm ready to show you how," Ben answered him. "And it's going to get bloody."

CHAPTER TWENTY: READY FOR BLOODY

"Good, I'm ready for bloody! First, I have to get Adain to safety." Mike grabbed the phone and dialled the number of Martha Treneglos, his close friend and Adain's godmother in Cornwall. They had sent Adain to stay with her only a few days ago when Mike had finally fallen prey to post-traumatic stress, though it seemed like an eternity ago. The flashbacks, the personality changes and depression coupled with the nightmares had taken their toll. His time as a helicopter pilot in war-torn Afghanistan had ended in a catastrophic crash which had taken his life, and only the skill of the medics had brought him back. Now, his new ability to see and communicate with spirits had taken another direction after Aberth, where his friend and mentor, Dai Bricks had been killed by the demon Astaroth.

He had killed the high-ranking demon and his 'bitch', to quote Dai, making him a high-profile target for every demon with a brain. Mike wasn't one to sit and wait for the fight, and now, with his family at threat, the fight was on.

Mike and Beth's daughter, Adain, was special. Very early on she had displayed telekinetic powers and had been a huge part in Mike's contact with Merlin as he searched for the ancient magician's manuscript. Adain had magic and it needed nurturing and controlling, which had begun behind the veil at Glastonbury on the ancient Isle of Avalon. Mike had no doubt whatsoever, that this is where Adain would be safest, and there was no one he would trust more to get her there than Martha.

The telephone rang in Martha's cottage in the village of

St Breward on the edge of Bodmin Moor. Mike could picture it, with its internal walls covered with Martha's precious books, that overflowed into neat piles wherever there was floor space. Adain adored Martha, as did he and Beth; in Crowsmoor, she had saved their lives in her no-nonsense headmistress way.

"Martha Treneglos." It was a statement, not an answer to the ringing, and Mike allowed himself the ghost of a smile.

He heaved a deep breath, trying to contain the wrath that was still sweeping through him. "Martha, it's Mike. I need your help; I'm sorry, but I'm bringing trouble to your door again."

"I rather thought so, Michael. If you hadn't called, I was about to call you. Adain has been very fretful over the last few hours, talking about 'something coming to get her' and 'something bad happening to her Mummy and Daddy'. What's going on, Michael?"

Mike swallowed the hard lump in his throat; already Adain had been affected by this. He told her the bare facts and then he cleared his throat and said in a husky voice, "They've taken Beth. And they tried to kill Jack. He's in a bad way, but it looks as though he's going to pull through it." He stopped short of the full story; there simply wasn't time to explain it all. He continued, "For God's sake don't let Addie know about this. I have to rely on you to take her to safety. And you. These sons-of-bitches are going for anything that I care about, and that includes you."

"I see. Do you have anywhere in mind?"

He could have hugged her for her calm acceptance of everything and allowed himself the passing thought that perhaps any demon trying to tackle Martha Treneglos would probably regret it. Even so, he wanted her as far away as possible. Then another thought took its place: if anything happened to him or had already happened to Beth, Adain was going to need Martha – for the rest of her life. Once again he allowed himself a moment to feel the intense guilt that underpinned his incandescent rage for doing what he did and thereby endangering not only himself, but everyone close to him. With difficulty he let it go; he had to. For now. Later, he would allow the guilt and the rage to blend into a cocktail of emotion that would drive him.

"Yes," he said. "There is only one place that I know of where you and she will be safe. I need you to take her to Morgana in Avalon; Adain is the daughter of the Pendragon and she is the future Lady of Avalon. There she will be protected and nurtured; she can stay with Jim and Rowan," he added, referring to his ex-policeman friend who had also found a home and a future on the Isle of Avalon. "And, as her guardian at this moment, you too will find a welcome there."

There was a pause before Martha said, "Spoken like the Pendragon, Michael. We'll leave immediately, though once Adain is settled I think I would rather come home. I have Cat to think about."

Mike's nemesis was Cat; the evil-eyed, lethal-clawed, thoroughly obnoxious, feline that shared Martha's cottage and her life.

"Take him with you. Martha, I mean it, I want you safe too. It's going to get bloody."

Mike could picture Martha standing to her full height, bulk, and considerable presence that had inspired instant obedience, or repentance, in her students as headmistress of the village school. "I think you know that you are mistaken, Michael, if for one single moment you believe that I will allow any foul creature, living or otherwise, to drive me from my home and my books. I will deliver Adain to safety, and I will return. You may have need of me here."

It was probably the longest speech that Martha had delivered for some time, being thrifty with both words and emotion, but he was left in no doubt of her intentions. He had no choice but to accept her decision, knowing from the start that he wasn't going to win this one.

"All right. Take her to Brighid's Mound on the edge of Glastonbury. Adain knows how to call the mists and the barge that will take you to Avalon. I have to go, Martha." He paused and swallowed the defiant hard lump in his throat again. "Give her a hug for me."

"Go and do what you do, Michael. And Michael ... get bloody, and don't spare any of them. And when it's over, tell Jack that I said he needs some Cornish air."

Mike knew what she meant; Martha loved Jack like a wayward son. He heaved a deep breath as he heard Martha disconnect the call at her end without further talk. And he also knew that already she would be talking to Adain about an exciting trip to Avalon to see Morgana again. At least two of the most precious people in his life were going to be safe for now. He couldn't allow himself the luxury of thinking any further ahead.

He breathed deeply and turned to Ben who had been watching and listening in silence. "I'm ready."

Ben's face was set in an expression of grim determination. "Not here," he said. "Take what you need and secure the cottage, Mike. You're going to be staying with me for a while."

"A while??" Mike demanded. "I don't have 'a while'! And what if Beth comes home?"

"Then your first lesson is this," Ben said in a quiet voice, "I'm the teacher here and it will take as long as it takes to get you ready for the battle that's ahead of you. Or would you prefer to rush in and get your head taken off at the first encounter? Up to you, of course, but I recommend you listen to me, or run like hell. And we both know you're not going to run, so shut up and listen up."

Mike's despair went soul-deep. He wanted to go after the demon that had Beth, but knew he didn't have a clue where to begin looking. He wanted to scream. He wanted to cry. He wanted to vomit. And he wanted to smash Ben in the face. He knew what he had to do, and he knew that

Ben was going to be the one to help him do it.

He suddenly realised that he had no clue as to how Ben had arrived at the cottage.

"How the hell did you get here? And right behind me too?"

"A friend lent me his bike. Now, let's go. I'll meet you at my place. And don't drive like a madman, you need to survive to at least fight these bastards."

Mike grabbed his car keys and locked the door behind him. He daren't look back; it would be the end of him. Night had fallen and Tank's beast stood gleaming in the moonlight, like some huge alien beast. Despite himself, Mike whistled as he took in the line of the bike and the over-sized tank that was custom-painted with the death's head.

"That's no bike. Jesus, Ben, that's a fucking work of art, a bloody masterpiece. You do this?" He asked.

Ben nodded; a half-smile of pride on his lips that disappeared, in his inherent modesty, almost immediately.

"Yes. Now, can we go?"

Mike got behind the wheel of his Volvo and a sudden realisation swept over him. He was going to need a different car. Something heavy and capable of anything, a 4x4, a tank, and it was going to need some customisation from Ben.

He tried to lighten his sorrow. "Race you," he said.

"You just dare and I'll kill you myself," Ben snapped back.

CHAPTER TWENTY-ONE: LOVECRAFT'S RULES

Ben reached his cottage on the edge of Skenfrith ten minutes ahead of Mike, and Fred, his faithful old Rottweiler, greeted his master joyfully, which turned to ecstasy when ten minutes later he saw his favourite visitor. Mike petted the dog and generally made a fuss of him, allowing the moment to distract him momentarily from his immediate situation.

Greetings over, Fred returned to his usual place in front of the old range to await further instructions while Mike started to fill the kettle; anything to put off the moment when he had to face the stark reality of what was ahead of him.

Ben shook his head. "Not tea. Something stronger I think," he said, as he opened the old dresser next to the range and took out a bottle of twelve-year-old single malt. "Courtesy of Jack."

Mike replaced the kettle and took two heavy tumblers from the draining board. "Can't argue with that," he said, as he went to put the glasses down on an old coffee table in front of the sofa by the hearth.

Ben put the whisky on the huge old pine table and pulled out a chair to sit down. "Don't think about getting comfortable. Over here. We're going to start with some basic rules. Lovecraft's Rules."

Mike raised an eyebrow.

"Lovecraft's Rule number one: Demons lie. Rule two: Demons lie. Rule three: If you think they're not lying, you're wrong and probably going to die. Never, ever forget these first three rules Mike; you're life, and your soul, will depend on it."

The atmosphere in the cottage was becoming charged with deadly intent and Mike's temporary respite from it ended abruptly. He nodded at Ben.

"I get it."

"Oh, we're just getting started. You need to burn Lovecraft's Rules into your very soul, Mike."

Mike was silent as he took a hefty belt of the mellow, smoky, whisky. Jack always did have good taste in booze. It warmed him from his core and he felt it spreading throughout his whole body, allowing him a moment of comfort that was short-lived.

"Rule number four?" he asked.

"Rule four," Ben replied, "Exorcism doesn't kill demons; it just sends them back to Hell. Only certain objects, religious or sacred objects, can kill a demon. You wasted Astaroth with such a weapon; the iron blade created from the hammered out nail from the crucifixion. We need to go and see Beckett, by the way; you're going to need that blade. Rule five: Demons lie. Rule six: Demons don't die quiet. Oh and Rule seven is - Demons lie. Beginning to get the picture?"

Mike took another mouthful of the whisky, needing the comforting warmth that did nothing to take the edge off his despair.

"Yeah, I get it, demons are lying sons-of-bitches."

Ben raised his voice. "Mike, I know you're hurting but I'm telling this: you take these rules seriously because ignoring them will probably cost you your life. And maybe someone else's as well."

Mike sobered, "I'm sorry. You're right, but where in God's name do I start looking for her? Tell me that! Tell me. Because I sure as hell don't know, and if you can't help me, where do I go from here? What do I do next?"

"What do you want to do?"

"I want to kill every goddamn one of them, show no mercy and, in your words, get bloody."

"Then that's the place to start. Mike, a demon has

taken Beth, so it's among the demons you have to look for her. Where do you find them? Every-fucking-where; but you need to be selective, and if you can waste a few others on the way - result! You're forgetting something: they are looking for you." Ben raised an eyebrow, prompting Mike to examine his words, suggesting an idea.

Mike was quiet for a moment as understanding came to him. "So I get them to come to me. Bait. Are they really that stupid?"

Ben poured another small whisky into each glass. "Sometimes. But right now, they know that you're no match for them. You understand ghosts, restless spirits and just plain evil spirits, and you've encountered a demon or two and come out on top - even killed one of their heavyweights. There is a difference between evil spirits and demons: evil spirits were once human but can potentially become a demon, most demons are spawned in Hell, demon-born. This isn't just about possession either; there are many forms of this filth, from necromancy to voodoo to good old-fashioned black magick. And there is something else: once a human host is possessed by a powerful demon, even after exorcism, they are destroyed; their humanity is gone, and you need to focus on that when you kill them. And you will have to kill some of them, or they will kill you. You need to process that. You need to be better armed, Mike. Armed with weapons and armed with knowledge. And this is where we start. You'll be no good to Beth dead. Or worse. Trust me, Mike."

Mike's penetrating stare reached deep into Ben's eyes. And he did trust him, and he understood what could be worse than 'dead'.

"You saved my life once before, Ben. I trust you to do it again. Besides, Dai told me that I was to learn from you. It's just so hard to sit here talking when she's out there somewhere, with ... that!"

Ben's heart went out to him, but there was still something that he needed to share with Mike; something from his ancient past and his agreement after his fall from grace. He waited until Mike swallowed another substantial measure of the whisky.

"I told you about how I fell from grace, Mike. I told you that I agreed to come down here and find my redemption, and that you are my redemption. I told you I have no powers, no wings, and no angelic nature. I'm human. I know I have been by your side in past skirmishes, but the war is yours and when you are ready you will understand why. There's a lot to learn, Mike. Magic, Latin, Fighting - I already told you, you fight like a girl. But they have delivered you a huge advantage by taking Beth; they have turned you into something else. You are a hunter; a killer. And there will be no turning back."

Mike's face was deadly serious. Then, without warning, Ben launched himself at Mike and hit him hard on the jaw, sending him sprawling, dazed, onto the kitchen floor.

"What the...?" Mike had his hand to his jaw, his head reeling. He tried to get to his feet but Ben sent him down again with another well-aimed blow.

Bewilderment gave way to his earlier fury but, before he could react, Ben reached down to him and hauled him to his feet and put his hand on his shoulder.

"First lesson: from here on in you can't relax. Don't trust anyone and don't let your guard down. Some of these bastards can alter their appearance to people we care about and trust. You ..."

Further words were taken from Ben as Mike span around and planted his fist under Ben's jaw. His head jerked back but the huge biker remained standing. He threw his head back and laughed.

"Better. But next time put more of that pent-up rage into it; demons can take a hell of a punch. And just in case you haven't realised it yet, you aren't going to be getting sleep anytime soon."

CHAPTER TWENTY-TWO: BOUND AND TIED

Beth opened her eyes to darkness. It was cold, it was damp, and there was the constant, echoing sound of water dripping into a puddle. There was a smell in her nostrils that was familiar and yet she couldn't quite identify it. Her head was foggy and she felt sick, a feeling that wasn't helped by the sour taste in her mouth.

The realisation that she was lying on the cold, damp surface slowly filtered through the fog. She struggled to get to her feet, an action which revealed another truth: she was bound at the wrists and ankles. Eventually she managed to sit up and lean against a wall; it too was cold and damp.

She fought the rising panic and failed, releasing the cry for help that was sticking in her throat, out into the world. It echoed and bounced around her until it fell silent. Gradually the fog in her brain was clearing and she tried to blank out the fear in an effort to rationalise her situation. How had she come to be in this place, wherever 'this place' was? Who had brought her here?

The last question was answered in her subconscious almost immediately; she remembered only a blinding pain in her temple – a pain she did not yet realise had been caused by a demon overpowering her mind. Panic began to give way to anger and then another wave of panic – where was Mike? When she had spoken to him he had insisted she keep the doors and windows locked, and she had, until she had believed it to be Mike at the door. She shivered as the possibilities began to formulate in her mind. She thanked every God and Goddess in the Universe that Adain was safe with Martha, and then the thankfulness succumbed to doubt; she was safe, wasn't

111

she?

Then Beth gave an involuntary cry as she remembered something, the last thing, before she had blacked out.

There had been a man standing in the doorway: a tall man, with sharp features and dark eyes; black eyes. And she knew enough to realise that this had been no man, at least no human man. This had been a demon, and she was now in the hands of one of the darkest and most malevolent beings.

Beth had been taken by a demon before, when she had given birth to Adain and the thing had tried to take Adain from her. She had been near death then and Mike had saved her; but that was then and this was now. She had no idea where she was, only that she was alive; the burning pain in her wrists and ankles from the ropes, in conjunction with the nausea, told her that.

She tried again to wrench her arms free and felt the warm stickiness of her blood welling up between her bound wrists, intensifying the pain, as the ropes bit further into her skin. Eventually she stopped struggling, but the wounds on her wrists were deep enough now to keep the blood oozing down into the palms of her hands.

She had hoped that her eyes would become accustomed to the dark and eventually make out at least the outlines of her surroundings, but the darkness was solid, and her eyes couldn't penetrate it. The floor was hard and, combined with the cold and damp, brought Beth to the belief that she was in a cellar somewhere. If only she could identify the smell that was now permeating her nostrils and setting up an irritation at the back of her throat.

She was suddenly alert, listening to a far-off sound like a strong wind in the distance, and then flinched as the sound grew louder; it was coming closer. She began to shiver uncontrollably as the temperature, already cold, began to plummet even further.

The voice that came through the black space in front of

her was human, and it startled her until she recalled that demons could possess a human body, or replicate one; she wasn't sure which this was. It made no difference; a demon was a demon. Whichever it was, Beth chose to remain silent. One thing she had learned from Mike was that demons liked the sound of their own voices and, if you listened closely, then maybe you could pick up clues as to their agenda or even, in her case, their location. Malgron moved closer again.

She felt him come right up to her, but still she could only just make out the demon's outline when it was right in front of her and she was sure it was the 'man' that had been in their house. Still she remained silent, battling with the scream in her throat, determined that it should remain there.

He sensed it. "It doesn't matter if you scream. No one can hear you. You're cold. And afraid. You should be afraid, because before I have finished with you, you will beg me to kill you, to end it. And your husband will know how terrified you were and how you suffered. And that it was his fault."

Beth choked back her angry response and remained silent.

"You think you can stay quiet? I don't think so."

He leaned over her and she felt a long fingernail on her throat, felt it dig into her skin and slowly trace its way downwards towards her chest. She felt the warmth of the thin trail of blood that seeped out of the shallow wound. And still she didn't cry out. He moved his hand back to her throat and began again, deeper this time, dragging the nail through skin and leaving the red trail in its wake. Deeper and harder, until Beth was biting her tongue, knowing that she was going to lose the battle and cry out.

He lifted his hand and grabbed at her shirt, ripping it away and exposing her breasts and abdomen, as the cold intensified further. Again the fingernail traced its red path down her chest, continuing to the top of her left breast.

113

She held her breath, feeling the nausea rising and the scream edging its way to her vocal chords. She closed her eyes.

The fingernail bit deep into her and clawed its way across her breast. And she screamed.

A soft laugh came from Malgron's mouth. "You see. I told you that you couldn't stay quiet. And I've only just started with you. I can see I'm going to enjoy breaking you. Sadly, I wasn't given the opportunity with the other one, but there is time yet. They very kindly brought him back from death, so now I can enjoy breaking him personally."

Beth's mind was flying as her scream became a sob somewhere under her ribcage. Who was he talking about? Jack? It had to be Jack. Mike had said that 'they' had tried to kill him but that Jack was going to make it.

Malgron read her mind and laughed again. "I see you have an agile mind. Good. It will make it all the more interesting for me as I take it from you piece by piece. Maybe I won't kill you, maybe I'll return you to him, a babbling, dribbling wreck; a constant reminder of his mistake in taking my brother."

Beth could remain silent no longer. "He'll see you in Hell first."

Malgron laughed again, a laugh that was dripping with malice and ice. "But my dear, I have been there and as you see, I am free. There is now an open portal and, I and many other demons are now free to walk the Earth. Oh, he can try to send me back there, but he will fail. Do you know why he will fail? Because I will take you with me if he tries. I'll leave you with that thought, but I will be back soon. In the meantime I don't want you to die of hypothermia; there would be no fun in that."

He pulled her shirt around her again and then she felt the sudden warmth of a heavy jacket around her shoulders. A heavy jacket that had the coppery taint of blood on it.

CHAPTER TWENTY-THREE: THE BASEMENT

Mike went to pour another whisky but Ben's huge fist was over his before he could lift the bottle.

"Sorry. You've had your last until you're ready. Time's not your friend Mike."

Mike felt the white-hot rage welling inside him again, whisky-fuelled. His priority was to find Beth and bring her home; she was alive, he believed that. He had to. The alternative was unthinkable. He wanted a drink badly, but equally, he knew that if he went after the demons unprepared, or worse, it would be bloody all right; but it would be his blood. And he'd be no good to Beth dead.

When he was in Afghanistan, he'd learned to lock away things he would rather not think about into a remote part of his mind and forget it until he could deal with it. Civilians being bombed, innocent children caught up in a bloody, senseless war, that sort of thing. All of which tumbled out when his Post Traumatic Stress Disorder had kicked in, all contributing to his near breakdown. But he couldn't afford that now.

Mike was aware of Ben watching him as his pain and hatred filled him and took on a life of its own; his own demon being born right there inside him.

The muscles in his cheek twitched, pulling his scar down into a tight, dark line as the changes took place inside him. He could afford no emotion, no weakness. If he was going to get Beth back, he would have to become something else; something dark, because that was where Beth was, and where his enemies were. In the dark places. And there was a dark place inside him now; a place from where he would draw his resolve and his distance from his actions.

"Then don't waste the time," he snapped at Ben.

Ben didn't acknowledge him; he just stood up from the table and shoved it sideways to the wall, and then yanked up the rug that covered the middle of the floor, revealing what appeared to be a trapdoor. He reached into the pocket of his leather trousers and took out a key, bent down and fitted it into a lock at the side of the trapdoor, turned it and pulled it open. Mike's expression was impassive as he crossed the floor and stared into a dark void with a set of steps leading down into Ben's cellar. He felt calm and centred, knowing that the journey to bringing Beth home began there, as Ben flicked a switch on the wall, illuminating the dark void.

Mike needed no prompting as he descended the steps into a huge cellar, larger than the footprint of Ben's cottage, and extending outwards at one end into a dark tunnel. Ben had followed him and began turning on light switches, still saying nothing, allowing Mike to look around and take in the walls lined with books that he had no doubt were rare occult works worth a small fortune; glass cabinets full of strange objects, and a padlocked cupboard that spanned ten feet along the wall opposite the books. In the middle of the floor was a table with a lamp in one corner and a pile of books in another.

"Where the hell did you get all this?" Mike asked in awe.

Ben shrugged, "Let's just say I knew where to look and how to persuade the owners that they no longer required them. I may be human now, but I remembered a lot."

"Dai was right about you. He said there was more to you than anyone knew. Except Jack," he said, with an almost bitter twist to his words.

Ben shook his head, "I haven't got around to sharing this with Jack yet. He's had enough to deal with trying to understand what I was and what I am now."

Mike didn't reply. He walked across to the bookshelves

and began to scan the gold-embossed leather spines, the linen spines, and the rolled up parchments, before examining the cellar itself.

"The cottage was once used as a shepherd's cottage, but before that it was something else. If you follow the tunnel you come out underneath the church. The entrance at that end is well hidden but it was used as an escape tunnel by priests in the days of their persecution."

"I'm guessing you didn't find it in this condition?"

"It was essentially sound, but I did a little work on it, electrics mainly, shoring up a few falls in the tunnel and strengthening the structure generally, putting in heaters, and this..." he crossed to the far wall and opened what appeared to be a cupboard and pulled down a fully made-up bed. "You're going to be staying here for a while and then it will be your bolt-hole. I've warded it against demons or anything else that can slither from the dark. You don't need to understand yet, just know that while you're down here no demon can get to you. It's had a lick of paint and then filled with things that shouldn't be on display for untrained eyes."

"Like mine," Mike said.

"For now, but when I've finished with you, your eyes will be far from untrained, and they are going to see things that will make you want to gouge them out." Ben reached out to the shelf nearest to him and took down two heavy tomes that looked as though they had only been in a museum or ancient library prior to their latest home. He put them on the table.

"Start with these. I'm going to make a call and brew some strong coffee. You need to stay awake." He turned without further conversation and climbed the steps into his kitchen.

Mike stared long and hard at his retreating figure. "I don't get you, Ben. All this and you do nothing with it."

"On the contrary, I did what I was supposed to do with it. Get it ready for you. Start reading." He carried on up the stairs without looking back at Mike.

The book on top looked and smelled of age and Mike was almost afraid to pick it up lest it disintegrate in his hands. It was bound in soft leather with gold tooling and lettering, entitled Lemegeton. The pages were brittle and the ink faded into the browning leaves which he turned with great care. His first thought was that it was in Latin and that he had no chance of reading it, a thought which annoyed him greatly as Ben knew damn well he couldn't read the dead language, but as he continued to leaf through it, he discovered page after page of demonic seals, similar to the one that was now burned onto Jack's arm. But these seals seemed to belong to the big boys in the team as he recognised the names Ba'al, Belial, Lucifer and the rest of the bad boys in the band.

He placed it carefully back onto the table and picked up the second book which appeared to have no title. On closer inspection, it was a handwritten copy of the first book, and without knowing why, he knew that it was written by Ben's hand.

Inside the book were instructions for summoning and dismissing demons and other works of ceremonial magick. Now he was confused. He was supposed to be out there to kill demons, not summon them to do his bidding. He picked up the book and climbed the stairs. Ben had some explaining to do.

Ben was on the phone and so Mike seated himself at the table. He was tired – no, he was exhausted – and to sit somewhere comfortable would have been disastrous. Ben acknowledged him by raising his hand as he continued his conversation.

"... No. That's right, the works, crash course. Thanks, I owe you; bring the bike in for some TLC on the house." He replaced the phone.

Mike instinctively realised that he had been the subject of the conversation, probably because Ben had been looking directly at him the whole time; he raised an eyebrow.

"An acquaintance of mine. He's going to teach you how to fight, Mike. I told you ..."

"Yeah, I fight like a girl! Well, pardon me for not having had to brawl my way through life! But I can take care of myself!"

"You may get by in a bar fight, but this is going to be no Saturday night punch-up in a pub car park. You were a pilot, Mike, and while you may have done some stuff in basic training, it was a long time ago. And you may have enough stored hatred in you now to start the explosion but you need to be able to finish it too. *And* you need to trust me. How many times do I need to remind you?"

Mike needed no reminder that Beth was missing, God knew where, in the hands of God knew what, and he had the good grace to give Ben a brief nod in submission.

"So, what? Martial arts, Judo? Karate? What?"

Ben's deep booming laugh filled the room. "Christ, Mike! Demons fight dirty, so I've got you a dirty fighter for a teacher. And by the way, you'll probably be hurting at the end of it."

"Cheers. So, what does this dirty fighter do?"

"He's an ex-SAS hand-to-hand combat instructor from Hereford. He won't have time to turn you out completely but he'll show you a trick or two. Harden you up a bit. Built a bike for him that would make his mother cry."

"My God you know some strange people! And I thought you'd be teaching me to pronounce Latin and exorcise the bastards, not this."

Ben sighed. "I told you, Mike, once a demon possesses a human body, all bets are off, he or she will manipulate that body to do the most damage to you, and if you're going to survive you need to be able to take the punches as well as deliver them. So, Lovecraft's Rules – what's Rule number one?"

"Demons lie. I get that."

"Good, well, here's a couple more. Engrave them on

119

your heart. Rule eight: It aint dead until it's *really* dead. And that usually means taking its goddamn head off. Rule nine: Demons can jump bodies - so try to make sure the bastard is still in there before you take some poor sod's head off."

"I thought you said they were as good as dead once they'd been possessed for any length of time."

"I did, but I also said that you had to defend yourself and others. If a demon is in front of you and you know it's a demon, waste it. Or get wasted. I told you this was going to get bloody, Mike. Walk away now if you're not up to it. But if you want to see Beth again, get used to the idea that before too much longer you are going to kill someone. I can see murder in your eyes. You've already crossed the line in your heart and I can't bring you back, but I can equip you for the journey. It's a lonely road you're taking, Mike, and my guess is you won't play well with others."

Mike's jaw set hard as the truth finally hit him. And that was okay with him; he would do what he had to do, even if it meant killing to save his own life long enough to save Beth.

Ben nodded towards the book in Mike's hand, "Questions?"

Mike suddenly felt foolish. He knew he was up for the fight but he also knew he was ill-equipped and that Ben was the one to get him in shape, in every way possible.

"No," he said, "Just came up for that coffee."

Before Ben could reply the telephone rang and he grabbed it. "Ben Lovecraft."

His face was unreadable and Mike realised that he was holding his breath. Jack?

"Get your coat; we're going to talk to a demon. Jack's awake."

CHAPTER TWENTY-FOUR: THE COLLIERS

Bevan Hughes was drunk; extremely drunk. But not drunk enough to take away the memory of what he had done, or why he had done it. In fact, he doubted if there was enough alcohol in the world that would cut it.

The image of Rob Jenkins' dead body was indelibly sketched into his memory banks; the dead-fish eyes, clouded well before they should have been; the gaping mouth; and the smell, dear God, the smell. Just dead, Rob looked as if he had been in the grave for days and smelled like it too. And then there was Bailey Shaw fixing him with eyes that were blacker than the coal that the miners were bringing up, ordering him to dispose of the body and himself with no will to argue or plead, just locked onto those eyes. Eyes that were no longer the property of the mine owner.

He hadn't stopped to think about Rob's size or the fact that he was a dead weight, literally. He hadn't stopped to consider where the hell he was going to dispose of the body; everything was done on autopilot as if he had been pre-programmed to carry out the ghastly deed.

The iron door was ready to replace but Bailey Shaw was having none of it, which had given the miners the reason they needed to walk out. Bevan himself had sent them home but Shaw was adamant: get new people who weren't afraid of a few shadows and rats. It was all a mess, but it had given Bevan access to the Demon's Hole, and although he couldn't recall having dragged Rob's body into the cage and out at pit bottom, then down the long tunnel, that is exactly where he found himself.

The hole in the floor was still loosely boarded and he

kicked out with his foot, hoping it would move. It collapsed inside the hole, releasing a huge blast of fetid air that made him stagger backwards, almost falling over the body. He threw his arm out against the wall of the tunnel, retching violently but bringing nothing up. He had begun to shiver and his teeth were chattering as he dragged the dead weight towards the edge of the hole, gave it a shove and watched, in slow motion, as Rob Jenkins rolled over and into the hole. Bevan listened for the thump as the body landed; none came.

His stomach heaved again and this time he vomited, lurching against the wall for support, when something on the floor against the wall caught his eye. He leaned heavily against the wet rock and bent to pick it up. It was a watch, and on the back was engraved the words *'Pete' Peterson, To Dad With Love from Joan.* The answer to what had happened to the deputy was in his hands. He looked down into the hole and, without further thought, tossed the watch in after Rob Jenkins.

Bevan turned to leave and then thought about the open hole. It should be covered to prevent someone falling into it; *or something climbing out of it.* The images were too much and he began to run back up the tunnel to pit bottom. He threw himself into the cage that took him back to the surface and he was still running when he reached his car.

He floored the accelerator, throwing up gravel as he screeched past the pit-head baths and down the valley. He didn't stop until he got to The Colliers.

Morgan Jenkins had been the landlord of The Colliers for thirty years and was known locally as Morgan the Drink, a tongue-in-cheek reference to the old valley ways of identifying a soul when many had the same first name. He was drying glasses when Bevan walked into the bar and he barely looked up in acknowledgement. Congenial host, Morgan the Drink wasn't, but he served a tidy pint and was more than persuadable to a lock-in. Despite the relaxation of the licensing laws, old habits died hard in the valley.

Bevan parked himself at the bar and ordered the first of more than a few pints, which went down in swift succession, followed by a rapid flow of large brandies. As the bar filled with regulars, Bevan's state of inebriation increased and he began talking to anyone who would listen and then to anyone who had the misfortune to be in ear-shot.

A hand gripped his shoulder and he spun around too quickly, almost losing his balance and falling from the bar stool. If it hadn't been for the iron grip on his shoulder he would have been heading for the floor.

"Steady, Bevan mun." Idris Roberts stood at Bevan's side, all six feet and eighteen stone of him, pint in his hand and concern on his brow. "You okay? Don't usually see you in here. Had a few, have you? And by the look of you it's not because you're celebrating."

Bevan squinted through his alcoholic haze and the sight of Idris simply served as a reminder that Peterson was missing. He knew there would be nobody to raise an alarm other than Idris; 'Pete' Peterson was a widower and his daughter lived in New Zealand. But Idris knew he was missing. Idris knew that he hadn't come back up from pit bottom. In fact, Bevan thought, Idris knew too much.

Bevan tried to shrug his hand from his shoulder but only succeeded in falling backwards, knocking Idris's pint out of his hand and landing in an ignominious heap in front of the bar. A few regulars looked over briefly then carried on their conversations. Idris brushed the excess best bitter from his jacket and hauled Bevan to his feet.

"Come on, you. You've had enough, I'll take you home."

Bevan tried to shrug him off again, unsuccessfully. Idris had an iron grip on him and dragged him outside into the car park where Bevan continued to try and release himself from Idris's fist.

"Stop that, Bevan mun. What the hell is wrong with

you?"

"Me? S'nuffing wrong with me. But there's sure as hell something wrong down the pit."

Idris pierced him with a flinty stare. "What?"

Conscious of the fact he'd said too much in just that short sentence, and to the wrong person. "Nothing. Don't mind me, I'm drunk. Did you know I'm drunk?"

"Yes, stinking. But that won't wash. You tell me what's wrong down the pit or I'll drag you back down there myself. Think of it as the night shift."

Bevan went pale and for a moment Idris thought he was going to spew up the beer and brandy onto his shoes so he took a step back, but held onto Bevan by the shoulder.

"I've a mind to do that anyway," he said. "Have you seen Pete yet?"

Drunk he may be, but Bevan's instinct for self-preservation was in the ascendant. "Yeah. He quit. Said he wasn't going to work in the Demons Hole, no matter what. Said he'd had an offer of a job over the mountain."

"What job?"

Bevan shrugged again. "How the hell should I know? A job; that's all he said."

Idris weighed him up. "Why do I think you're a lying bastard, Bevan?"

"'Cos you're a suspicious, trouble-making asshole?"

The words were hardly over his lips before Bevan regretted them. The bulky miner gripped him tighter with both hands, lifting him from his feet like a rag doll, and Bevan needed no quick assessment to tell him he would lose if things turned violent. He was a thinker, not a fighter. 'Use your brain, Bevan' his mother had said, 'Use your brain and you won't have to use your fists.' Sound advice most of the time, but looking into Idris's angry face, he wished that he'd had a bit of practice, at least.

"C'mon. We're going down and you can tell me what you know. Or at least, what you think you know. Because

I'm telling you now, that iron door was put up for a reason. And it needs to go back. But I want to have a good look down there first. And you're coming with me."

CHAPTER TWENTY-FIVE:
DEMONOLOGY 101

Thoughtful silences were now a thing of the past between Ben and Mike, every moment needed to be spent in teaching and listening, so the journey over to Abergavenny and Nevill Hall Hospital was given over to theory.

Mike had met with and dealt with numerous troublesome spirits, learning the hard way: by experience. He had encountered a demon twice; the first time Ben had helped him and the second time, Mike had actually killed the demon. But he wasn't stupid enough to believe he had the ability to tackle every piece of filth from the pit alone. Knowledge was power in this case, and the more he knew and understood about demons the better. Besides, thoughtful silences only gave way to thoughts of one thing; - Beth - and he couldn't afford to lose his focus because then he was in danger of losing her for good. The darkness inside him was growing like a cancer, but he had to nurture it, control it and direct it, because it was this darkness, fuelled by his rage and despair, which he would use as his most powerful weapon. He didn't have the luxury of expressing the rage in any other way.

"So, Demonology 101," he said as calmly as he could manage.

"Well, the first thing is, they are not all-powerful. Don't get me wrong, some of the fuckers are mean sons-of-bitches that will rip you apart and take your soul in the blink of an eye. But some of them are stupid, like I said, and that's where you have the advantage. Even the low-ranking, stupid ones are a nuisance and can cause damage, but you'll find they are the ones that will respond best to a bit of heavy persuasion."

"By heavy persuasion I take it you mean torture?" Mike asked in an even tone.

"If that's what you'd like to call it. But make no mistake, Mike, they are evil. Don't waste any compassion on them."

Mike made a noise somewhere between a laugh and a snort of derision, "I don't think that's going to be an issue."

Ben frowned. "Try not to enjoy it too much. You need to at least *try* to keep your own soul intact!" His voice was sharp and censoring.

He continued, "Remember, not every troublesome spirit is a demon. The first one can be exorcised and released, the second one can be sent back to Hell or killed, but to kill it you have to know how and have the right weapons in your arsenal - physical and spiritual. You need to be able to intone the Latin rite of exorcism correctly; mispronounce it and the demon will see you as an amateur and pounce on you. You need to memorise the rite. There will be times when you are reciting the exorcism and fighting for your life at the same time, so holding books is out. And it's another sign to the demon that you're less than proficient at it and it will take full advantage of the fact. Many of the demons were once human and they have their own personalities, likes and dislikes and even their manner of speech, but don't believe for a moment they are still human and can be saved. You can't save a demon, Mike."

"I don't have time to learn Latin!"

"You don't have to learn it, just how to pronounce it and memorise it. I've put it on a tape for you and written out the translation so you know what you're saying. You need to know that to have a rock-solid belief in what you're doing; a moment's doubt, a second's hesitation, and if it's a demon worth its salt it will turn you inside out."

Mike allowed himself a smile at Ben's reference to a tape. Technology wasn't in his skill set, and he used a hand-held tape recorder that utilised small magnetic tapes instead of the new digital kind.

"Demand to know its name," Ben said. "Names have power and once you have its name, you level the playing field a bit. But keep in mind Lovecraft's Rules."

"Yeah, demons lie. So how do I know it's giving me its real name?"

"Because, you will command it in the name of God. *The* God; the creator of all things, not just the Christian God, or the Jewish God or any other God. Just God. Once you have the upper hand, it will plead and wheedle and curse, and that's when you know you're going to win, as long as you don't give it an inch."

Mike thought that he was unlikely to be giving it anything, except a close haircut that started at the neck. It comforted him a little. Not much, but a little, and he said nothing.

The entrance to Nevill Hall Hospital was on them and Mike sensed a change in Ben's mood immediately. Jack was his closest friend and he was anxious about him, but Ben was on a whole different level, and Mike knew there were no words that wouldn't sound trite so he let it go.

They were met at the door of the Critical Care Unit by Jason Ryan, the Charge Nurse.

"Glad you're here; he's asking for you both constantly and we were afraid we'd have to sedate him again. We don't want to do that unless we have to; he needs to begin his recovery naturally now."

Ben smiled at him and put his huge hand on the nurse's arm. "We'll try and calm him down. How is he doing?"

Jason seemed to hesitate before saying, "He's doing as well as can be expected. I believe that's the phrase I'm supposed to use but, frankly, we don't know why he's even alive. So we're taking things slowly and keeping a close eye on him. We ... we did a scan this morning, and it seems we were mistaken in believing that Jack had massive internal injuries. Apart from some heavy duty bruising, all his internal organs appear intact."

Ben beamed at him, "Well, that's good news. Thanks for all you're doing for him."

Jason Ryan shook his head, "That's just it: we're doing very little for him, except keeping him hydrated and fed. He's on a heavy dose of antibiotic as a precaution but he's refusing all pain medication, insisting he isn't in any pain. Does he have a naturally high pain threshold?"

Mike grimaced and quickly pulled his expression back into neutral. He had long teased Jack about being a pussy when it came to pain. A headache was interpreted by Jack as a brain tumour. A nick on his hand needed instant stitches and don't go there when it was cold and 'flu season. He had a moment's unease; if there was this change in Jack, what other significant changes would there be?

Ben was obviously keeping pace with him on it, and Mike could read his expression like yesterday's newspaper. "Jack's full of surprises," was all he could think of to say.

"Well, you can visit for as long as you like, but don't tire him. We've asked the policeman that was in the waiting room to come back tomorrow; we don't want Jack upset."

Ben and Mike hadn't given D.I. Gareth Jones another thought after they had left the hospital. Beth's disappearance and Mike's fast-track learning schedule had taken him from their minds.

"Does he need to come back?" Ben asked.

Jason shrugged. "He said there were some questions he needed answers to, but that they could wait. If you'll excuse me, I'm a little busy." He turned, almost as an afterthought, "Jack's been saying some pretty wild things. It's probably trauma based, but I thought you should know, and not be alarmed. If it continues we'll have another doctor come take a look at him."

Read 'shrink' for 'another doctor', Mike thought, and a glance at Ben told him that he was on the same wavelength.

They thanked the nurse and walked over to Jack's room without another word.

Jack was sitting up in bed, wires on his chest, a needle in his arm, and his head still in bandages. He looked anything but relaxed and calm, agitation showing in every pore. His expression changed the instant he saw them approaching.

"Jesus Christ, Ben, Mike, what the fuck has happened to me?"

Mike chose his words carefully. "You were in an accident, Jack. But you're going to be OK." He tried to sound casual but only succeeded in sounding pathetic.

"Goddamn it! I don't mean the accident. I mean, what the hell has happened to me since? What the hell have they done to me?" His voice was raised and there was a high colour appearing on his cheeks.

"Calm down, Jack. I mean it," Ben said, in a slow deliberate voice. "You need to calm down or they'll be sending you up to the locked ward. Understand?"

Jack took a deep breath in and his face relaxed a little, allowing his usual handsome features to fall back into place. Ben and Nike's presence were reassuring to some degree.

Mike and Ben had discussed whether or not to tell Jack about Bazaliel and concluded that it was probably best not, until they really had to. Mike thought that time had come and he spoke before Ben could stop him.

"They've done nothing to you, Jack. But you should know something. We allowed a demon to possess you."

Jack's face was a picture of shock and disbelief, then, as he saw the impassive expressions on both of them, his reaction went nuclear.

"*Really? Fucking really?*"

CHAPTER TWENTY-SIX: OPENING THE PORTAL

Idris Roberts kept a firm grip on Bevan as they descended in the cage to pit bottom.

"I'm telling you, Idris, this isn't a good idea. There's something bad going on down here. Real bad."

Idris didn't reply, just propelled him forwards towards the tunnel that led to the Demon's hole. The iron door still lay on its side waiting to be put back into place. Bevan shivered as Idris pulled him through the opening into the Demon's Hole. He cast a wary glance around him. *Was there any sign of Rob Jenkins demise? Was there anything to link him to the disposal of the body? Was there any sign of 'Pete' Peterson?* Satisfied that there was nothing to arouse Idris' suspicions he relaxed a little.

Idris steered him towards the gaping hole in the floor. "Do you know why I brought you here?"

Bevan shook his head.

"Because you're weak. Because you weren't strong enough to hold me. You pushed the body of my first host back into hell, and you ran. And now you are going to join him and the other one."

Bevan's mouth went slack and his eyes widened as he stared into the black holes that had been the eyes of Idris Roberts. He made an inarticulate noise in his throat as his balance went, sending him headlong through the gaping hole; the Demon's Hole, and the last thing he saw was the real face of the demon that now inhabited the body of Idris.

Idris Roberts, the real Idris Roberts, had known nothing other than being down the mine, working at the coal-face since he left school. He'd been a union man, not fanatical, but fair until roused, and when the strike in 1984 put a strangle-hold on the industry in Wales, culminating in the death of the pits, he capitalised on his large frame and worked as a bouncer in the clubs of Cardiff and Newport. Only the very stupid or the very drunk argued with him, and those that did regretted it instantly.

Now he stood staring into the Demon's Hole, knowing what he had just done without control of his body. He sensed the hitch-hiking demon, was aware of its actions, and could do nothing to stop it or evict it. He felt as if he was sleepwalking through a nightmare and for the first time in Idris's life he was helpless.

He had followed Bailey Shaw into his office to demand that the iron door be replaced. He remembered the stories about his name-sake and how he had become a babbling wreck after seeing God-alone-knew-what. All they could get out of him was 'Ysbryd Du', Black Ghost.

Now Idris had seen for himself the swirling black dust that the demon had used to manifest before taking possession of a human host. Rob Jenkins had been the first and he wouldn't be the last; the open Demon's Hole was too good an opportunity to be missed. He lowered his head and drew power from the gate to Hell itself and invoked the demons to rise up.

Venite ista Daemonia conspirata corruptione; Invocationem veneris ad propinquos meos! Via patet ad vos. Manifestus veniet!

Come you Demons of the Pit; Come at my invocation. The way is open to you. Come manifest!

Quia potestates tenebrarum terra ambulare iterum. Venite Daemones. Egredere de corruptione aeterno et manifesta. Venite!

So shall the Powers of Darkness walk the Earth once more. Come Demons. Leave the Pit of Eternal Suffering and manifest! Come!

A howling wind rose from the open hole and a blast of icy air was borne upon it. Idris raised his head again, his eyes now glinting with evil behind the black holes in their sockets. The howling wind grew in force and rose from the hole, gathering the coal dust with it that the demons would use to take form. The black cloud grew in size until it towered above him, and then it separated into the many demons that had answered his call. Each one of them sped towards the tunnel that led to pit bottom and from there they sped up the shaft and out into the sleeping valley.

The sound of a heavy footfall behind him made him turn around. Bailey Shaw stood in the entrance to the Demon's Hole, his eyes blacker than the darkest night. He simply nodded to Idris, words unnecessary as his thoughts found their home. *You have done well.* He turned away and left with Idris close behind.

Further down the valley at The Colliers, Morgan the Drink was concerned. He didn't normally interfere with his customers lives, preferring to stay aloof and behind the bar, answering only in monosyllables to their requests. Their business was their business – but lately his customers had been dwindling; not just his customers but his regulars, and that was hitting him in the pocket. Rob Jenkins, always voluble in the bar, hadn't been in that night, nor had 'Pete' Peterson. On a weeknight he may have dismissed the fact, but it was a Friday night and their presence was a given, right up until they had their fill and went home. And there was something else: Bevan Hughes never put in an appearance unless it was to a wake, and that night he had drunk himself senseless and been dragged off the premises by Idris Roberts; Idris, of all people. Idris, who always minded his own business, had taken it upon himself to haul the very drunk Bevan from the floor and yank him outside. Something was amiss and at this rate, his profits were going to disappear quickly. He made a decision to call time at eleven and go to see for himself what had happened to his most loyal of regulars before it spread. God forbid they had taken their custom to The Forge Hammer down the valley. If that bastard

Evan Griffiths was poaching his trade, there would be hell to pay.

Eleven-thirty brought Morgan Jenkins to the front door of Rob Jenkins terraced house; it was in darkness. He hammered on the door, his concern deepening. A deep growl made him halt his banging, and he turned slowly to face Sultan, Rob's huge German Shepherd.

"Easy boy," he said in what he hoped was a soothing voice that belied his trepidation. "Easy now. Where's your master, then?"

Sultan's low growl changed to a whimper as the dog decided that Morgan was friend and not foe.

"I'm going to have a look round the back, you going to come with me?"

He took a step towards the passage that went between Rob's house and the house next door. Sultan hesitated and then trotted behind him, keeping a wary eye on the intruder. Morgan was in no doubt that one false move would lead to a sudden and fateful conclusion to the encounter, and that he would not come out the winner.

The rear of the house was equally dark and anyone that knew Rob Jenkins knew that if he wasn't home he was at The Colliers, or down the pit. Morgan knew he wasn't at either. He tried the back door; it was locked.

Returning to the front he lifted the letter-box and called out "Rob? Rob, you home?"

The action was clearly not approved of by Sultan who began to growl again. Deciding that discretion was indeed the better part of valour, he stepped away from the door and took another avenue of investigation by knocking on the next-door neighbour's door.

It was answered by an elderly woman who Morgan believed was called Maggie, though he wasn't sure.

"Sorry to bother you so late, lovely," he said. "But I was wondering if you knew where Rob might be?"

She obviously knew who Morgan was, "You're from The Colliers, isn't it? Well if he's not at the pub, I can't say.

Haven't seen or heard from him since he went on shift this morning."

Morgan smiled and nodded at her. "Don't suppose you'd care to watch his dog until he gets back?" he asked tentatively. Her scowl was response enough. "No, all right then. I'll be away now."

The door closed without further conversation but the curtain at the adjacent window twitched, and he knew he was being watched until the old girl was satisfied that he'd actually left. Sultan followed him.

"Hungry are you?" he asked the dog, as if he expected the mutt to reply, 'Yeah, bloody starving!' "Okay then, you'd best come with me. Get in," he said as he opened the car door wide. "And don't piss in my car or I'll skin you alive." He got into the driver's seat and hesitated before starting the engine. What if Rob came back and found the dog missing? He rummaged around in the glove compartment and found a scrap of paper and pencil and scrawled a quick note. 'Rob, I've got your dog at the pub. Morgan the Drink.'

Twitching curtain; old Maggie was still doing her bit for Neighbourhood Watch. He shoved the note through the door and drove away, wondering how long the old woman would stay at the window.

'Pete' Peterson's cottage at the end of the village was similarly dark. Morgan frowned. Both were grown men and to report them missing would probably get him laughed out of the cop shop, but both were creatures of habit and there was something causing a nag in his stomach. He decided to risk the ridicule. After all, there may have been an accident at the pit; but then everyone would be talking about it. No; something wasn't right.

CHAPTER TWENTY-SEVEN: INVESTIGATION

D.I. Gareth Jones looked up from his lukewarm coffee and laid the report back on his desk. He'd seen the report almost by accident as he searched the internal report on Jack's accident. If he couldn't get to speak to Jack, then he'd get as much information as he could before going back to the hospital. There was little more in the sparse report than he already knew, but as he flicked through other incident reports he came across something that made him sit up and read it very carefully.

Men were going missing in a newly re-opened coal mine not far from the mountain road which had been the scene of Jack's incident. He read it again and then made a decision.

He downloaded the files and claimed the investigation; to hell with the Super. No one else had shown any interest; these were grown men that hadn't been missing for twenty-four hours yet. And yet there was something that was making his teeth itch. For no reason that he could think of, he knew the two were connected.

The landlord of The Colliers seemed genuinely surprised to see him.

"Felt a bit daft, after," he said. "They made an official report because I insisted but they said that nothing would be done until they were officially missing for forty-eight hours. I mean, a lot can happen in two days." His eyes narrowed in suspicion. "So, why are you here now?"

"Let's just say I'm interested, that's all. Can you tell me if anything out of the ordinary happened, other than these two men going missing ... if they are missing."

Morgan the Drink shook his head. "Not as far as I

know. He hesitated. "There was one thing, but I can't see as how it's the same thing."

"Perhaps I should be the judge of that," replied Gareth, his teeth on edge again.

"Well, it was the same night; Bevan Hughes came in, looking weird he was, scared of something if you ask me. Well, he sat there and got slaughtered, didn't he? I was about to call time on him when Idris Roberts starts talking to him, quiet like. Then the next thing, Bevan's on the floor. Idris yanked him to his feet and dragged him outside."

Gareth considered it. "So, why was that particularly unusual? Friday night, the boys having a few too many, and a potential scrap?"

"What's unusual is Bevan Hughes doesn't come in here drinking unless it's a funeral or a wedding; and then only has a couple. And as for Idris Roberts, well, he never says a word to anybody. Sits in the corner minding his own business, has two pints and then goes home."

Gareth nodded to him. "Do you have the address of either of them?"

"Not addresses as such but Bevan lives in one of the new houses just before the main road. Idris lives in a miner's terrace, or was a miner's terrace 'til they closed the pits. Down the road on the left, somewhere in the middle. Anyone round there will tell you which one. So, do you think it's connected then? With 'Pete' Peterson and Rob Jenkins?"

Gareth ignored the question, thanked him and left, aware of the landlord's stare at the middle of his back right up until he had closed the door behind him. He sat in his car for a few minutes, thinking. Could the two be linked? He decided to pursue it; he had nothing better to do until he could get to see Jack. Mike and Ben had looked rough when he last saw them and, given the harrowing death of Dai Bricks in Aberth, he thought they could do with some time. Not too much time though; those teeth of his were in need of a mighty good scratch!

Enquiries pointed him to Bevan Hughes' house. There was no one home, but a neighbour told him that Bevan was probably at the pit, and gave him directions. Before that, however, he wanted to see if Idris was home. The itchy teeth had given way to stomach acid; now he knew there was something going on here that had the sickly sweet odour of something rotten about it.

Half expecting the same empty house, Gareth was surprised when Idris opened the door to him, filling the frame with his impressive bulk.

"Yes?"

Gareth flashed his warrant card. "D.I. Jones, Monmouthshire police. I'd like to ask you a couple of questions if that's all right?"

Idris didn't reply; he stood expressionless in the doorway, staring at him. Gareth persisted, stomach acid starting to give his ulcer jip.

"I understand you had an argument in the pub with Bevan Hughes; is that correct?"

A shadow flitted across Idris' face and was gone. "So? Against the law to have a difference of opinion now is it? Last I hear we had free speech in this country, bugger all else mind you. What if I did have a few words with him. Drunk as a skunk he was, thought I'd save Morgan the job of throwing him out. I took him into the car park because he looked as if he was going to throw up all over the bar. Stayed with him a minute, made sure he wasn't going anywhere in his car and left him to it."

"Would you mind telling me what the argument was about?"

"Yes, I would, but it looks like you're not going to give me any peace until I do, so I might as well tell you. It was nothing. He was getting drunker by the minute and it was pissing me off, all right? I go to The Colliers for a quiet drink and object to someone getting lary and spoiling the peace and quiet. Nothing more."

For a fraction of a second Gareth thought he saw a change in Idris' eyes. Maybe it was the light, or maybe not, but for an instant he thought that Idris' eyes had turned black. He'd seen that look before. In Aberth. In a demon.

He hadn't made D.I. without being able to think on his feet. Quickly.

He took a step backwards as Idris took one forwards, his eyes obviously black now. Gareth stood his ground, staring in to the black holes in Idris' eye sockets.

"Thanks then. If there's anything else, I'll call back. That seems satisfactory for now."

Gareth's heart was doing the can-can and his mind was in frantic search-mode for an explanation of the phenomenon. Was it something to do with working down the mine? Was it a rare eye-disease? Was it a demon? He remembered Aberth and the demons that had infested that village, and he remembered how, before that, he didn't believe in ghosts, ghouls, or anything else that went bump in the night. He preferred that blind innocence.

But this was obviously turning into an investigation rather than an enquiry, and he was well aware that he needed help from his newly-acquired outside source: Mike Travis. Men were missing, he was sure of that now, and Idris Roberts had more black inside him than coal dust. He dialled Mike's home number and let it ring for almost five minutes before hitting the call end button and cursed himself for not having his mobile number.

He looked at his watch; it was late; too late to go wandering down the valley to the pit, but he'd be back first thing. In the meantime, he needed to spend some quality time with a take-away, beer, and the internet; he needed to know as much as he could about the valley, the village and the pit.

CHAPTER TWENTY-EIGHT:
BREAKING THE NEWS TO JACK

Jack's voice was loud and panicked. "What do you mean; you allowed a demon to possess me? Christ Almighty!"

Mike put a restraining hand on his arm. "Calm down, Jack. You'll get us thrown out and you put back to sleep at best; or you'll have a bloody heart attack at worst. Let us explain."

Jack's eyes were wide and staring, his colour heightened, his breathing rapid and irregular.

"Listen to us, Jack," Ben said in as soothing a tone as he could muster.

Jack took a deep breath and settled back against the pillows. "Well, you'd better get on and exorcise the fucking thing!" he said. "You can explain later!"

"No," Ben continued, "I can't; if you'll just listen a minute."

"Can't! What do you mean *can't?*"

"I mean that if I exorcise this demon from you, you will almost certainly die." His voice was cold and harsh, displaying his own distaste and feeling of helplessness. "Jack, you were as good as dead. The doctors were ready to switch off the life-support. We'd been told to come and say our goodbyes. There was nothing more they could do for you."

Jack was silent, staring at both of them, waiting for them to say they were just kidding. As bad a joke as it would have been, it was preferable to it being the truth.

"This is important, Jack," Mike interrupted. "What can you remember about the crash?"

Jack closed his eyes, his breathing coming fast and deep, the monitor beside him replicating it in digital beeps.

Mike looked at it, and then back at Jack. "You have to calm down, mate. We need to talk to you and if you can't calm down we're going to be shown the door." Jack seemed to respond and the beeping slowed down to a steady rhythm.

Mike continued. "There is no time for us to explain the finer details now, but trust me when I tell you: it was the only way to save you. The demon inside you is called Bazaliel and he's there to keep you alive until you can heal yourself, *if* you can heal yourself. Look at your arm Jack."

Jack looked down at his arm as if he was seeing it for the first time. "What the hell?"

Mike tried to keep his voice low and calm. "It's the demon's seal, Jack. It means you have control over it. It can do nothing, influence you in no way, not speak, nor act in any way unless you instruct it to; just use its powers to keep you alive and help you to heal. And it's on its best behaviour, because if you decide you'd rather die than be host to it, it has to leave immediately and Ben will send it back to Hell."

"So why is a demon concerned with my welfare? Are you sure this is real? Am I hallucinating? They pumped enough drugs into me to keep me tripping for months. Are you even real?" There was an element of panic in his voice, reflected in his eyes.

Mike's face clouded over with compassion for his friend and an overwhelming sense of guilt; because, however he looked at it, it all boiled down to the fact that the demons were targeting him through people he loved.

"I'm afraid it's all too real, Jack. I wish it wasn't. Look, I know it's hard for you but you need to tell us what you can remember about the crash. And … afterwards … if you can."

Already pale, Jack's face lost the last of its colour. "I wasn't driving particularly fast; it was the mountain road, for God's sake. I don't have a death wish." His words hit a raw nerve and he swallowed hard and carried on.

"Anyway, all of a sudden, I had no control over the steering and the car just veered towards the edge of the mountain. I couldn't open the door and the key wouldn't turn the ignition off. I don't remember too much after that. I ..." He stopped and his voice cracked. "Oh my God, I *do* remember some stuff. I remember being out of my body and yelling for help. I was on the road and calling the paramedics and no one heard me. Then nothing until ... until I woke up and everyone was running round like headless chickens. Why can't I feel the demon? I don't feel any different. Oh God, what shall I do?"

Ben put his hand on Jack's shoulder. "Nothing. Just you concentrate on getting well and leave us to sort this out. But there's something we need you to do for us." His voice was low and caring, and his eyes told Jack that what he was about to ask was big.

"What?"

"We need you to allow the demon to speak to us."

"Are you fucking kidding me???" His voice climbed several octaves.

Mike felt the muscle twitching in his cheek as he fought to control his emotions and his voice. "Jack, they've taken Beth."

Jack's reaction was quiet and instantaneous. "Oh, Jesus. What do you want me to do?"

"I only know the theory behind this, I haven't tried it before," Ben replied, "But I want you to concentrate and mentally instruct him to communicate with us. Then you will feel as though you are asleep, but you will be aware of everything that he says. When you want to, you can cut the communication at any time just by thinking it. You have his seal, Jack. You are in control."

Jack closed his eyes. "You sure this demon ... Bazawotsit ... is not going to drag me to hell?"

"Not unless he wants to spend the rest of eternity down there with you. We made a deal, Jack, his release from the pit in return for him saving your life. It's a deal

145

we can break and send him back there at any time, and part of the deal was that if you didn't want any part of this, if you wanted to die, then he would be on the next train back there. You only have to say the word."

"And if I do, I die, right?"

Ben nodded. "Probably. Apparently you were a mess in there." He gave Jack a wry smile.

Despite himself, Jack laughed. "Then I guess I'm going to have company awhile then." He turned to Mike. "Whatever I can do to help get Beth back, you know I will. I love her too, you know."

"Just try and relax, and order him to speak to me, remember you have the control. He may have some answers, because right now we have no idea where to start looking for Beth," Ben said.

Jack looked scared but he closed his eyes again and appeared to be asleep. When he opened them again they were black as midnight in a moonless sky. Mike gave an involuntary gasp; seeing his best friend like this rocked him to the core. Ben gave him a warning look; they had to appear to have the upper hand with Bazaliel or they stood the chance of getting nothing from him. In any case, they were dealing with a demon and Lovecraft's Rule number one was uppermost in their heads; demons lie.

Mike shivered as Jack's vocal chord's changed in tone and timbre and the voice of the demon came from his lips. He wanted to be sick, he wanted to scream at Ben to send Bazaliel back to hell, to release Jack from the hold of the foul creature inside him; but he couldn't bear the thought of Jack in death, and he badly needed some information, any information, which might help him find Beth.

Ben's voice was harsh and commanding, and Mike could see that he too was having difficulty in looking at Jack without wondering if they had done the right thing.

"Demon, you will answer my questions and you will not lie. Is that understood? You know the consequences. Bazaliel, you will answer me. Where is Beth Travis and who has her?"

There was silence from the demon for several seconds and then he said, "The demon that has her, has her cloaked. I can't see her. But I can tell you his name, and you should tremble. Malgron has the wife of the demon hunter." He almost spat the words 'demon hunter', and Mike flinched; partly because the hatred in the tone of voice coming from Jack's mouth was directed at him and, partly because, despite the label, he was far from being a demon hunter worthy of the title. Yet. But there was a sudden lift in his heart. Bazaliel had said that the demon had her cloaked; that surely meant Beth was alive.

"I knew she was alive," he said.

The black eyes looked at him. "For now. Though, when Malgron is finished with her, she may wish she wasn't."

Mike lunged forwards, "Why, you son-of-a-bitch!"

Ben restrained him. "Demon! You had better be speaking the truth. I ask you again, where is Beth Travis? You know I have the power to send you back into the darkest corner of the pit!"

"And watch your friend die? Though he isn't strictly your 'friend', is he, Priest? Oh yes, I know you now, because I know my host. I know your secrets, Fallen Angel; only a heartbeat away from Hell yourself. But I have spoken the truth because I know you can do what you say you can."

"And what of Jack? You have saved him, now can you heal him?"

"Perhaps, but it will take a long time. But while I share his body, broken as it is, he has that time."

"Look again. Look for Beth," Mike demanded.

Again the black holes in Jack's eye sockets pierced Mike's own eyes. "All I can tell you is that I sense it's cold; cold and damp and dark. I cannot see where she is, Hunter."

Mike had reached his limit and couldn't bear to look at

Jack with those eyes any longer. "Stop calling me that! And you need to do better!"

"Easy, Mike," Ben said in a suddenly gentle voice, which changed the instant he addressed Bazaliel. "You may go. But know this, you will use your dark powers to heal this man, and if you harm him in any way, *any* way, you will be out of there and back downstairs before you can say 'demon'. Are we clear? Because, if you think I won't let Jack die then think again. I know he would rather be dead than share his body with evil. So, you had better keep your side of the bargain, demon. If you want your soul back, that is."

Mike was about to protest; to insist that Ben push the demon further – but, one look at Jack's expression as he struggled to push Bazaliel back into the furthest reaches of his psyche, made him back down. The two most important people, vulnerable in all this, were Jack and Beth. He had to keep that focus; it would drive him and ensure his survival and, hopefully, his victory.

Ben's expression and tone were deadly serious as he dismissed the demon in Latin. "Dimittam te, dæmonium habentem. Iterum vocatus respondere parati. Sub sigillo vestro permanebis." *I dismiss you, demon. Be ready to answer my call again. You remain under the control of your seal.*

Jack looked at them both with his own eyes, eyes that had the hint of a tear in them. "I'm sorry, Mike. He wasn't very helpful. You're no closer to finding Beth."

Mike frowned. "You heard what he said?"

"I heard everything. And you're right, Ben. I *would* rather die than share my body with evil. But right now I don't feel it and, besides, while there's a chance in hell, pardon the pun, that this thing can help then leave it be."

Ben nodded but said nothing. He simply leaned over the bed and planted a kiss on top of Jack's head, then stood back clearing his throat. But all of them knew that if it came to it, Ben wouldn't hesitate and, in some strange way, it was a comfort.

Jason Ryan brought their visit to an end, appearing with another sedative. The erratic behaviour of Jack's monitor and its rapid beeping had made his decision. It was time for Jack to sleep again. And this time, he had no protest from his patient.

As they drove away, Mike was quiet, brooding on what the demon had said. When his thoughts found voice, he said, "Jack was right, we're no further forward."

"On the contrary, we know that Malgron has her.

"So?"

"So, we have his name. Names have power, Mike. Remember? And we know all this is related to Aberth; Malgron is the brother of Astaroth, so we know what pushes his buttons. And ..."

"And?"

"And now we know what we're dealing with: one of the highest-ranking demons. Malgron is a powerful, evil, bastard. He's from the Malebolg; the darkest level of Hell; a class of demon called the Malebranche. So you'd better be ready."

CHAPTER TWENTY-NINE: STEEP LEARNING CURVE

Back at Ben's cottage, they were greeted in the usual adoring way by Fred, who always seemed to make his loved ones think they had been gone for a century. It didn't take long for Ben to encourage the range to flare back into life and the embers in the hearth to produce the reds and oranges of a welcome fire. It was not unduly cold for the time of the year, but they were chilled to the bone.

"Don't get cosy," Ben said. "You need to hit the books. I'll brew some coffee to keep you awake." Ben's coffee was dark and thick and reminiscent of a cowboy's brew, but it would do the trick and keep Mike alert for the next few hours.

Ben followed him down to the basement, steaming mugs in hand.

"Start with the exorcism. You need to get it right; otherwise the demons will just laugh at you before trying to take your head off."

Mike stared down at the book in front of him and his heart sank. "Why Latin? Surely the same words in my mother-tongue will do the same thing."

"Maybe. But do you really want to risk it? Listen to me for the pronunciation." He began to recite the words of the rite of exorcism from the Catholic Roman Ritual.

"Exorcizamus te, omnis immundus spiritus, omnis satanica potestas, omnis incursio infernalis adversarii, omnis legio, omnis congregation et secta diabolica."

I exorcise you, every impure spirit, every satanic power, every incursion of the infernal adversary, every legion, every congregation and diabolical sect.

He continued, slowly and deliberately, through to the

end of the rite with Mike repeating it after him until he was word perfect and understanding the meaning of his words; because without understanding there could be no self-belief in his actions, and without that, he was - proverbially - stuffed.

"One question," Mike said.

"Which is?"

"Does this have the same effect not coming from an ordained priest? I mean, you were ordained, whether or not you left the Church."

"The Church would have you believe not, but that isn't the case. Never, ever doubt that, Mike, or you may as well start running now. Time for you to get some sleep but, before you do, I want to show you something."

He crossed the room to the huge cupboard against the wall, which still remained locked courtesy of a large padlock. Ben took the key from his pocket and opened the doors wide.

Mike made no sound as he stood staring at the contents of the cupboard; a veritable arsenal, totally illegal, and undoubtedly lethal. Eventually he gave a low whistle.

"No wonder you keep that locked. Where in God's name did you get all this stuff?"

Ben's expression was deathly serious. "In God's name, yes. Where doesn't concern you; what does concern you is that you get used to the idea that you will use them; some of them, maybe all of them. This isn't going to end overnight and it won't end once you have Beth back, because you're marked. Your life won't be the same from here on in. You're a hunter now, Mike, and when it comes to kill or be killed; you'll kill. This is a war, Mike, and there will be collateral damage. Put your military head back on; it will help you survive. It is a case of get them before they get you; get used to it or, like I said, head for the hills."

Mike took in the array of weapons in front of him; assorted knives, guns, a crossbow, several strange objects and blades of various shapes and sizes, an axe, bottles, crucifixes and rosaries, a dreamcatcher and a blade attached to a leather strap and mechanism. He picked up the latter.

"It's a wrist-activated blade. Twisting your wrist against the pressure point in the mechanism brings the blade out into your hand. Useful in a close-up fight for your life, but you need to mind your fingers, if you want to keep them," said Ben.

Mike strapped it above his hand and twisted his wrist. The blade flew out ready for action. His fingers remained intact. He turned to Ben.

"Why are you doing all this for me?"

"I already told you, I was given the chance to come down here as a human to help a human in his fight against the demons. You, Mike, I've been collecting this lot ever since."

"Then why aren't you a hunter, Ben?"

"Because if I was, the chances are I might not be here for you now. Demon hunters don't have a lengthy life expectancy."

"Cheers."

"Besides which, my instructions were clear: mentor you, teach you, provide you with information and resources. I can exorcise demons but can't kill them. If I do, I blow it and my deal is off. There will be no way back for me. It's your journey, Mike. What I mean is, you were always going to walk this path, and I was always going to be here to help you, I just didn't know it was you until you came here looking for an exorcist."

"So, what made you think it was me? You were looking for a hunter; I was a paranormal investigator that didn't know an exorcism from a Christmas carol."

"I just knew. And I was right. So let's get on with it. Try and get some sleep. You've got a hard day tomorrow. Ex-Lieutenant Paul Burryan is arriving at five to take you on a cross-country run before breakfast. Then, when he's finished with you, after some hand-to-hand training, we need to talk about your car."

"Sleep? Now? Who are you kidding?" His mind was in freefall at the information overload, the implications of what was ahead of him and, always there, Beth being held captive by some shit piece of hellspawn.

Ben shrugged. "Suit yourself, but if you want to survive the day with Paul you should think again."

Despite himself, Mike fell asleep; physically, mentally and emotionally drained. But, even in sleep, he found no peace.

He could hear Beth calling him in the distance and he was running towards her, but every step he took brought him no nearer to her. Then he was surrounded in flames; fierce, intense flames with tormented faces swirling around in them, and he knew this was Hell. His ears took over then, and he could hear a cacophony of screaming and wailing. He balled his fists and pushed them hard against his ears but the sounds were inside his head, leaving him no escape from the torment.

The image of Beth writhing in agony in the flames brought a scream from his throat that echoed into eternity.

"Noooooooo!"

Perspiration ran from his face and soaked his pillow as he tossed his head from side to side, mumbling incoherent words which ended in her name. Something grabbed him then, and his survival instinct kicked in from a great height. His fist flew up under the demon's chin, but it didn't move, let alone loose its hold on him. It was shaking him and worst of all – it knew his name.

"Mike! Mike! Wake up." Ben was leaning over him, his powerful hands gripping Mike by the shoulders and shaking him gently.

Gradually the demon's face drifted away as his consciousness took hold, replacing the demon's face with Ben's concerned expression that was seeping even into his straggly red beard.

"Mike, wake up, damn you!"

Mike put a hand out. "I'm awake, and I think you're too late; I'm already damned."

"If you're going to talk shite, you can talk to yourself. No one is damned unless they damn themselves." He let go of Mike who was on his feet in an instant. "You're on the side of the good guys, and you'd better not forget that."

"I've got a feeling I'm going to have to remind myself of that a lot." He looked at his watch. It was four o'clock. "Well I guess I should be getting up anyway. Any chance of bacon and all the trimmings?"

Ben grinned at him. "Not unless you want to be throwing up in a hedge. Can't say that would impress Paul much.

A mug of Ben's thick, dark, cowboy coffee stood steaming on the kitchen table next to a pile of old books; Ben obviously hadn't been to bed. Mike picked up the coffee and took a gulp, ignoring the burning in his throat.

"What've you been looking at?"

Ben grabbed his coffee from the edge of the range and joined him at the table. "I've been trying to get information about Malgron. He *is* Astaroth's brother; the meaner half. And that's saying something. As I thought, he's a Malebranche from the Malebolg; the deepest level of Hell. Which means …"

"Which means," Mike interrupted, "I need to know how to kill this mother."

Ben sighed. "Which *means* he'll be using the lower demons to do his dirty work. If I'm right, there will be a lot more demons roaming around up here than there were before. If they've found a way out, and they obviously have, they'll be making the most of their freedom and God help anyone who they fancy for a host. As for Malgron, he'll be watching and waiting, as the demons wreak havoc up here. And you …"

Mike interrupted again, "And I will know that innocent people will be dying because this stinking pile of filth wants me to know that it's my fault. But you know what? It isn't. It *bloody well isn't!* I didn't let the bastards out, but I'm damn sure I'm going to put them back in – if they survive.

CHAPTER THIRTY: MOVING BETH

Beth opened her eyes again, still groggy and disorientated. There was a heavy, sick feeling in the pit of her stomach and she gave a dry heave as she remembered her situation. She strained to listen, pushing all her senses outward in search of information.

She was alone; she was sure of it. Her preliminary struggle had let her know she was still tightly bound, and trying to pull her hands free only served to open up the wounds on her wrists; she felt the warm trickle of blood over the caked red rivulets that already streaked her hands and wrists, felt it pool around the fingers, slick under her wedding ring. The feel of it brought Mike to the forefront of her thoughts. He'd be searching for her. He'd be looking everywhere, and eventually he would come there and find her.

But what if he was too late? What if the demon moved her? She needed to leave him something to tell him she had been there. Straining to get her fingers together, she hooked her nail under her ring and pushed as hard as the ropes would allow. She felt the ring move up sharply against the slick of blood beneath it, and suddenly it was off, hitting the ground with a metallic clink. She stopped struggling against the ropes, but her mind was still working.

The words of the Rite of Exorcism were beginning to play around in her head. She had been a priest, but had lost her faith in the Church and its hypocrisies. Could she still use the prayers? Surely if they came from the very soul, they wouldn't be ignored. Beth had been an Anglican priest, where the Roman Catholic rites of exorcism were considered too extreme, and there had developed a watered-down version in the forms of blessings and prayers for peace. But there hadn't been anyone in her group in college that hadn't delved into the Roman Ritual at some time or other. Her included. She struggled now to bring those Latin words to the forefront of her mind.

The sound of heavy footsteps approaching and a plummet in the already cold atmosphere sent any warmth from her body which had managed to survive out into the frigid air.

Malgron had a taste for the theatrical and had decided to let Beth see his true form because, after all, he was going to kill her eventually. But he wanted to have fun first; he wanted to see how long it would take her to lose her mind.

She tried to swallow but couldn't; every part of her was paralysed at the sight of him.

Humanoid in form, with a dark, red, leathery skin, he stood over seven feet tall. His face and skull were triangular with spines protruding along both sides. He opened his mouth and his long forked tongued licked towards her, making her shut her eyes and flinch for just a second, before she fought back with every ounce of inner strength.

She forced herself to look at Malgron again. His reptilian skin continued from his head down over his entire body, with spines protruding at intervals over the red surface that was studded with pustules. His hands and feet both ended in filthy talons that would take out an eye in a heartbeat, and a heart in the blink of an eye.

She drew a deep breath and began to recite the words that were slowly coming back to her in their English translation.

"I exorcise you, unclean …"

Talons flexed, Malgron's hand came flying through the air and connected with her lower jaw, sending her flying back against the damp wall.

"… unclean spirit …"

Another blow rendered her senseless and totally compliant as Malgron assumed the human form of Bailey Shaw again. He leaned over Beth's inert body and placed his hand centrally on her forehead, sending her into a deep oblivion that would last many hours. Word had got around the valley faster than smoke on the wind, and everyone was talking about 'Pete' Peterson going missing and no one had seen Bevan Hughes either. Had to be the Demon's Hole, they said. Malgron knew it was time to relocate and he needed her so deeply unconscious that he'd be able to transport her with ease - his only regret that, whilst she was unconscious, she wasn't suffering.

He was angry; this had been a perfect place to keep her. No one was going to venture back near the Demon's Hole for some time to come, if ever. He'd have peace to carry out his perverted tortures – or, would have before someone had interfered and brought the police to Idris' door. It would only be a matter of time before they poked their heads down the mine.

He heaved her upright, her head lolling onto her chest in her unconsciousness, and tossed her over his shoulder as if she had been a thin summer jacket.

He reached out and yanked the doors of the cage shut, leaving them rimed with a coating of ice. At the surface, all was in darkness with only the security light throwing a small pool of light around the door. He was through it and at Bailey Shaw's Mercedes before any human eye could process movement. He flung Beth across the rear seat and took off. He knew exactly where he was going to take her. There were several adits and air shafts surfacing on the mountain known locally as 'The British'. Apart from dog walkers, few and far between at this time of year, he was more or less guaranteed invisibility.

But first he was going to pay a visit with one of the lower demons to the interfering landlord of The Colliers.

CHAPTER THIRTY-ONE: HAND-TO-HAND COMBAT

Whatever Mike's expectations of Paul Burryan had been, they were way off.

Instead of a hulking man, the ex-special forces Lieutenant was around five feet eight with a muscular build, sinews taut in his arms like piano wires. He was tanned and exuded rude health and hidden strength. His hands were hard as they gripped Mike's.

"Ready for a run, then? Let's see what stamina you've got? Ben told me you're on a fast-track to some decent fighting skills, so show me what you're made of."

Officer training and then pilot training had taken Mike's fitness to another level. To be a fighter pilot required skills and traits other than being able to fly the helicopter; he had to be alert, quick-thinking, quick-reacting, and at the peak of fitness. His accident and subsequent civilian life with a damaged leg, had practically wiped that out. He was still reasonably fit, his reactions were still sharp and thanks to the healing arts of Avalon, his leg was now strong again, so he was confident that he wouldn't embarrass himself totally.

It was an opinion that disappeared rapidly as the former SAS instructor took him on a punishing run across open countryside, rocky outcrops, through hedges and ditches and back over rough terrain. They were gone for just over two hours.

Inside Ben's cottage, Mike collapsed in a breathless heap onto the sofa in front of the fireplace.

Paul nodded at him. "You should have done that in just under an hour. But I'll give you one thing: you didn't give up. You'll do. Ten minutes to get your breath back, and then you can have breakfast before the serious stuff begins."

He turned to Ben. "He'll be fine, but he needs to build up some stamina; he needs to do that run every day."

"He will. Thanks, Paul; I owe you."

"We're even; I seem to remember you wouldn't take squat for fixing my bike a few months back."

"Ten-minute job; it hardly compares."

Paul Burryan dismissed the conversation with, "Even."

Ten minutes later, Mike sat at Ben's table with a plate of steak and eggs as per Paul's instructions; he was going to need every ounce of energy and strength before the day was over.

In the clearing of the small wood behind Ben's cottage, Paul demonstrated some of the basic hand-to-hand combat techniques. There was no way that he was going to get Mike up to anywhere near trained in the time-frame given by Ben, but he could at least show him enough to hold his own in a straight fight and maybe buy himself enough time to bring weapons into play. Fighting with a demon inhabiting a human being brings its own challenges; the host is imbued with tremendous strength, and a weedy paper-pusher can become a force that will send you flying into walls at twice the speed limit. Self-defence often means killing the host.

"Go for the most vulnerable areas," Paul said. "No Queensbury rules; use your whole body; kick, punch, gouge, whatever it takes to disable your attacker. Throw your punches from the shoulder, not the fist, use your whole body-weight behind it. The eyes and throat are particularly vulnerable, as are the delicate parts in the trousers; if you can land some good kicks or punches in any of them you will have the advantage. Momentarily. Ben said that demons recover almost instantly and are usually even more pissed off with you so, if you get the advantage, use express delivery on the weapon front. Follow through with your wrist-blade or crossbow. Nice equipment, by the way." He grinned at Mike. "Come on then, let's get this show on the road."

Mike was surprised at Paul's easy mention of demons but had no time to dwell on it, spending the best part of the next two hours on his back, with livid bruises appearing where his defensive tactics had failed. He was slowly getting things right when Paul threw him a punch that took him off his feet and he landed flat on his back, winded.

Paul yanked him to his feet, and continued the onslaught, peppered now with taunts.

"You think fighting like this will get your wife back? The demons have her, right? Can you imagine what they are doing to her? So, show me what you've got!"

Mike's rage erupted and his legs and arms found their targets, sending Paul to the floor, hard and heavy. He was on his feet again instantly but, with Mike's fury still in control of the fists, he was floored again pretty quickly.

"That's better. Use your rage as a focus, Mike. Refine it, hone it, and direct it like a bullet."

Another hour and Mike was exhausted. He'd hardly slept and the cross-country run had stretched his energy reserves to the max, now after three hours of what was essentially a one-sided fight, he was way past ready to call it a day.

Ben put another plate of hot food in front of him, which he devoured like a starving beggar, but if you'd asked him what he'd eaten, Mike couldn't have told you.

Late autumn dusk had arrived early, and brought with it tendrils of mist that draped the ground in a swirling carpet. It was damp and chill outside but Mike needed to be there, however briefly, to send Beth a message from his heart. *'I'm coming, love. I'll find you and come for you. And kill the bastards that took you.'*

Inside, Paul Burryan was taking his leave of Ben. "He'll be OK. He's no wimp, that's for sure, he's gutsy and above all he's driven. I'll be back tomorrow for another session, then it's up to him to keep training. "

With Paul gone and Mike too tired for study, Ben made a pot of tea and indicated that they should sit by the fire.

"You're too tired to study effectively, but we can talk about your car."

Mike sat down with gratitude, hurting in places that were a whole new experience for him. "I know what you're going to say. I need to change it. I already realised that. What do you suggest?"

"Got to be a four-by-four; you may have to drive over rough terrain to get to something – or away from something. And you may have to do it fast."

"You're talking a high-performance off-roader."

"Essentially yes, but with some 'modifications'."

"Such as?" Mike queried.

"Such as stuff that will get you arrested if you ever get involved in a stop and search."

Mike nodded, too exhausted to listen and too knackered to care.

"I've got the very thing in mind for you. There's the perfect vehicle at the car dealership on the Hereford road, about ten miles up. It's five years old and seen some wear and tear but nothing I can't fix and improve on. It's sturdy, manoeuvrable and it'll take something to catch it. I already called them; they'll take yours in part-exchange, the balance isn't stupid either."

Mike didn't reply; he was asleep sitting up with his cup in his hand.

Ben took the cup away and put his legs up on the sofa, covering him with a blanket before turning the lamp down and heading for bed. If they were going to have a cat in hell's chance of finding and saving Beth, they all had to be on top of their game. And demons don't play by the rules.

But he knew he wouldn't sleep, so he built up the fire and made another strong brew. There was a book he needed to consult; one that he hadn't been able to read since the day he 'acquired' it. It was ancient and written in

Enochian, the language of the angels. Since his fall he had shunned the connection to his old life but he knew that one day he would have to reach into his past and read the Enochian script. That day had come.

CHAPTER THIRTY-TWO: DI JONES

Men had gathered at the entrance to the mine well before their shift began at six. Their voices were mingled in various levels of aggression. They wanted the work right enough, but who was going to look after their families if they bought it, down in the Demon's Hole? Who was going to speak to Bailey Shaw for them now there was no Union? Was it worth the risk? Maybe Shaw would pay them a bonus for being down there. Rumours had spread already, and they were all muttering about 'Pete' Peterson and Rob Jenkins. They knew that Morgan the Drink had reported them missing, but they knew too that the police would do nothing until they had been missing for long enough to convince them that they *were* in fact missing. This was the mood of the miners when D.I. Gareth Jones arrived.

He flashed his warrant card at the nearest of the group.

"D.I. Jones, Monmouthshire police. I'm conducting enquiries with regard to a missing person's report. Do any of you know the whereabouts of Don Peterson? Or Rob Jenkins?"

"You mean Pete; he's known as 'Pete' Peterson. And while you're about it, you'd better add Bevan Hughes to your list. No one's seen him since last night either," the most belligerent said.

Gareth walked over to him. "And that would be unusual?"

The belligerent one sneered. "Hell, yeah. He's always smarming up to the boss - in early, working late, Shaw's lackey he is. Left early yesterday, got pissed in The Colliers, never made it home apparently. There's been nothing but trouble ever since they opened her up."

Gareth's questioning expression brought venom, "The Demon's Hole! Goddamn it, its name should be enough, but, oh no! The boss wants more profits so down we go. Well we aint going back down there. Not until that iron door is back up at any rate."

Gareth assessed the mood of the crowd and decided to go for the top. "Can you direct me to Mr Shaw's office?"

Belligerent One spat on the ground, narrowly missing Gareth's shoes. "Aye. Follow me, I want a word with him anyway; on behalf of the boys like." He strode off, with Gareth close behind him.

The miners were looking for trouble, that was certain, but was it justified? The mention of the Demon's Hole had sounded his alarm bells. There was too much going on to be coincidence and too many demons in the vicinity to be ignored. He needed to speak with Mike, but first he was going to have a look around, just in case.

Bailey Shaw's door was open and, after a cursory knock Gareth followed Belligerent One into the office.

"Police to see you, Shaw."

"*Mister Shaw*, if you please. You can go."

"I'll be waiting outside, if it's all the same to you. The boys want me to speak for them. So I'll be waiting."

Shaw nodded his dismissal and the door closed, none too gently. "How can I help you, Officer?"

Instant dislike and itchy teeth put Gareth immediately on the defensive. "Inspector, actually. Detective Inspector Jones. We've received a report that some of your workers are missing. I'd like to take a look around if that's all right?"

Malgron, inside Shaw, bathed in his self-preservation smugness. He had moved Beth; had spent the night sealing the entrance. Any demons who hadn't taken advantage of the portal being open by now didn't deserve freedom.

His cold eyes fastened onto Gareth as his lips stretched into the parody of a smile.

"Of course. Any help I can be. But 'missing' is a bit

premature, don't you think? I mean they're grown men with chips on their shoulders and they got paid yesterday, so I'm guessing they'll be back later with sore heads and empty pockets. Well, that's all right, it means they'll be back on shift again. Where would you like to go first?"

Gareth had the overwhelming desire to punch Shaw's lights out, but he said instead, "I'd like to go into the mine where they were working, please?" He knew he had no search warrant and it would be the devil's own job to get the Super to sign one; he decided to wing it.

"I've a warrant in the car, if you'd care to see it," he said with confident determination.

Whether it was Gareth's confidence or his own smugness didn't matter, the end result was the same: after a second's thought Shaw nodded and indicated that Gareth should follow him.

The easy acquiescence made Gareth wary; he knew he was on his own with this one. They made a stop at the safety office and Shaw gave Gareth a safety hat with a lamp in the centre and he gave him a self-rescuer to aid breathing in case of emergency. None of it made Gareth feel any better.

The journey down to pit bottom took a lot longer than he had anticipated and was silent except for the clanking and whirring of the cage and, as it juddered to a halt at pit bottom he was more than glad to step out of it.

"Which tunnel were they working?" he asked Shaw.

Malgron, inside Shaw, was assessing the threat level again. This copper nosing about was irritating him, but he knew that he couldn't get rid of him like the others; too many people knew he was there. He mentally scanned the scene again; there was nothing to connect him with anything down there. Rob Jenkins had disposed of Peterson, Bevan Hughes had done the same to Jenkins and Idris Roberts had been responsible for Bevan Hughes. Nice and tidy, no leads to him.

He was pointing towards the Meadow Vein tunnel and

its offshoot, the Demon's Hole, when the cage juddered into life again; someone had called it from the top. When it came back down again, Belligerent One stepped out; he wasn't going to let his quarry go.

Shaw turned his attention to him and Gareth saw his opportunity to make his way into the tunnel.

Christ! Men were working down there in the cold and damp, water trickling down the walls and he just knew the skittering sounds were rats running for cover. He shivered.

There was nothing to see in the tunnel and he had come to a huge iron door lying on its side; he stopped to have a closer look. Nothing jumped out at him so his pressed on; the tunnel forked just in front of him with the Meadow Vein stretching out into the distance; this meant that the fork in the tunnel must lead to the Demon's Hole. He took it.

'Hole' was about the right word for this dark cavernous opening. He shone his light around the walls and ceiling, finding nothing of interest; the same with the floor. He stopped his beam over a concrete patch right at the edge, bent down over it and ran two fingers across its surface. They came away damp with traces of concrete clinging to his fingertips. It was recent. Maybe this was what he was looking for.

He stood up and shone his torch around once more; better to be sure. He could hear Bailey Shaw's footsteps approaching and turned to meet him. As he moved his head, the torch beam from his safety hat caught something glittering on the floor against the wall. Without hesitation, he broke the cardinal rule of forensic investigation; he removed a piece of evidence from the scene, knowing without reasoning that it would be better if Shaw didn't see it. He grabbed at it and shoved it into his pocket, a second before Shaw stepped into the Demon's Hole.

"If you've finished here, I need to go back to the surface. It seems I have a rebellion to quell. I'm afraid that safety reasons mean I can't leave you here on your own, so if you wouldn't mind coming back up top with me."

A last look around the hole with his torch-beam satisfied him and Shaw that there was nothing to see; the blood had washed away hours ago. He nodded his agreement and followed Shaw back to the cage where Belligerent One was waiting. In the ride back to the surface Gareth couldn't help fingering the object in his pocket. It was a ring, a small ring and therefore a woman's ring. Way out of place down a coal mine.

His face was trained to remain impassive but the fingering of the object had not gone unnoticed by Malgron. Frustration made it difficult to keep his true-self from emerging; he would have to wait for his opportunity and, when it did, he was going to relish it. But in that fraction of a second, in the half-light of the elevator, Gareth caught a glimpse of the anthracite pools in Shaw's eye-sockets.

CHAPTER THIRTY-THREE: NOT THE FIRST COPPER

Mike's home number was still ringing unanswered, so Gareth resorted to everyday police work. In minutes he had the address of Ben Lovecraft, the other tour-de-force in the Aberth debacle; hopefully he would know how to contact Mike.

His number was unlisted and Gareth had no valid reason for demanding a warrant to obtain it, which left his only option to drive over to Skenfrith and hope that Ben was at home.

Mike had begun a repeat of the day before with a gruelling cross-country run, except that the breakfast, compliments of Ben, was absent. Mike scanned the kitchen and found the note that Ben had left for him. It was short and to the point, in Ben's characteristic way. 'Gone to hospital, Jack trying to sign himself out. Ben'

Mike cursed under his breath. Of all the times for this to happen, in his last session with Paul Burryan! He'd been pleased with his performance, making the run in an hour and a half; half an hour up on the previous day. He felt good and ready for further instruction, or punishment, to follow. Now he was torn. Should he go to the hospital, or carry on as planned? Ben was more than capable of handling Jack, he reasoned, and, with Beth still missing, his priority had to be her.

He grabbed orange juice from Ben's fridge and fried three eggs while Paul took a phone call.

"Don't rush breakfast," he said. "I have to go for an hour or so." He grinned. "You've got a reprieve."

Mike's reprieve didn't last long, as Gareth Jones appeared at the door, relieved to find Mike there. He didn't waste too much time with preamble.

"There's something happening down Pontypool way; a newly re-opened mine to be exact. Men are missing and I'm sure this is your thing." He paused, "You okay? You look kind of distracted."

"Sorry. What do you mean 'my thing'?"

"Never thought I'd hear myself say this, but there's some kind of evil down there. You know, supernatural kind of evil. I caught a glimpse of it in the owner's eyes. Black holes, just like in the movies." He dug his hand into his pocket. "I found this."

Mike stared at the ring in Gareth's hand, at first refusing to believe what he was seeing, and then he took it with a shaking hand.

His voice was ice. "This belongs to my wife. Take me there. Now."

Gareth frowned, understanding still a million miles away. "You sure?"

"I think I know the ring I put on her hand when I married her."

"Jesus Christ, Mike! What the hell …?"

"I need to get a few things together. You may not want to see." Mike pushed the table back and pulled up the rug and hinged door. Gareth seemed to accept the sight of steps leading down into a huge cellar as perfectly normal and then followed Mike close behind.

He gave a low whistle as Mike unlocked the cupboard doors and began throwing knives and a crossbow into a holdall. He threw in a rosary and a bible for good measure.

"You were right; I wish I hadn't seen this."

Mike spoke as he fastened the leather strap of the pressure-release blade onto his wrist. "So arrest me; only do it later. Beth was taken by demons yesterday and this is the first lead I've had as to where she is. Tell me what's been happening there, in detail."

Before Gareth could reply, there was a disturbance in the air and Mike spun around, on high alert and ready to lash out.

"Hold it, boy! It's me, isn'it?" Dai Bricks stood before him in all his spectral glory, brushing himself down as if he'd come through a rainstorm. "Still getting used to it, see. Listen to me, and listen fast. There's demons onto you, and they're coming here. Where's Ben?"

"With Jack. Dai, they've got Beth. I know where they were keeping her."

"You've got more pressing problems. You'd better pray you can remember what you've learned so far."

The temperature dropped rapidly in the cellar and they could see their breath. Gareth had felt the energy shift when Dai appeared but couldn't see him, though from listening to Mike - and he congratulated himself on this fact - he realised who he was speaking to and didn't show any reaction.

"That was Dai, right? The old chap that died in Aberth?"

Mike nodded and made for the steps, "Yeah, but he's not keen on the 'old'. Now if you want to stay and help, please do. If not, you'd better haul your arse out of here; there are demons on the way."

"Tell me what to do."

Mike gave a harsh laugh,"If I knew that, we wouldn't be having this conversation."

They had just pushed the table back over the rug when Fred went ballistic, barking and growling and snapping; then Ben's front door splintered inwards and crashed flat on the floor. Mike raised the pistol he'd grabbed from the holdall, as a tall, rough-looking man stepped onto the flattened door and into the room, one arm tight around Beth's throat, the other holding a knife directly under her chin. Fred launched himself at him, only to be floored by a single gesture of the demon's head. He lay at Mike's feet, whimpering.

Mike had no clean shot; any bullet fired would stand a chance of hitting her and, as the man's eyes turned to jet, he knew that a bullet would be useless anyway.

"Beth!"

"Steady Mike!" yelled Gareth, "He'll do it!"

She tried to lift her head and he could see a gash on her cheek and the already-purple bruise spreading across her eye. Red rage fired him forwards as the demon shoved the knife upwards and Beth fell to the floor, bleeding into a fast-spreading, red pool. Mike was on the demon in a heartbeat, bringing him down to the floor. A flick of his wrist brought out the blade and without a second's hesitation he sliced open the demon's throat and. like lightening grabbed his holdall, brought out a machete and took its head off in one clean blow.

Gareth and Mike both dropped to their knees instantly at Beth's side, just as she opened her eyes and started spitting and hissing at Mike.

"You filthy, foul, fucking pile of shit! How dare you take her form?" he roared, as the machete sliced through the air and severed Beth's head from her body.

"Jesus H Christ! What the …?" Gareth jumped back to avoid the blood shower.

Mike turned, splatters of dark black blood covering his chest, neck and face. "That's not Beth," he snarled. "It's a demon taking her form. Look at her hand."

Gareth followed Mike's pointing finger and his eyes rested on an identical ring to the one he'd found, which Mike had now claimed. So much for interfering with evidence.

Mike raised his finger on which he had forced Beth's ring, her tiny fingers even smaller than his little finger. "*This* is Beth's ring. There's a tiny nick in it just on the left of the stone where she caught it in the car door. Almost lost her finger. And then there's Rule number eight: It aint dead until it's really dead."

"Well, I think that they *are* really dead. I underestimated you Mike Travis. I won't be doing that again. Are they …? Were they …?" He shrugged, not knowing the right words.

Mike was shaking and his voice trembled, but he wasn't aware of it, running on a reserve, coming from he knew not where. "Were they human? Well, she wasn't, for sure. That was a demon with the ability to shape-shift; some of them can. As for him, I'm not sure. I think probably yes. Would you rather I waited for him to take off my head?"

Mike considered what had just happened and how he had reacted instantly, using his new weapons instinctively. It did nothing to make him feel any better as he looked down at the decapitated demon wearing Beth's appearance. He grabbed the rug from under the table and threw it over its head.

A foul-smelling vapour was wafting up from the decapitated bodies making them gag.

"It's probably better if you left now, before you can be an accessory. I need to get rid of these; they're already stinking up the place."

Gareth stared into Mike's eyes, searching for any sign that the horror that had just played out had had an effect on him. He found none. His voice was even again and his face expressionless. And that worried him.

"I'm already an accessory. But I'm not ready to defend you by saying you killed demons. They'll have me in the funny farm before I can blink. So I'll take that advice. Do what you have to do … and I don't want to know … . I'll wait for you at the end of the lane leading to Cwmpergwm colliery. It's on the sat nav, so you'll find it easily. Take your time and don't leave any traces. Jeesus! Listen to me, maybe I should check myself in anyway. Oh, and: I wasn't here!"

Mike smiled despite himself and the mess on the floor. "Don't worry, Gareth. You won't be the first copper to help me get rid of a body."

Gareth weighed him up, unsure if he was joking or not. Suddenly he *was* sure, and it scared the hell out of him.

CHAPTER THIRTY-FOUR: A DEMON-BEACON

Dai had remained silent during the bloodbath. He didn't even have time to tell Mike that it wasn't Beth before Mike realised it for himself. And his subsequent action had left Dai in no doubt that Mike was a quick learner with a hair-trigger, a burning rage, and now, because of Beth, no guilt.

"Low graders, see," said Dai. "No finesse, and no plan. They thought to torture you by him cutting her in front of you. I wonder if you hadn't got her ring on your finger would you have known it wasn't her? Would you have been so fast? Not all demons are easy to tell apart from the human they copy, or the human they inhabit, look. Chalk this one up to 'bloody lucky'."

Mike was breathing hard and fast, his heart pounding in his chest, the adrenaline still surging through him, his molten lava of rage slowly cooling to steel.

"Those demon marks on your chest are sending out a bloody beacon, isn'it? You want to hunt them instead of being hunted? You need to get rid of them, see. Holy oil masks them a bit, but it's not enough."

"Get rid of them how? They're permanent black scars inches deep, Dai. You know that."

Dai pushed his spectral cap back and scratched his head. "Aye, well I'm thinking you're going to have to burn them off. Or cut them out. I don't know! I do know that while you have them, you're a sitting duck. Whichever way you do it, you should do it sooner rather than later."

Mike's face was grim. He marched over to Ben's range where a selection of kitchen knives sat in their block. He grabbed the sharpest one and a couple of tea towels, ready to staunch the blood. Then he took hold of the half empty whisky bottle.

Dai nodded. "Yes, best be safe and disinfect it, isn'it."

Mike ignored the remark, pulled the cork from the bottle with his teeth and spat it onto the table, and then took a hefty swig from it and then poured some over the knife-blade. He placed the knife over the largest of the demon marks.

"Stop! What in God's name are you doing! You bloody idiot!" Ben's voice boomed out through the room.

He stood in his doorless doorway, Jack at his side looking unnervingly well apart from his pallor which, given his normal tan, was very evident.

"What the fuck happened to my door? Jesus, Mike! I left you in capable hands and come home to Armageddon! And what the hell on earth were you about to do?"

Fred, recognised his master's voice; and got to his feet with an expression that said he'd hit a brick wall and the mess on the floor had nothing to do with him. Ben petted him, his eyes dangerously dark.

Mike stood up and went over to them, arms outstretched. "Jack, this is the first and the last hug I'm gonna give you. You should still be in hospital, you idiot, but it's good to see you home." He turned to Ben. "I'm okay, thanks for asking. I need to get rid of these things," he said, prodding his chest. "You call me a hunter? Well, so be it, but I'm damned if I'll be the hunted, *and* easy prey, because I've got a demon-beacon on my chest! Dai's here. He's saying I need to cut them out or burn them out."

Dai stood beside Mike, nodding, when Jack beamed at him and came over.

"Hello, Old Man!"

Mike narrowed his eyes. "You can see him?"

Jack nodded. "Yep. Don't ask me how."

Ben growled, "It's obvious how! It's the bastard demon that's inside you that's seeing Dai. Spirit to spirit. But the fact that you can see him means he's out of bounds! And

180

Dai's right to a certain degree, Mike. You have to burn them out. Evil can only be completely destroyed by fire. You cut it out; some of it stays and grows and festers. We need to clean this mess up and then we'll do it. And then I have business with Bazaliel!"

Dai had slowly vanished in a shimmer and Mike's adrenaline flow was returning to normal. It was then that the enormity of what had happened, and the knowledge that he had faced his first demon solo, and beaten it, washed over him like a tepid bath.

The telephone rang and Ben answered it immediately. It was a very one-sided conversation, ending with Ben's 'I'm sorry. Thanks.' He put the phone down slowly, choosing the right words.

"That was Paul Burryan. Someone made a hoax call to him while he was here. Apparently, to get him away so that you were on your own when the demons came and, also, to keep him out of the picture so that he can't help you any more. He called me from the hospital; his car was run off the road and he's lying in the emergency department waiting to have two broken legs put into casts."

"One more!" Mike snapped. "Just one bloody more, that's all! And I'll take myself to their patch, walk right into hell and waste every goddamn one of them!"

Ben's tone was even when he replied, "In the meantime, you'd better give us a hand."

He and Jack had begun to haul the bodies of the demons out of the front door on the bloodied rug where they'd fallen. Mike took one side of the rug and hauled with them. The smell was intensifying and Jack's pallor was tinged with grey. They took the bodies to the rear of the cottage where the garden adjoined woodland. The bodies had to be burned, Ben said. And as they could hardly take them to the nearest crematorium; it had to be done there. Fortunately, demon's bodies incinerated at a lower heat than human flesh; they were probably combustible from being in the fires of hell for so long, Mike thought.

With no shortage of wood or petrol, there was an almost immediate conflagration. Ben and Mike watched as the charred remains burned to ash; bones too, proving Mike's assessment that they were demons that had shape-shifted and not possessed human bodies. Even the teeth had turned to ash. Ash which Ben would bury under concrete.

Inside the cottage, they found Jack sitting in front of the fire with Fred watching him warily, growling low, confused that one of his family looked the same, but there was something in him that was setting his hackles rising. He was looking at the Jack he loved, but he could smell something different. He continued the low growl despite Ben's chiding.

Mike suddenly realised that he hadn't told Ben and Jack about his lead, so he quickly brought them up to speed, talking as he was pulling off his bloodstained shirt and dragging a roll-neck over his head.

"Hold on," Ben interrupted him. "You're going nowhere until we've got rid of those." He nodded to the black scars on Mike's chest. "We deal with them before anything else. I should have made you do it before now."

He poked the flames in the hearth into a brighter blaze and then stuck the poker into heart of the fire; the significance of which didn't reach Jack until Ben pulled it out, glowing bright red and orange.

Jack stood up in alarm. "Really? *Fucking really?* You're kidding me?" Fred was on his feet too.

Mike shook his head and sat back onto the sofa, gripping the arm until his knuckles were white. "Got to be done, Jack. Okay, Ben."

Mike lost consciousness before the scream of agony had time to get past his lips and was spared the smell of his own burning flesh.

CHAPTER THIRY-FIVE: MIKE'S BEEN STUDYING

Jack's face was still tinged with grey. "Shit, Ben, was that really necessary?"

"Not only necessary, but overdue. He'll come round in a minute. How're you feeling? I wish to hell and back you'd stayed in hospital, Jack. At least until I know what to do about that goddamn demon making a nest inside you. There has to be a way out of this mess, and I'll find it if it kills me."

Without thinking, he looked over at the book on the table that was filled with Enochian writings. It had taken the better part of the previous night to even recall the meaning of the symbols and sigils, and he hadn't completely translated the spell that he needed to perform to protect Mike; to protect them all. Jack was especially vulnerable and, above all, he wanted to free him from Bazaliel. Only angel magic would do that and, without his angelic powers, he wasn't sure he'd have the juice to bring it off. He needed more time, and time was at a premium.

Jack was on the defensive. "I couldn't stay there; they were treating me like some kind of freak back from the dead. I even heard one of them refer to me as Lazarus."

Ben couldn't prevent the involuntary laugh that broke from his lips and it broke his dark mood. "You still need to rest. Look, I've got to go and see Beckett. It's all well and good that Mike at least has the rudiments of effective fighting, and his weapons will stand him in good stead, but he needs that blade. I'll have to beg Beckett for a long-term loan."

Jack looked puzzled. "Fighting? Mike? From memory I have to say he ..."

183

"Fights like a girl? Not any more he doesn't."

"And weapons??"

Ben's smile reached his eyes. "Come on. Let me show you the basement. I haven't kept it from you deliberately, it just never seemed the right time." He shoved the table to one side and pulled the rug from under it. Jack's instant interest was obvious and, just for one second, Ben wondered if it was indeed Jack, or was it Bazaliel that was interested? He hesitated, and then opened the trapdoor. It was too late to think again without hurting Jack, and it would only be a matter of time before he would see it anyway. And he couldn't bear the thought that he could no longer trust him without thinking first.

Jack followed him down the steps in silence and grinned at what he saw when Ben switched on the light. His gaze travelled to the pile of old tomes on the table.

"Mike's been studying?"

"He hasn't scratched the surface, but, yeah, he's been studying. It's a good job he's a quick learner."

Jack nodded, "He always came top of the class. I could never beat him." He started to stroll around the room, looking at the books and other arcane objects. "What's in the cupboard?"

Ben opened the doors wide.

"Holy shit!"

Mike's voice made them both spin around. "They're my toys, so hands off."

Ben went over to him immediately, his eyes on the scorched skin of his chest. "I'm sorry, Mike. It was the only way. You okay?"

Mike nodded without expression, despite the searing pain from the burns. "I'm going to meet Gareth at the mine. You should stay with Jack." It seemed neither of them was happy to leave Jack alone with his squatter. He sauntered over to the cupboard, almost too casually, and took out a sawn-off shotgun.

"Just in case," he muttered.

"Well, it won't kill a demon, but it will take the head off any host. Be sure, Mike."

"I'll be sure."

Jack's face became sombre the moment Mike had left. "Ben, I want you to promise me something. Promise me that if I lose control of this thing, you know, if I go all Night of the Living Dead on you, promise me you'll use that thing on me."

Ben turned away, unable to look into his eyes, unable to process the possibility. His voice was gruff, "It won't come to that; I'm working on it."

"But if it does .. ."

"It won't!"

Back in front of the fire, Fred seemed to have made his peace with Jack, but he kept wary eyes on him. One false move from the demon and he would go Cujo on it. Inside Jack, Bazaliel knew it too.

The enormity of what had happened to him, suddenly hit Jack head-on and he began to shake uncontrollably, and then he began to realise the truth of what they were all still facing. "Do you think she's still alive?"

Ben didn't answer for a moment, and then he said in a quiet voice. "Yes. But perhaps it would be better if she wasn't."

"Ben!"

"The only reason she is still alive is for Malgron to use her to make Mike suffer. He will be planning some exquisite torture, no doubt; if he hasn't started on her already. When Mike finds her, and he will find her, there's no guarantee that it will be Beth he gets back."

Jack's voice broke. "Have you told him?"

Ben shook his head. "No, but I don't think I need to; he's not stupid. If you won't go to bed and rest, at least put your feet up. I'm going to re-hang the door and then go to Beckett. I won't be long." He had no desire to continue the conversation that lodged emotions in his chest like a brick. There was a lot to be said for being human. This wasn't it.

Mike was grateful for the pain from the burns on his chest; it gave him a focus while he drove to meet Gareth. He knew that Beth was no longer down the mine, but his hopes were on finding some clue as to where she may be now. He didn't want to dwell on any other possibility, so the constant, searing pain was a welcome distraction from the dark thoughts of how this had all come to be. And, ultimately, how he had brought it to their door.

Gareth's car was parked at the end of the lane, where he said he would be.

Mike grabbed the holdall from the passenger seat and slammed the door of his Volvo, the thought passing through his head that it was another problem to be sorted. This was no suitable vehicle for his new purpose. He let the thought drift away as Gareth came up to him.

"I take it you've sorted out the mess back there?"

"Do you really want the details?"

Gareth shook his head. "No, thanks. It's enough to know it's done. I've been watching things here pretty closely. The guy with the demon eyes isn't here. There was a ruckus with the miners and he left. Most of the men left just after him but one or two of them are inside."

"You didn't follow him?" Mike demanded.

"No, I didn't follow the guy who I believe is a demon, because I don't know how to deal with it, and I didn't fancy having my arse reamed all over the valley. I thought it better to wait for someone who does know what he's doing."

"Well, sorry to disappoint you, but that's not me. If you haven't got the stomach for it, you should leave." He realised instantly that he was being grossly unfair to the obviously stressed D.I. "Look, I'm sorry, that wasn't fair. You've been brilliant, but this is going to get bloody, very soon. If you'd rather put some distance between you and it, I understand."

"*Going* to get bloody? Mate, I think that ship sailed out

of the harbour when you decapitated those two. I … er …suppose that was necessary, was it? Yes, stupid question. Come on, I'll take you down to where I found the ring."

"Did you say there were still some men working in there?"

"Yes, though it was strange really. The one who was protesting the most, and being a mouthpiece for the others, was one of the ones who stayed."

Mike clamped his jaws together and spoke through gritted teeth. "Well, I'm thinking his shift is almost over."

"What do you mean?"

"I mean, if there was a portal opened, then more than one demon is probably prowling around out here looking for a body. If he's possessed - depending on the demon - then he's long gone. If you're staying, you need these." He thrust a pistol into Gareth's hand, and a flask of clear liquid. "The gun won't kill the demon, but it may slow the host down, depending how much of him there is left, and that's holy water; aim at the face, preferably the eyes."

CHAPTER THIRTY-SIX: ONE MISSED PHRASE

Regardless of his protests about not being tired, Jack fell asleep soon after Ben had left. Fred was still unsure what had happened to one of his loved ones but had no intention of moving from his side. Jack was sleeping deeply and had been that way for over an hour.

A sudden and loud knock on the door startled both of them. Fred went to the door, alert and ready.

Before Jack could get to his feet, the door opened and Martha Treneglos stood in the entrance, looking like one of the Furies in tweeds and sensible shoes. She entered the room like a ship in full sail and covered Jack in an ample hug that ended as abruptly as it was given, Martha having no time for an excess of emotion, but she pinned him with her gimlet eyes that defied the whitest lie.

"What are you doing here? Michael led me to believe you were on death's door!"

"Hello, Martha," he treated her to his best grin and watched her get flustered for all of a second. She returned the greeting with her best *I'm the headmistress and you are in trouble'* look.

"Hello, dear boy. Well, are you going to tell me what's going on around here? And where are Michael and Benjamin? Leaving you alone when you're clearly in need of looking after! It's outrageous. They will have a piece of my mind. Well, it's just as well I'm here; now I can look after you."

Jack felt immediately cheered at Martha's appearance, in no doubt that she doted on him as much as Adain, seeing him as a loveable, roguish adopted nephew that had the unique ability to make her blush. In turn he adored her

189

like a favourite aunt.

"Come and sit down and I'll tell you everything." His face clouded over. "Addie is safe in Avalon, isn't she?"

Martha snorted, "Of course. What do you take me for? Now, what are you doing here? Why aren't you in hospital?"

He looked sheepish, knowing his answer was going to bring her wrath down on him. "I, erm, signed myself out."

"Stupid boy!"

"Martha it's complicated."

"When is it ever *not* complicated with you two? So, what happened, and is there any news of Beth? Start talking. I'll make you some tea."

She strode over to the range and put the kettle back on the hob, secretly delighted to see Jack alive and obviously on the mend, but unwilling to lose the air of authority. The boy needed taking in hand.

As the tea brewed she settled next to Jack on the sofa. "I'm not a fool, Jack. There is something very seriously evil going on here and you'd better tell me now rather than later, because you know you will tell me in the end."

Jack chose his words carefully. "It all started when we lost Dai."

Martha lowered her head. "Yes, I was very sorry to hear about that. We got on."

Jack smiled. There were very few mortals that fell into that category; Martha was economical in her relationships.

"What happened to you? Start with that."

He gave her the full tour, omitting nothing. She sat by his side, implacable throughout, and then something happened; something terrible. Martha Treneglos had tears in her eyes. She sniffed and put her hand on Jack's leg and patted him. "Well, it's a good job I'm here. Someone needs to care for you boys." She patted him again, unnerving Jack; he had never seen her like this. "Beth will be all right. Michael will find her and bring her back. How is he? How is he holding up? Blaming himself no doubt. Some people are called to deal with the evil in this world; Michael is one of them. Beth knows that. She always has, and she understands."

Wanting to change the subject, Jack asked her, "How's Cat?"

"Hmph. He's extremely displeased. My neighbour is looking after him and Cat is not speaking to me. A couple of cans of tuna will sort him out, deep down he knows better."

Jack laughed, the first genuine laugh he had managed since the crash.

"Good to see someone can make you laugh." Ben entered the room bearing a polished wooden box. He went straight to Martha and planted a kiss on her cheek. "Well, as you're in such good hands, I'll take this straight to Mike." He smiled at her with the genuine affection of an old friend, despite their fairly recent meeting; if he was going to leave Jack with anyone, he couldn't find better than Martha.

She cast a glance at the box. "Yes, dear, go to Michael. And tell him that I expect to see him back here unharmed. And Benjamin, watch him."

"Of course."

Ben wasted no time and headed straight out again. Mike's instruction for him to stay with Jack was born from his concern for his friend, and now that Martha was watching over him, his anxiety was for Mike.

"What did you mean by that - 'watch him'?" Jack asked, on edge again.

"There's a darkness growing inside him that he needs to control."

"He's possessed by a demon??"

She gave him a rare smile. "Only his own."
***

Gareth was aware of the change in Mike's breathing, as it became slower and heavier, almost deliberate; his demeanour was ocean-deep dark, and the jaded copper was mightily glad that Mike was on his side. The entrance to the pit was deserted and there were very few lights switched on. They had expected it to be cold, but the freezing air hit their lungs and came out again in a frigid fog.

It took a lot to unnerve Gareth but the utter quiet and feeling of desolation, combined with the freezing air, made him wish he was at home in front of the TV with a beer and a curry. "Should it be this cold in here?"

"Yes. It means there are demons here. Be quiet." The instruction was redundant and Mike knew it, the demons would already know they were there; they would smell them, but he wanted to focus his mind. The temperature dropped again as he jabbed at the button to call the cage to take them to pit bottom.

As it juddered to a noisy halt, he yanked open the cage door and strode out towards the man that Gareth had dubbed the Belligerent One as he crept out of the shadows; shadows that had not been there a moment before.

"So, you have come, demon hunter. That was foolish; but welcome." His eyes were coals, at home in their environment, and fixed on Mike; the voice thick and guttural - not the voice of the pissed-off miner that Gareth had heard previously. He felt his hand tighten on the pistol at his side.

The involuntary movement wasn't lost on the demon but before it could react, Mike had hurled holy water in its eyes, which resulted in the demon screaming in agony and rage - mostly rage; rage that brought the demon's hand flying out, pointing towards Gareth, who grabbed at his chest and fell forwards. Mike's reaction was swift and his first bullet opened a gaping hole between its eyes before Gareth hit the floor.

In a slithering motion, the demon lurched upright. "Can you do no better than that, so-called demon hunter?" His laugh lodged in the centre of Mike's brain and sent signals about tightening his bladder muscles to the relevant department. It was on its feet and coming in fast, and the sounds coming from the tunnel meant that other demons were coming to join the party; each wanting to claim him to present to Malgron; all of him preferably, but they would settle for parts.

Mike could feel the demon's icy breath as he twisted his wrist and extended his arm across the demon's throat. There was a look of surprise at first, and then, as a fine black-red line appeared at its throat, it staggered backwards. Mike aimed his foot centrally and, in a moment of insanity, its head wobbled and fell, rolling towards the oncoming demons.

There were three of them; Mike launched himself forwards, aware of Gareth getting to his feet, swearing like an accomplished trooper. His blade, already out and bloody, found its home quickly and dispatched the nearest demon in like manner. His confidence boosted, he spun around to meet the onslaught.

The other two halted and began to back off and, in a swirl of ice-cold air, their hosts fell to the floor as the demons left in a pall of coal dust.

The adrenaline was pumping through Mike's veins and arteries in a torrent as he grabbed Gareth by arm. "Go!" he yelled at him. "Get yourself out of here." And before Gareth could answer him he was running down the tunnel towards the retreating black miasma. For a second, Gareth considered doing just that, but apparently, his legs didn't agree and he was down the tunnel in Mike's wake before his brain could argue. He caught up with Mike just as he began to recite the words of exorcism.

"Exorcizamus te, spiritus, omnis satanica potestas, omnis incursio infernalis adversarii, omnis legio, omnis congregation et secta diabolica."

I exorcise you, every satanic power, every incursion of the infernal adversary, every legion, every congregation and diabolical sect.

Too late, Mike realised that he had missed a phrase

from the exorcism. The swirling black cloud was above their heads and from its core came a shriek of pure hatred. Gareth stood transfixed as the bank of coal dust separated and an arm of it flew into his face and disappeared. The other half fell to the floor and shot off into the tunnel which forked ahead of them into pitch dark.

Mike had sensed Gareth behind him and turned to repeat his warning, his words not finding voice as Gareth raised the pistol to Mike's face. His face was contorted into a mask of pain and confusion.

Ben's voice thundered from the entrance of the tunnel.

"Exorcizamus te, omnis immundus spiritus, omnis satanica potestas, omnis incursio infernalis adversarii, omnis legio, omnis congregation et secta diabolica."

I exorcise you, every impure spirit, every satanic power, every incursion of the infernal adversary, every legion, every congregation and diabolical sect.

The dull thud as Gareth's back hit the tunnel wall made Mike cringe, and when his body began to rise up against the cold rock and scrabble its way across the ceiling, something inside him grew a shade darker.

Gareth was crouched in the bend of the roof, hissing and snarling down at them. His crab-like movements were contorted and the sounds that were passing across his vocal chords could only have been spawned in hell.

Ben hadn't missed a beat as he continued the exorcism.

"Ergo draco maledicte et omnis legio diabolica adjuramus te. Cessa decipere humanas creaturas, eisque aeternae Perditionais venenum propinare."

Thus cursed demon and every diabolical legion I adjure you. Cease to deceive human creatures and to give to them the poison of eternal Perdition.

More snarls and guttural profanities spat from Gareth's mouth.

Ben's voice grew louder and more commanding as he fought the demon with his will.

"Vade Satana, inventor et magister omnis fallaciae,

hostis humanae salutis. Humiliare sub potenti manu dei, contremisce et effuge, invocato a nobis sancto et terribili nominee, quem inferi tremunt!"

Go away Satan, the inventor and master of all deceit, the enemy of humanity's salvation. Be humble under the powerful hand of God, tremble and flee – I invoke by the sacred and terrible name at which those down below tremble!

More obscenity and skittering crab-like movements accompanied a stream of foul-smelling viscous matter aimed at them from above. Mike felt his gorge rise; the pea soup moment that he had dreaded had arrived.

Amid the torrent of taunts and abuse also being hurled at them, the miasma of black dust poured out of Gareth's mouth and nose and in a second it fell to their feet, just coal dust once more. Mercifully, his body hit the deck only after slithering part way down the wall.

Mike was bent over him in a heartbeat, hauling him to his feet.

"Take him out of here. I'll be right behind you."

Mike's eyes tracked Ben's hand as he pulled what Mike concluded to be explosive, from his pocket. "I said, take him out of here."

Mike hauled Gareth forwards as quickly as he could, hearing the snap of the lighter as it fired into life. He was practically dragging Gareth and just made it to the cage. He dropped Gareth onto the middle of the floor, straining his ears for any sound of Ben returning, hearing nothing. Then, heavy, running footsteps brought Ben to the cage and he hurled himself inside. Mike slammed his hand against the red button that brought the welcome sounds of wheels and cogs which inspired a judder in the cage before taking it to the surface.

Ben hooked his arm under Gareth's shoulder and they both heaved him outside, semi-conscious and incoherent. They released him to slump onto the back seat of Mike's car just as an underground explosion sent a tremor under their feet. The entrance to the mine belched rock and stone dust in a filthy cloud as they sped away from the site.

As the cloud of dust began to settle, an accumulation of coal dust followed it, its particles beginning to find each other, slowly taking on the form of Idris Roberts.

CHAPTER THIRTY-SEVEN: FINGERS IN HER HAIR

Malgron's instructions had been crystal clear: "Watch her until I come for her, restrain her if you have to, but she stays alive. The longer she's alive, the more he suffers. This place is not safe."

"Where will you take her?"

Malgron fixed him with his most terrible countenance, said nothing, and left.

The demon inside Idris Robert's body smiled to himself. Malgron had said he could restrain her, not kill her; but he never said anything about not having a little fun. He put his head on one side watching her in her unconsciousness, wondering how loud he could make her scream. It was almost as satisfying just thinking about it - he was in no rush; he'd leave her unconscious for a while yet.

Her pounding head and the pain in her whole body from lying on the cold rock were slowly filtering through as Beth began her rise through the levels of unconsciousness. There were voices. One voice she knew only too well, but the other was new to her. She kept her eyes closed and strained to hear what they were saying.

So, they had moved her and were going to move her again. The one with the familiar voice was obviously in charge and her spirits lifted when she realised he was leaving. Perhaps the one he left watching her wouldn't be as powerful. Her mind was working overtime; there was St Patrick's breastplate; the prayer that had saved her once before. Then there was the rite of exorcism; she would do nothing until she could remember the words in their entirety.

She heard Malgron leave, and then she sensed the proximity of the other one; too close just to be watching her. The chill that started around her heart, spread throughout her body. The foulness of the demon made her stomach turn and she fought to control the threatened heaving that would give away the fact that she was awake.

He leaned over her and it took all her will to keep her eyes closed and her breathing slow and deep. And then she felt his fingers in her hair.

As the words of the opening prayer in St Michael's exorcism were live-streaming through her mind, she brought her tied-together legs up in the air and kicked out. The howl of pain was accompanied by a back-handed slap across her face, tearing the delicate skin over her cheekbone, followed immediately with another.

She knew the demon's instructions had been to not kill her, but just how far she could push this one, she didn't know. She guessed it wasn't far. His hands were in her hair again and she could smell his foul breath on her face and something else, something familiar. The connection came suddenly; she smelt coal dust. So, she had been in a coal mine, and now she could smell it again. It was powerful on the demon but more subtle in the environment, but enough to make her realise that she was still in part of one.

She closed her eyes and strove to divert her will away from what was happening towards sending her soul out in search of help. The prayer to St Michael the Archangel was searing itself into her brain and found her voice of its own volition.

"Most glorious Prince of the Heavenly Armies, Saint Michael the Archangel, defend us in our battle against principalities and powers, against the rulers of this world of darkness, against the spirits of wickedness in the high places."

The hand was across her face again. "Shut your mouth, whore!"

"Most glorious Prince of the Heavenly Armies, Saint

Michael the Archangel, defend us in our battle against principalities and powers, against the rulers of this world of darkness, against the spirits of wickedness in the high places."

He let her see his true form then and her scream died in her throat as she mercifully surrendered her consciousness again.

The demon's smile soon faded. Malgron stood beside him, fury emblazoned on his true face.

"You were told to watch her, not enjoy her! That pleasure is mine." He made a miniscule gesture with his hand and Idris Robert's body was flung to the end of the adit where it crashed into the rock face.

A dog was barking somewhere near the entrance to the adit. Then a whistle and the owner's voice calling the dog. It continued to bark. Malgron was furious; he hadn't wanted to take her to his territory just yet, but now it seemed as if he had no choice. He picked Beth up as if she were a doll and disappeared into the darkness of the small tunnel that would eventually open out into the main shaft and then back to the Demon's Hole. Travis and the copper had already been there with the ex-priest and he had lost two of his lackeys, and one of them had blown up the entrance to the Demon's Hole and therefore the portal. But there was another way in, and Malgron knew it. After all, he had taken the thoughts and memories of Bailey Shaw when he had possessed him; he had a blueprint of the mine in his head. He had to go back there, because that was where the portal was, and that was where he was taking Beth.

To Hell.

CHAPTER THIRTY-EIGHT: THE PEA SOUP MOMENT

Mike drove away from the colliery with his foot down as hard as he dare on the rough lane; Ben overtook him on his bike and waved at him to pull in when he could. That wasn't until they were back on the main road running through the village.

In the back of Mike's car, Gareth was moaning quietly, interspersed with profanity, and when Mike leaned in to help him, he flailed his arms in a windmill of wild agitation, pushing himself back against the seat in an effort to back away. Ben opened the door behind him and pulled him out of the car.

"Gareth! Detective Inspector! Stop. It's all right, everything is all right; you're safe."

Gareth eyed them with a wild stare, froze for a moment and then bent over, heaving.

Eventually he shook his head, "Thank you," he said, "It felt like I was in a morass of black treacle and I could see and hear everything, but I had no control over my body."

Mike sighed. "I kind of gathered that when you were crouching on the ceiling spitting pea soup. I messed up; I'm sorry. You have Ben to thank for pulling your arse out of there."

"From what I remember, you did pretty well with that bloody blade up your sleeve."

Ben nodded his agreement to that. "Yes, though you do need to smarten up on your Latin exorcism. One missed phrase was all it took, and that's because you haven't got faith in it yet."

"I do now."

"I don't want to bring you down, Mike, but those were

really minor league demons. You wouldn't have found the big boys that easy. And we're no nearer to finding Beth."

"You don't have to tell me that."

"I wouldn't be too sure about that," Gareth interrupted.

Two heads spun around in his direction.

"I don't know how or why but, for one minute, I found myself sharing the demon's thoughts. He was thinking about delivering you on a plate to Malgron and his train of thought went to Beth. She's still around coal, Mike, I could smell it, but it's not deep, I could feel fresh air and see daylight."

"Sounds like an adit," Ben offered.

Mike and Gareth both shot a questioning glance.

"It's an entrance to an underground mine which is horizontal or nearly horizontal, by which the mine can be entered, drained of water and ventilated. There must be a load of them scattered about up on the mountain. What we need is a map or chart of them; there should be one in the office back there. And I've been incredibly stupid. I forgot about adits when I blew up the tunnel; there are still ways in and out of the Demon's Hole through them. Damn!"

Mike was already climbing back into his car. "Stay here and wait for us," he said to Gareth, "You shouldn't drive yet, but you should be safe waiting in your car."

Gareth pulled open the passenger door and sat beside Mike by way of reply and buckled up. "Wherever you and he are going, I'm coming with you."

Mike took that to mean, *'If you think I'm staying by myself you have to be crazy.'*

It took only a minute to return to the entrance to the mine. Everything was eerily quiet as they tried the main door; no one had locked it after they left. Inside the mine everything was in darkness, but darkness has a variety of depths and the corridors were bathed in shadows. Gareth didn't move more than a couple of inches from Mike or

Ben, his face still pale and greasy with sweat.

Mike tried the door to Bailey Shaw's office; it was locked, and before Ben could utter a sound, Mike's boot connected hard with the lock and the door splintered open. The room was in darkness but there were moving shadows, swirling into a cloud of black dust, and they could smell and taste coal particles.

Out of the middle of the black dust-cloud, red eyes were forming and beginning to blaze out of the face that was manifesting; the face of Idris Roberts, his eyes now pitch, and obviously bearing a grudge.

He fully formed in a second, gaining strength and power by the heartbeat. He flew at them, fury - fuelled by his recent humiliation by Malgron - driving him, and a guttural roar emanating from somewhere deep inside.

Ben threw the light switch and bright light flooded the office, momentarily blinding the demon who threw his arm up to shield his eyes whilst roaring profound and disturbing obscenities. Ben then lunged at him and threw holy water into his screaming mouth, following straight away with a binding incantation.

Demon claudicatis! In nomine Dei et angelorum et in omnibus planis entia, lumen, meum et nunc absolvo vos manebit, donec religatos!

Halt Demon! In the name of God and his angels and all high beings of light, you are now in my power and will remain bound in this place until I release you!

He pulled a small wooden box from inside his jacket and grabbed the crucifixion blade nestling inside, and was on the temporarily blinded demon before Gareth could process it, or Mike get to it first, the ancient and sacred iron blade pressed hard into the demon's throat causing it to scream in agony as the iron seared itself into the skin.

"Tell me your name, demon!"

"Fuck you!" the demon growled.

"Tell me your name, demon!"

"Benjamin Lovecraft."

Ben pushed a little harder on the blade, bringing forth more screams and curses in a lava stream of obscenity.

"Tell me your name!" Ben roared, pressing the blade deeper. Blood so dark it was almost black began to stream down its neck. The demon opened its eyes wide and spat at Mike. He stepped back before the vile stuff reached him and, in autopilot, he slammed his fist into what had been Idris Roberts face.

"What are you waiting for?" Mike yelled at Ben, "Finish the bastard!"

Ben pressed harder and the blood flowed swifter. "Name!!"

"Buriel; my name is Buriel."

Ben's face contorted into the semblance of a grin; he looked at Mike with an expression that said, 'Back off, I've got this.'

"The wandering Duke, eh? No wonder you don't like bright light! One of the most despised of the demons, even by your own kind. Buriel! In nomine Dei et angelorum et in omnibus planis entia, lumen, meum et nunc absolvo vos manebit, donec religatos!

Buriel! In the name of God and his angels and all high beings of light, you are now in my power and will remain bound in this place until I release you!

"Go fuck yourself!"

Gareth paled as Ben's blade bit deeper into tissue causing the demon to writhe in agony and scream more foul curses on their heads.

"I command you to tell me where Malgron has taken Beth Travis!"

A sneer spread across the demon's face. "To Hell of course. Where else?" He gave a rough, coarse laugh. "Where you'll never find her, Hunter!"

Mike gave no warning as his body sprang into action and he thrust both of his hands over Ben's and pushed hard. There was a momentary strangled cry from the demon before the black blood began to pour forth in great gouts.

"Holy Mother of God!" Gareth steadied himself against the wall.

"Jesus Mike! I might have got more from him still."

Mike shook his head. "I heard enough. And the sight of him was an offence to decency."

Ben let the lifeless, defiled body of Idris Roberts fall to the floor. He looked across at Gareth's frozen expression and said, "Don't worry, I'll clean this mess up."

Mike turned on his heels and walked away.

"Where the hell are you going?" Ben called after him.

"Exactly. That's exactly where I'm going. To Hell."

CHAPTER THIRTY-NINE: IN HELL

Beth awoke to the sound of screaming; bone-chilling, soul-freezing, screaming. Howling. Wailing. In the dark. In the shadows.

Layer upon layer of the sounds of torment assailed her ears and she clapped her hands over them to try and obliterate the sickening cacophony of screams and wails, but nothing would take them from her brain. She suddenly realised that her hands and legs were unshackled.

And she knew where she was.

Hell is no place for living, breathing humans; they can't survive there. Maybe she was dead? Maybe she hadn't survived. Why else would Malgron have freed her?

She stood on shaky legs that had been shackled too long. Gradually her eyes accustomed to the dark and shadow, and her heart froze.

She had heard of the Hounds of Hell, but nothing she could have imagined came anywhere near to the terrible truth. Slavering and drooling, interspersed with menacing growls, the Hound stood before her, equal to her in height, with the body of a huge wolf and the head of a rabid pitbull. It pawed the ground, holding a posture ready to spring; once it did, it would be game over.

But it didn't spring; it just kept staring at her with red, baleful eyes, snarling and growling, and obviously appreciative of the lunch menu. Beth tottered backwards, expecting the Hound to be on her ready to devour her at any second. A sharp pain in her chest reminded her to breathe; not dead after all! She heaved a huge breath and it made her dizzy. She put out a hand to steady herself and found no support. And still the Hound stayed put.

A sucking sound and movement caught her attention.

She didn't want to take her eyes from the Hound but something was moving out of the shadows, something low to the ground, slithering towards her, writhing and winding and coiling it's body as it's head reared up, it's flat head all eyes, forked tongue and fangs; a Serpent of the Abyss.

Thoughts and images of her approaching death ran through her mind, galvanising her into action. She did the only thing that her body would comply with; she turned away from the horrors and ran.

But, she didn't run far. An invisible barrier brought her to a sudden halt, rebounding as if from a rubber wall that she couldn't see. She spun around, expecting to see giant, slavering jaws and slithering, coiling venom, ready to strike.

Neither had moved forwards, both were making threatening gestures and noises but neither of them had come any nearer. She processed the information, slowly at first and then, finding a hook to hold on to, she followed the train of thought.

Her eyes travelled to the ground.

She was standing in the middle of an inscribed circle, filled with sigils of dark magic. The impenetrable force-field made sense now, and why the Hound of Hell and Serpent of the Abyss had not made her today's special. They couldn't cross the circle. And neither could she. She was as much a prisoner as when she had been shackled down the coal mine. Only this time, she was in Hell, and she had no idea how she had come to be there, how she could escape, or even how she was still alive. She could ponder the metaphysics of it later but, in the immediate moment, she needed to find a way out of the imprisoning circle of dark magic.

But once she found a way, she would be immediate prey to the waiting Hound and Serpent. Not a win-win situation. Her thoughts went to Mike and Adain and hot tears found their release. She brushed them away impatiently. Tears would not free her. Nevertheless they continued to stream down her face.

Almost as one, Hound and the Serpent drew back from the perimeter of the circle. There was a subtle change in the atmosphere, as it became charged with icy malice. Rasping breath and heavy footsteps came from the shadows. Something was coming; something that scared a Hound of Hell and a Serpent of the Abyss. She was icy cold and shivering, her teeth chattering together, her eyes wide and searching.

She felt her heart seize and then respond to her body's need for it to resume it's pumping, her eyes filled with a horror that she would never be able to erase from her mind.

Malgron emerged from the gloom in his true form. He stood at seven feet tall, with toad-like skin erupting in vile pustules. His head was semi-human with large ragged ears and jowls and four horns protruding from the top. His arms were hefty and strong, ending in filthy talons; his legs and feet the same. As if his appearance alone wasn't enough to send her mind reeling, one of his arms was dragging behind him the limp body of Adain. He dropped her at the edge of the circle and, for one heartbeat, Beth believed her daughter dead; and then slowly, very slowly, Adain began to move. She picked herself from the floor and stood wide-eyed in front of Malgron, powerless under his gaze and in a dream-like state. Beth screamed her name.

Adain turned her eyes to her mother; eyes that pleaded 'Help me, Mummy.'

Beth rushed towards the edge of the circle and was once again rebuffed by the dark force that guarded it. Malgron's mouth twisted into the parody of a smile, exposing huge, pointed and rotting teeth, which he then sank into Adain's throat.

Beth's scream was silent; her vocal chords no match for the horror in front of her. Then from nowhere the knowledge came to her, seconds before her mind was to be lost forever.

This wasn't Adain. She was safe in Avalon where no demon, however powerful, could get to her, protected by the magic of the ancients and under the watchful eye of Morgana. This was an illusion created to drive her mad.

She stood tall and forced herself to make eye-contact with the foul creature, shivering and shaking, but giving no ground. If she was going to die, she wasn't going to do it crying and snivelling. Malgron made a move towards the circle's perimeter and stretched one of the foul talons to the ground and gouged a break in the integrity of the circle.

Beth sensed the force-field disintegrate, suddenly feeling naked and exposed. As one, and in response to Malgron's silent instruction, the Serpent's forked tongue flicked in and out, something white and viscous dripping from its fangs, as it raised itself high above her ready to launch its attack. The Hound threw back its head and howled in anticipation of its victory.

CHAPTER FORTY: A FRIEND

If Hell is no place for angels, then it is certainly no place for the dead who have no business being there.

He had no idea how he had found his way there; all he could remember was a penetrating, electric-blue light, that had temporarily blinded him. He shielded his eyes and his head filled with images and sounds that would be enough to drive a living soul into an asylum.

Not the stereotypical Being of Light, he pushed his cap to the back of his head and swore with imagination and flare.

In life, Dai Morgan, 'Dai Bricks' to most, had been a rational man; a rational man whose life had been embroiled with spiritual evil. In death, swiftly administered by the demon Astaroth, he had found himself at a crossroads in the afterlife. Should he move on and up to the higher levels of light, or should he hang around the lower levels of the heaven in order to carry on helping Mike? Apparently, at that moment he was in neither.

His innate rationality took over, and he quickly surveyed his surroundings, the other side of him reaching an unwelcome understanding of his whereabouts. Then he became aware of a bright light. He looked around for the source but could find none.

He took several tentative steps forwards, and the light went with him. Realisation flooded him; he was the source of the light. He couldn't resist a low chuckle. "Well, I'll be ...!"

His voice echoed around the dark corner of Hell in which he had found himself, as it rolled and bounced from the dark grey nothingness, '... I'll be ...be ... be ...' until it faded away.

What was he doing there? How had he been brought there – because, brought, or sent, he must have been? He stilled his consciousness and reached into it, scanning recent memory files.

The dazzling light had come from nowhere, bringing him to his knees, and at the centre of it he saw her. And heard her scream; silent it may have been but it was heard in the heavens. He knew he had no way of getting her out or, for that matter, a way back for him, but at least he could be with her and hopefully fend off some of what was crawling, sliding and slithering towards her. Some, not all; he was, after all, a rational man.

The darkness seemed endless beyond the pool of light that was emanating from him, and he heard and sensed several of the lower entities of the Abyss, hiss, curse and spit before backing off. Light was anathema to them.

His confidence grew as he wandered through moving shadows filled with spectral nastiness and dark grey clouds that roiled and boiled with evil. He sensed them, saw their faces, felt their malice, as he pushed on, reaching out to her, willing her to know that he was coming. That, if she were to die, she wouldn't die alone.

Beyond the halo of light, in the gloom ahead of him, Beth fell to her knees as a Serpent of the Abyss drew back its head ready to strike, and the slavering jaws of the Hound of Hell champed together.

The voice was in his head now, telling him what to do, guiding him towards the evolving scene of carnage that was overshadowed by the furious face of Malgron. He closed his eyes and raised his hand in silent communication with whichever being was guiding him. Pulling in his light, he fed it, fuelled it and charged it with every fibre of his being.

The light dimmed around him and he felt its energy surging into his outstretched arm. He grinned. He'd seen this in the movies; it was where the good guy blasted the evil one from existence. He flicked his hand to release the laser-like light energy and direct it straight at the Serpent and Hound, expecting them to combust or explode into tiny fragments. They didn't.

He frowned. "Huh."

They didn't explode, but they did hesitate. Malgron was engulfed in rage and raised his hand to Beth, throwing a sideways glance of fury at his hesitating servants. It was long enough for Dai to throw himself forwards to stand in front of her. She grabbed him, unable to speak in her distress, as Dai concentrated his consciousness into the stream of light, expanding it by the power of his will to bathe them both in a pool of illumination. He put out a protective hand and stepped back, forcing Beth to step back also. Another step, and once again he threw out the light in his hand, this time directing it into Malgron's eyes. The demon roared and lunged forwards but he was blinded by the incandescent beam, doubling over instead and shielding his eyes once more.

"You need to run, my lovely. That piece of shite will soon be back on us, see."

Still speechless, Beth nodded her understanding and ran in the direction that Dai was indicating. He was right behind her, pushing her on, not giving her an inch.

Finally, Beth could run no further and she dropped to the floor, scraping her knees, exhausted and terrified. Her breath was coming in long heaves, gradually settling into a frightened gasp.

"Dai!" she sobbed. "I don't ... ." Lost for words she subsided into a desperate silence, her eyes pleading with his for an explanation.

"It was a surprise to me too," he replied to her unvoiced questions. "And Beth, you shouldn't think I'm the rescue party. That was my ultimate trick and it won't last long. I'm not sure I have the energy to replicate it. Batteries running low. I can't get you out of here, lass, but I'm going to stay with you, isn't it."

"How am I still alive, Dai? I mean, this *is* Hell, right?

Unless … am I dead?"

Dai shook his head and smiled into her eyes. "No lass, you're not dead. And how you are still alive and in Hell is beyond me. The only explanation is that the demon Malgron brought you here." His consciousness was ahead of his words and he was thankful his last thoughts weren't voiced. He knew that a living soul would never survive long in Hell. Alive she may be, but that situation was kind of time sensitive.

Whatever Ben and Mike were doing, they had better do it quickly.

"We must keep moving. Malgron isn't the demon to piss off, if you'll pardon my language. "Malgron was the demon that had you prisoner in the coal mine and it was him that was about to send you into the realm of insanity, before allowing his servants to satisfy their hunger. Sorry to be blunt, see, but that's the truth of it. Now, we have to move."

He caught her under the shoulder and pulled her to him, his light fading but still glowing enough to repel the hideous lower entities that came close in the hope of a free meal.

Gradually, the screams and wails had filtered back into her hearing, having been silenced by her own terror. Now, they returned, louder and more soul-chilling than before.

Dai had absolutely no idea where he was heading, the guiding voice fading with his light. In fact, they had been close to the portal, but now they were heading away from it, further into the darkest realms of Hell, further from help. And Beth's time was probably on count-down.

CHAPTER FORTY-ONE: THE KEY OF SOLOMON

Ben's expression was rigid. "And just how do you propose to get into Hell?"

Mike stopped and turned to him. "Whatever it takes, I'll do it. Tell me how and I'm gone."

"I get it, Mike. I do. But the portal needs to be re-opened; not just whatever is sealing the entrance, but the portal itself."

"So, tell me."

Ben lowered his head, fighting the sense of defeat that was rising in him. Was he to fail so early in the mission? "It's not that easy. It has to be opened from that side. Opened by a demon, Mike - in Hell."

Mike ground his teeth together, a gesture that was becoming a part of him. "So, we summon one!" he snarled.

Gareth was too quiet, his mind processing the events of moments ago that he still saw in slow-motion, running through scenarios in his head that would lead to successful disposal of Idris Robert's body, oblivious to the heated conversation going on around him.

"Hey!"

Gareth jumped, his mind still lost in a fog of horror and its consequences.

"Hey!" Ben repeated. "We need to go. I already told you, I would fix this. I will. Look, if you don't mind me saying this, you're out of your depth here. You should go home, turn on all the lights and drink until you pass out. This is our territory now. There are no arrest warrants or handcuffs that will stop this bastard."

Gareth thought momentarily about refusing and

insisting he go wherever they were going, but he knew Ben was right; he was in way over his head and he needed to come up for air. He nodded and followed them from the building.

Ben grabbed Mike's arm. "That was foolish in there. We might have got more information from him."

"It was taking too long; he was never going to give anything up."

But we had a demon in our hands, Mike. We could have made him go back down there and open the portal."

The enormity of his action dawned on him, to which he responded by yanking open his car door, roughly turning the key in the ignition until the engine screamed in protest.

"I'll see you back at yours," he said, slamming the car door. He threw the car into gear and screeched away. Ben mentally willed him to calm down; the last thing they needed was for Mike to crash the car and, in his frame of mind, he was a perfect target for a demon looking to hitch-hike.

His anxiety levels didn't drop until he turned the throttle of his bike and caught up with Mike, who was now still driving fast but without the suicidal numbers on the speedometer. He nodded as he past him, and then slowed down in front of him, forcing him to do the same. The lanes were narrow, as was the fateful mountain road, so there was little chance of Mike overtaking. This way he could at least make sure Mike got back to his cottage in one piece.

Thoughts of his cottage led inevitably to Jack. He couldn't believe he had allowed the demon, Bazaliel, to infest him, but the alternative was just too much agony to contemplate.

Since he had become human, Ben had experienced many emotions, but grief wasn't one of them. Until the moment he had been advised to say his good-byes to Jack. In that moment he understood humanity in all its frailties, and so he had rejected common sense and chosen the path of the lesser evil, relatively speaking. He had to live with that.

He pushed the thoughts away as he sensed familiarity around him. They were only a mile or so from home; from home, from warmth, from sanity, and from information. There had to be some way to open the portal from this side, and if there was it would surely be in one of the hundreds of occult books in his possession. And he thought he knew where to look.

He dismounted the bike and wheeled it around the back of the cottage. From inside, it was obvious that Fred had discerned the return of his adored one, and was barking fit to raise the roof. But there were also raised voices.

Mike pulled his car into the small lay-by at the front of the cottage and made his way through the small wood to Ben's open door. As he approached he heard the argument in full swing. He frowned. Jack and Martha? Couldn't be.

He and Ben entered at the same time; Mike through the front door, Ben through the back, both puzzled and anxious to quell the loud quarrel, whatever its cause.

Ben strode between them. Martha was on her feet in full pissed-off headmistress mode and Jack was sitting, arms folded, a picture of belligerence.

Martha spun around, a whirlwind of tweeds and fury. "Michael, Benjamin, speak to the boy! I can't get any sense into him!"

"What's going on?" – Mike and Ben in stereo.

Jack and Martha both started talking together.

Ben put up a hand. "Whoa, whoa. One at a time. For the love of God, we've enough problems without turning on each other. Martha, tell me, *quietly*, what the hell is going on."

Martha drew herself up to her full five feet and a couple of inches of quiet authority.

"It seems he's been communicating with that atrocity

inside him, and between them they have come up with craziness."

Ben turned on Jack. "Jack! You know you can't listen to Bazaliel! You can't trust him."

Jack raised a defensive hand. "I know, I know. But you've got to let me help. I can't sit back and do nothing while Beth is missing. Bazaliel can help find her."

"No. I absolutely forbid it. He's already breaking the deal by even communicating with you. Jack, you have to stop. Besides, we know where Beth is." His voice petered out on his last words.

Mike looked away as both Jack and Martha fixed Ben with a stare.

Mike cleared his throat. "She's in Hell. Literally. I mean she's down there in Hell with that son-of-a-bitch Malgron and all the other filthy spawn f the devil, and I'm going in to find her and bring her back. So if you two would kiss and make up, I'd be much obliged."

There was silence for a moment, Jack's head was tilted slightly to one side and he had a look of deep concentration. Ben reached him in two strides, took him by the shoulders and shook him. "Jack! Stop! I know you're listening to the foul creature; you have to stop. Jesus! I knew this was a bad idea, but I wasn't going to let you just die like that! We'll figure this out, but first we need to get Beth before it's too late! But you have to stop letting him through!"

Jack's eyes cleared and he sat bolt upright. "What do you mean, before it's too late?"

Eyes on Ben. Ben's eyes on Mike.

He took a deep breath, almost a sigh. "A living soul can't survive long in Hell. It's the nature of it; it will suck out the life-force and overpower it with darkness, and the horrors down there will take the mind. We can't waste a minute. It begins gradually, with fatigue, confusion, then hallucinations, and as the mind succumbs to the horrors down there, the will to survive is lost."

Eyes on Mike.

"We have to find a way to open the portal from the other side. That means summoning a demon and binding it to obey and open the portal. It's the only way in."

"You can't be serious, Michael! There must be another way. In all of these ancient books, I refuse to believe there isn't another way. I'll get right on it."

"We don't have the luxury of time, Martha, love. This is the surest, quickest way."

Jack stood up. "No. It isn't. You have a demon right here. I will instruct Bazaliel; he has to obey, I have his seal."

Three voices chimed together. "No!"

"Then I'm coming with you, Mike."

Mike shook his head. "No. Enough people I care about have been hurt, badly, you included because of my fight. It ends here."

Bazaliel allowed himself a grin. This was just the opportunity he had waited for. He could easily persuade Jack Carter to release his seal to allow him to return to Hell and open the portal. But of course, he would do no such thing. He would have his freedom and he would have Mike Travis to give to Malgron. All in all, not a bad plan.

Jack had allowed him in once and now he had access to his thoughts. He began immediately.

"This conversation isn't over, Mike. In the meantime, tell me what I can do."

"Just get better, so that we can get rid of that thing once and for all."

Bazaliel frowned. So, he would have to hurry.

Martha was obviously distraught, a condition she was unused to, and she gave way to expressing it as anger. Things were out of her control and that was just not her way, but this time, there was nothing she could do. She turned on Jack as a coping strategy.

"I am not letting you out of my sight, young man. Where you go, I will be right behind you. Mike's right, though not in the way he thinks. We have lost enough without you being taken too. And when Beth comes back, and she will come back, how will she feel if she knows her life was at the expense of yours? Hmm? Tell me."

Mike and Ben had disappeared into the basement. Ben went straight to an old book among those in a glass cabinet. He pulled it out and took it to the desk.

"I don't like this idea, Mike. Summoning a demon? It's insane; we've got enough trouble with the sons-of-bitches as it is. And it's dangerous. You know the Rules. What scares me more is the fact that I know you're going to do it anyway. So you'd better do it right."

He opened the book, entitled in Latin, 'Clavem Solomon'; The Key of Solomon. "There are many dodgy translations of this work, and many dark magicians who have used those translations and found themselves either devoured by the demon they seek to control, or off their heads. This is the real deal."

"How do you know?"

"Because I took it from him."

"Him?"

"Solomon. Before Michael took the ring from me to give to him, I took his work. He reproduced it, of course, but I have the original."

Mike stared at the ancient pages covered in sigils and diagrams and strange words. "Have you never been tempted?"

"Are you crazy? Only a madman will summon a demon."

Mike's voice was quiet. "Or a desperate one. Ben, you know I'm going to do this. I can't leave her there. I can't lose her."

"I know. And that's why I'm going to do it, not you. One mistake, just one, and it's game over."

"I can't ask you to do that. It's my responsibility."

"And you're mine, so are we going to waste time arguing over this? I think not. So let's get on with it, there's much to do first. You've got one chance at this."

Martha's voice interrupted them.

"You'd better come," she said in a tight tone. "It's Jack."

CHAPTER FORTY-TWO: COMMUNICATION

Beth couldn't go any further. Dai had been pulling her along using every ounce of his strength and light to move them both along, now she stumbled and fell to her knees.

"I can't Dai. I'm so tired."

He bent down to her. "Try, lass. Come on, isn't.it."

She tried to stand and immediately fell back to the floor. Her eyelids were drooping as he tried to pick her up, limp in his arms. He cast around for a better place for her to rest, hoping it was just tiredness that had overcome her, but knowing the truth; her life-force was being drained away. She was going no further.

He carried her like an oversized rag doll into a corner where he could see anyone or anything that might come near them, sitting with his back to the corner and cradling her head on his chest. He didn't know how much of his light remained, or if he had the strength to defeat them. But he was going to protect her with what he had left. She wasn't going to lose this alone.

There was a faraway look in her eyes when she eventually opened them. Dai let fall a tiny sigh of relief.

"Dai, you should go while you have the chance."

His massive affection was apparent as he looked into her misty eyes, the kind of look from a father to a sleepy daughter. He stroked her hair out of her face.

"Tawelwch, lass," he said in his mother Welsh; *Hush, lass*. "Save your strength. I'm staying with you, isn't.it. And you don't have the strength to stop me, so, hush now."

She smiled dreamily at him, and he wondered where her mind was; wherever it was he hoped it stayed for a long time. Besides, he had no clue as to how to get out of there anyway.

"Okay, Dai," she murmured.

Dai let her drift in and out of sleep - he had no choice - but he continued to hold her tight. His mind was on another tack. Beth had been kept within the circle of dark magic. That did two things: it kept her a prisoner and it protected her at the same time from other demons that may take an interest in a feast. Now she was out of the circle, she was fair game. Malgron had obviously been keeping her for some purpose and now he had let her go. That could only mean he was fed up of toying with his food, now he was going for the main course: Mike.

Beth's thoughts were of a very different nature. From a warm and fuzzy distance she was watching Adain silently climbing the Tor, Morgana just behind her. Their tread was solemn and ritualistic. Time passed as they wound their way upwards to the stone circle at the summit, and Beth watched dreamily, following their progress.

At the top, Morgana summoned the mists and they fell at her call, enveloping the stones and obliterating them from sight. Beth's breathing became laboured as she waited impatiently for sight of her daughter again. Dai stroked her hair every time she murmured, "Addie."

Eventually she became calmer and the anxious lines on her face faded into a mask of peace; peace that was short-lived as she sat up with a start. Her eyes were glazed and there was a look of panic on her face. The panic increased as she began to look around wildly, until her gaze settled on Dai. Her brows knitted as she tried to place his face into context; Dai was dead, what was he doing there? Where *was* there?

He raised his arm slowly, "It's all right, Beth. You're all right, lass." He knew that she was fading, succumbing to the Hell's hunger for living souls, her confusion mounting by the minute.

Her hand was in her hair, twisting tendrils around her finger. "Mike will be home any minute, Dai," she said. "I'll make some tea." She seemed to drift off into semi-oblivion then, alternating between half-mumbled sentences and staring around through wild eyes and furrowed brows.

Her time was running out, he knew it, and he also knew that he had been sent there to protect her until Mike or Ben could find a way to get her out of there.

Realisation came in an answer to his unspoken prayer: they had been going in the wrong direction. His revelation was interrupted as he sat bolt upright, listening. The unmistakeable slithering, sucking sound was accompanied by a spine-freezing, low growl and snuffling sound. The Serpent of the Abyss and the Hound of Hell were closing in.

He made a quick assessment of the geography. They needed to move straight ahead and the revolting sounds of approaching terror were off to the far right.

But there was something else happening directly in front of them. Shadows had begun swirling, and thickening, into a writhing mass that was slowly taking form and emerging from the darkening gloom. Another serpent, an even uglier version of the first, slithered towards them, raising all three of its heads; heads that had human faces with serpent's eyes. All three forked-tongues flicked in and out of its fanged jaws.

Dai's heart sank; he had nothing left.

CHAPTER FORTY-THREE: BROKEN SEAL

Bazaliel was jubilant. He had found Jack's weakness; his fierce love for his friend and Beth. This was his opportunity and he took it, coaxing and persuading, showing him scenes of torture in Hell, playing the awful sounds of screaming and wailing into his head, and finally, giving him the solution: his offer.

If they released him, they would need no demon on the inside; he, Bazaliel, knew how to open the portal from this side. He would take Mike into Hell and - as he knew it so well - he would be a help to Mike in finding Beth. Azrael would never agree of course, but then Azrael wasn't there, and after all, it was Jack's decision. He didn't want to push Jack, but it was time-sensitive and they didn't have the luxury of wasting a second on debate; it was now or never.

He waited as Jack assimilated the offer, connected with his thought processes, becoming more and more satisfied as he followed Jack's thoughts and emotions; he was about to gain his freedom and please Malgron at the same time by handing him Mike Travis; he was going to walk him right into Hell.

Jack's mind fixed on the images of torture with the backing-track of torment. He felt his heart swell and unbidden tears well in his eyes. If it was in his power to save her, no matter what the cost, he would do it in a heartbeat.

Martha had watched the distress building on Jack's face and he wasn't answering her, he wasn't hearing her, but before she could call out to Mike he became calm again. He stood with his back to the fire and said, "Yes."

That's all; "Yes."

Martha was on her feet and down the steps with uncustomary haste, returning in seconds with Mike and Ben in her vast, tweedy, wake. Jack was standing at the kitchen sink without his shirt, Ben's sharpest knife in his hand. They halted abruptly.

Mike spoke softly, "Jack? What's up? Put the knife down and come and sit with me. We can talk about it, whatever it is."

Jack gave him a blank stare.

"Jack, it's us; Mike and Ben. Jack?"

Ben took a step forwards and Jack turned the knife on himself. "Stop! Stay where you are, Ben."

"Jack, please, stop listening to that foul creature. Whatever it is he's telling you, it's lies! He's broken through to you somehow and you have to stop listening to him. We'll sort this out, Jack, I promise you."

"I'm sorry, Ben, I have to do this." The knife went closer.

Before either of them could stop her, Martha was walking towards Jack, the epitome of a walking nemesis.

Her voice was iced with cold authority. "Jack Carter, what do you think you are doing? Hand me that knife at once and go and sit down." She held out her hand and kept walking towards him. Mike and Ben held their breath; it was too late to stop her, and if they tried it may tip Jack over the edge. They had tried the soft approach and the logical approach, but maybe he would respond to Martha's brand of persuasion, but what if the demon made Jack harm her?

For a moment, Jack looked confused.

Martha was almost in front of him, her hand still outstretched. "At once, do you hear?"

Jack's expression was fluid, rippling between confusion and high anxiety. Martha read his emotions and halted; he was on the precipice of tragedy. Unspoken pleas and prayers hung in the air like thick smoke, no one was moving.

Jack's expression cleared and he spoke; with the voice of the demon.

"It seems that you don't share your friend's desire to save your wife," he said, staring at Mike. "At least listen. You need a way into Hell and I can get you in there. I will come with you and help you find her. Jack has already agreed to my proposal."

"Liar!" Ben yelled. "You're a goddamn liar, Bazaliel! You just want your freedom, well, not while I have a breath in my body." He took another step forwards.

"Stay there or Jack might do something that we will all regret."

Ben halted, balling his fists at his side. "I will make you regret this Bazaliel."

"If we agree - then Jack dies, right?" snarled Mike.

Ben turned on him. "What? No! We can't agree. Are you crazy?"

Bazaliel raised his voice. "Shut up! First, Jack Carter has healed sufficiently inside for him to survive my ejection. Second, you have very little choice."

Jack took a sudden step back, the point of the knife pressing into his chest, a droplet of blood forming at the tip. He raised the knife.

Everything became lost in time then, played out like a slow-motion movie-clip. Their cries mingled. "No! Jack!!" Mike and Ben sprang forward and Martha tried to grab the knife.

But Jack was quicker. The knife glinted in the firelight as he swung it high and brought it down over Bazaliel's seal, taking a chunk from the outer circle. Blood gushed down his arm and the knife fell to the floor.

Relief was instant and short-lived. They had all believed that Jack was about to kill himself, instead he had hacked a wide gash on his arm. Ben grabbed a tea-towel and was binding the jagged wound before Jack could react, slightly dazed and staggered forwards. Mike grabbed him and together they steered him onto the sofa as Martha picked up a woollen throw from the back of a chair and wrapped it around him, bending then to put another log on the fire.

"Keep him warm," she said. "Shock." She busied herself further with filling the kettle.

Mike was visibly shaken. "Jack, what the hell?"

Ben's expression was stone. "He cut the seal. Once the seal is broken it returns to its owner. Jack no longer has any control over Bazaliel. None."

There was nothing but pain and anguish written on Jack's face for several moments and then it cleared, as quickly as it had appeared. His eyes rolled back in his head.

"Et nunc absolvo vos", he said, in his own voice, repeating Bazaliel's instructions. *I release you.*

In that moment Bazaliel had been swamped with Jack's emotions, his love, his loyalty and his easy sacrifice. He would never understand humans.

Dark grey shadows began to pour from Jack's mouth, nose and eyes; deep, dark shadows that drifted to the floor, where they joined together in a mass that undulated and twisted, growing taller at frightening speed. Ben lunged forwards at it, screaming the words of exorcism that fell impotent from his lips.

The shadow became denser and darker, taking form.

Then Jack collapsed.

CHAPTER FORTY-FOUR: HALLUCINATIONS

Dai placed himself between Beth and the three-headed serpent; not that it would do much good, ultimately, but his instinct was to shield her. The serpent reared up and all three of its heads were pulled back ready for the strike, venom dripping from its three mouths, and coming ever closer were the terrible sounds of the Serpent and the Hound.

There was a rush of air as The Serpent of the Abyss came into view, coils thrashing and heaving as it lunged towards the three-header. In a flurry of writhing coils and hissing, the two were entangled in a lethal battle. Three-header had trespassed onto the Serpent's territory and its dinner table.

The Hound of Hell was right behind the writhing, coiling mass of Hell's reptiles, its access to Beth and Dai blocked by the violent fight to the death. Dai acted swiftly, dragging Beth to her feet and pulling her in her confusion in the opposite direction.

A terrifying baying came from their backs as the frustrated Hound sought for a path to pursue them. If Dai had been in his live human form, he would have found running difficult and brief; in his spirit body, he moved by the supreme effort of his remaining strength and will, and moved faster than he could ever have run. He put distance between them and the unholy fracas, although the sounds of wounded and dying demon snakes and the baying Hound still reached them, echoing around them like a tormenting siren.

Beth pulled away from him and sank to the floor in a heap, "I can't. I can't go any further."

231

Dai sat down next to her; he had been surprised at her ability to run as she had, but the exhaustion was now in every cell of her body. It was the end of the road. Suddenly she was staring about her with wild eyes again. Her knees came up, her hands in front of her face, screaming and thrashing about, arms flailing, like something feral caught in a net.

"Get away! Get away from me," she screamed, as she backed herself into another corner. The look in her eyes portrayed the terror she was experiencing at something that wasn't there. She was in the final stages; hallucinations had overtaken her. He made soothing noises to her which only had the effect of making her scream even louder. He backed away, removing at least one source of her horror, because whatever she was seeing, it wasn't Dai.

He reached deep within, searching for any remaining glimmer of his light that would serve as a source of comfort to Beth in her torment and, finding a spark he drew on it, willing it out to her. She appeared to calm although she continued to stare about wildly and kept her hands in front of her face as if to ward off sight of anything that came to torture her.

Sheer bodily and emotional exhaustion overcame her terror and she leaned back against Dai, her screaming subsiding to a frightened whimper. The hallucinations were extreme and violent and all manner of demonic entities had paraded themselves in front of her horrified eyes, taunting her, coming close enough to touch her.

There was mist in front of her then, swirling, welcoming mist - perhaps she was supposed to walk into it? Perhaps this was what death was like; just walking off into the mist.

But this mist was different and yet somehow familiar. She followed the line of it and saw something that made her gasp: the crown of the stone circle in Avalon. The mists continued to move and thin and from out of them came her daughter.

"Addie?"

"Hello Mummy. I can't stay long because I'm not very good at this yet, though Morgana said I was a natural. What does that mean? Morgana said I was to try and reach you now I can do this a little, and tell you to be strong and to hold on, though she didn't say what you had to hold on to. She said …"

The image of her daughter shimmered and faded away.

"Addie!" she yelled.

Dai caught hold of her arm, "It's all right, Beth. You're all right."

Her voice was slurred, "S'okay Dai … was Addie … she said to hold on …"

And with that her eyes closed and she fell unconscious against Dai's chest. He put his arm around her shoulder; there was nothing else he could do. He had no idea what the Hound of Hell could do to a spirit but he was sure it was nothing pleasant.

CHAPTER FORTY-FIVE: A DEBT FROM THE DISTANT PAST

Ben had his fingers on the weakening pulse in Jack's throat, his face ashen. Mike stood in front of them as the demon manifested before them all. Martha's face expressed her revulsion at the face of Bazaliel, the Shadow Demon, and her mouth followed suit.

"In the name of God you're ugly," she said, her voice low and even.

The demon's twisted features settled into place. "I will take a more acceptable appearance but, once back in Hell, I will assume my true form - if we are to survive, that is. The other demons may see my agreement with Azrael as nothing less than betrayal and I will have to reassert my position. I can only do that in my true form."

Ben's fury was blatant as he spat hatred, "If you think you can possess any one of us you are so far from the truth you won't know it until you're dead." He turned to Martha, "Call an ambulance!"

Her fingers had already hit the first two nines.

"Shit! I can hardly feel his pulse!"

Martha was now in deep and urgent conversation with the ambulance hub.

Bazaliel ignored the chaos surrounding them with his attention on Mike.

"You have to come now. Your wife won't last much longer there."

"Go," Ben said. "Go, we'll stay with Jack. Rule number one, Mike, remember it! And Rule number nine is;- There are more monsters in Hell than demons. Go, and God go with you." He turned on Mike and surprised him with a bear hug. Mike nodded at him, re-adjusted his jacket and bent forwards to rest his arm on Jack, his chest rising and falling as if the bellows of Hell were pumping his lungs, and then he abruptly left with the Shadow Demon who had now assumed human form; an unattractive human form, but one that made Mike less likely to knife him where he stood.

"There's a delay; they said maybe half an hour." Martha's face was pale.

Ben's hands were in his hair. "He won't make it that long."

Martha had expected heroics from Ben, the kind that involved chest compressions and mouth-to-mouth, but what he did surprised her, although her face remained impassive. There was an aura of trust between them that made her stand back.

Ben picked up the knife that Jack had dropped, ran the blade across his forearm and allowed the blood to fall onto Jack's naked chest. He put his head back and his voice boomed through the cottage like thunder.

"Azrael! Azrael, you son-of-a-bitch! *You owe me!* I haven't forgotten Egypt! Time to repay! Azrael!! Get your self-righteous arse down here, now! ***Azrael!!!***"

The front door opened, but no angel stood there, instead Gareth Jones stepped over the threshold, looking as if he'd had no sleep for a month and arrived there via every hedge and ditch.

"I couldn't stay away," he began, then, seeing Jack he strode over to the sofa, his phone already in his hand.

"Half an hour the ambulance dispatcher said." This from Martha.

Gareth was already speaking into his phone. "DI Jones, Monmouthshire police. Requesting a priority on the call to the ambulance hub to this address." He repeated the address and listened to the distant voice. "Thank you." He put the phone back in his pocket. "On their way," he said. "How's he doing?"

Ben stubbornly refused to move as Gareth approached.

"Not good; he's barely breathing and I can only just feel his pulse. Thank you for that." He nodded towards Gareth's pocket.

Azrael was suddenly among them.

"As you say, Seraquel: I owe you. I'm only surprised you made no mention of it when last we met. I thought perhaps you had no memory of your past. I see I was wrong."

"I was saving it. Now we're even. And the name is Benjamin Lovecraft."

"Indeed. Now, if you will step away, Jack Carter is about to have a heart attack. I take it you'd rather I stayed until your paramedics arrive. Bazaliel has gone rogue, I take it?"

"You know damn well, you bastard!"

"On the contrary, I believed that he would do as he promised; it was after all in his own interests. I have no illusion that it was out of humanitarian affection."

"And Gareth?"

"Unharmed. He will be confused when I leave but he will get over it." His tone brooked no challenge. He had come to pay a debt and, by the colour of Jack's face, it would be at any moment.

Ben moved aside. Azrael placed his hand on Jack's chest, listening, searching. Suddenly, Jack arched his back, barely whispered a shallow breath, and then his heart stopped.

Azrael raised his hand and brought it down hard on Jack's chest, the familiar blue angel-light streaming from his palm. Moments later Jack's lips had lost their blue tinge as his heart once more began to circulate precious oxygen around his body.

"The doctors will see that he has had a small heart attack and treat him accordingly. You have no need of me now."

"Before you leave, tell me the truth: did you use Jack as a tool to get Bazaliel to agree terms?"

"Of course. There is no room for sentiment in the affairs of humans. They have enough of their own; it is their weakness. Your weakness. Remember, my debt is paid."

There was a sudden blue light and then darkness as they became temporarily blinded. Azrael had gone.

Gareth Jones scanned around him. "Where the hell am I?"

CHAPTER FORTY-SIX: THE SECOND PORTAL

Outside Ben's cottage Mike's face was set grim. "Just so we're clear on this, demon: I will gut you like a fish if you so much as breathe the wrong way. Understood?"

"I'm surprised at such hostility from someone whose friend I saved."

"Shove it. From what I've just seen, there's still a question mark over that. Now, where exactly are we going? As I recall, the entrance to the portal is blocked from the mine side, so how are we going to get in there?"

"You think there is only one way in? The gateway can be opened from this side in many places, you just need to know where to look and have the right invocation and a blood offering."

"Let me guess; my blood, right?" Mike guessed that he didn't mean a prick on the finger. He sighed; he didn't care about his own blood being spilled, but all too much of innocent blood had been wasted already. He was going to stop it.

Bazaliel gave him a deprecating look which did nothing to enhance his unwholesome countenance. "Fortunately, there is such a portal not far from here. It was re-opened about sixty years ago by a black magician, name of Aleister Crowley. He and a group of his acolytes were prone to getting their jollies in this place and used to often stay close by. Llanthony Priory was built over one of the oldest portals, and as it's now in ruins, and was back then, access to it is easy. Unfortunately, the portal was closed again some years ago now, by someone of your persuasion. They paid for it."

"Thanks for the history lesson; I just want to know

where. That's enough. Get in the car. Or are you going to use magic to get us there?"

Bazaliel eyed him with uncertainty. Mike was becoming stronger and more determined, uncaring of the danger, just focussed on the result. He would have to be careful; in this state the guy could become unpredictable.

"*I* can be there in moments. Transporting you, on the other hand, will take more juice than I care to waste. Drive."

Mike threw the car into reverse and spun it around in the road, heading out towards the village of Pandy and on to Llanthony. The journey would take around forty minutes at normal driving speed; flooring the accelerator Mike intended to do it in thirty. That was thirty minutes too long. Beth's time down there was limited and every minute wasted was a minute less likely that she would survive. He pushed his foot down harder.

Bazaliel picked up on his thoughts; Mike was rattled; good, he may make a mistake and hand himself over on a plate.

Mike refused to acknowledge Bazaliel for the remainder of the journey, regulating his breathing, remembering things that he had learned and focussing on one thing above all else: getting Beth back. He didn't trust Bazaliel an inch, but he was going to have to give him the benefit of the doubt if he wanted to get into Hell. And quickly. Once he had her, all bets were off and, if the demons had declared war on him, they hadn't seen anything yet. More blood would be spilled, but demon blood, and that was all right with him.

There was something else too; his own time in Hell would be limited before he too would fall prey to its hunger. He ground his teeth and forced his mind from the negative thoughts that threatened to knock him off balance. Stay focussed.

The ruins of the Augustine priory of Llanthony lay in the secluded Vale of Ewyas at the foot of the Black

Mountains, almost on the border between Wales and England and, as Mike drove towards the ruins of the abbey, they reared up into the darkening sky like arthritic fingers. In daylight it was a place of beauty, now in the falling dusk it filled him with foreboding. Thunder chose that moment to clap overhead. Appropriate, he thought.

He parked the car before he got to the visitor's car park, not wanting to attract unwanted attention, closing the car door carefully. This was it; he was going into Hell.

Bazaliel was quiet, thoughtful, preparing to do the unthinkable; open up a portal to Hell itself. They gained access to the ruins almost too easily and within minutes found themselves walking through the parade of gothic arches and crumbled architecture. At the heart of the ruins Bazaliel halted.

Mike looked around, seeing nothing significant, nothing that resembled a portal. But then what did he expect? A tourist map saying 'You are here: The Gateway to Hell.'

Bazaliel had begun walking backwards in a circle around what appeared to be a stone slab - which was, in fact, a tombstone. He was muttering low under his breath.

Mike was at his side in an instant. "You're going nowhere without me, so watch what you're doing!"

Bazaliel gave him a withering look and proceeded with the enchantment, all his demonic energy flowing into the ground below the tombstone. He stopped abruptly.

"Time for the blood offering."

Mike felt a warm comfort emanating against his side but he ignored it decisively. "I take it you have something."

Bazaliel's smile reminded him of something that slithered in slime as he conjured a dagger, seemingly from thin air. "You have to do it; let it fall over the stone."

Mike took the blade that had an unholy glint to it, pushed up his sleeve and drew it straight across his arm, all without taking his eyes from the demon. Blood flowed quickly and plentifully from the gaping wound that had appeared under the force of the blade. It ran, rather than dripped, onto the ancient tombstone.

Bazaliel's eyes lit with a fire that could only have been spawned in the darkest reaches of the underworld. He threw his arms on high and began the Latin incantation.

"Conjuro potestate Luciferi portam inferni oblatione sanguinis istud!"

I conjure the power of Lucifer to open the gate of Hell, by the offering of blood, shall this be.

He continued in an arcane and unintelligible language, whilst Mike kept his eyes unwaveringly upon him. More and more arcane incantations, and then he stopped abruptly.

Was that a hint of a tremor in the earth? Was he expecting a thunderbolt? A lightning strike? The earth to open into a monstrous cavern with a fire-pit in the middle? Mike suddenly realised how little he knew. But when he had Beth back, that would change.

There was an unmistakeable tremor under his feet, followed by a loud crack as the tombstone split in two, then three, then crazed and crumbled into dust which fell down into the blackness of a void.

Tendrils of shadow snaked up from the blackness and the full realisation of what was happening suddenly became clear. The portal was a two-way street. They were going to enter Hell through it, but things were entering the world from the other direction.

"You can shut it once we're in, right?"

Bazaliel shook his head. "Sorry, not unless you intend to spend a very long time down there, and you don't do you? Snatch and grab, as I understand it. But then you don't have long, do you? So, if you'd care to follow me."

"You son-of-a-bitch."

Bazaliel stepped into the void and disappeared. Mike closed his eyes and stepped after him.

If he'd been alive in the nineteen-sixties when the

psychedelic drug scene was at its height, this is how he would have imagined it would have been. He remained in his body but his consciousness was on a break. Falling, floating, expanding and shrinking, were all the sensations that hit him in waves of pleasure and pain in equal intensity. Then, nothing. Nothing but blackness.

And then the sounds of the tormented reached him; layer upon layer of howls, screams, wails and sobs.

"Open your eyes." Bazaliel was standing over him in the gloom. Mike obeyed.

"Not how it looks in the movies," he said, spitting something distasteful from his mouth.

"This is just the outer region, the edges; there are nine regions, each one of them worse than the last. Malgron's domain is the eighth region but he walks freely in all. This is the most desolate; this is the region of the lost souls and the lower entities of the Abyss; unintelligent and grotesque."

"Talking of grotesque, you forget I've seen your true form Bazaliel. Now, where do we start looking for Beth?"

"Malgron would have brought her here, to the outer region, after that we just have to look."

All too aware that Beth's time was running out, Mike said nothing, but his clamped jaws, sending ripples into his cheek muscles and stretching his scar, were sufficiently eloquent.

"Close the portal," he snarled at Bazaliel.

The demon's face darkened and he appeared ready to deny Mike's command.

"I said, close the portal."

Bazaliel hesitated further and then began a low incantation, once again in an arcane language that made no sense to Mike. He had no idea if Bazaliel was obeying him; he didn't trust the demon, remembering Lovecraft's Rule number one, and there was nothing he could do about it; it was all about finding Beth now.

Bazaliel moved off further into the darkness and

swirling shadows, seemingly immune to the cries of torment that were running rampant in Mike's head. Mike hated the feeling of helplessness that had overwhelmed him since Beth had been taken, and it wasn't getting any easier. He tried to shut out the peripheral sights and sounds and took a step back as Bazaliel began to morph once more into a morass of whirling shadow, slowly manifesting his true nature. He was around the same height as Mike, but with leprous skin and the head of a reptile, almost dragon-like, a forked tongue flickered across the leathery lips that sat above a lethal horn protruding from his chin. His body was partly covered in pustules; the remainder in scales. He pulled on the shadows until he was clothed in a grey pall; the Shadow Demon again.

Mike was glad Bazaliel was on his side; well, hoped he was. Lovecraft's Rules were playing in his head in an endless loop of background reminders of lies and treachery. He had no choice; he followed him into the darkness.

The demon stopped suddenly, putting out a scaly arm to bring Mike to a halt. On high alert since the moment he had opened his eyes, Mike felt the adrenaline rushing through him in a dizzying torrent.

"What?" he demanded.

Bazaliel was listening intently, and then Mike heard it too; a distant low growl alternating with a soul-chilling bay. And it was coming closer.

"There are dogs down here?" he demanded.

Bazaliel shook his reptilian head. "Not like any dogs you know. They are the Hounds of Hell. And they take no prisoners."

From the darkness there came the sound of something else moving in closer; a slithering, rhythmic sound accompanied by an acid hiss that would strip paint off a car. Mike stepped back a pace.

"A Serpent of the Abyss," said Bazaliel.

"Of course it is."

Without further warning the Hound was on them. It appeared to hesitate as its luminescent eyes alighted on Bazaliel; pondering, assessing; and then chaos erupted as it opened its slavering jaws and leaped at them. Bazaliel was screaming at it, still using the language from a past so ancient it was forgotten before the Flood. But word of his betrayal had spread and the Hound knew a good breakfast when he saw it.

Suddenly it was a flurry of bodies, scales and fur; and blood. The adrenaline in Mike bypassed common sense and he hurled himself into the fray, reaching into the inside pocket of his jacket and bringing out the blade the size of a small machete that he had kept out of Bazaliel's sight.

He had been surprised back at the cottage by Ben's sudden bear hug; until he had felt Ben pressing the blade into his pocket, along with something else. Something smaller, warmer; sharp and lethal. The crucifixion nail, honed and beaten into a weapon that would stand against all evil.

Curses and growls filled the air around him; blood spatters ran down his face, pooling in the hollow of his throat. He could taste the coppery tang and spat onto the ground as he raised the machete high above his head, praying it would find the right target. It came down with all the force he could muster, resulting in an eardrum-splitting yelp. There was a momentary stillness and then the Hound was on its feet again and Bazaliel was gathering himself ready to finish it.

He didn't get the opportunity. Mike slashed out at the Hound, bringing forth more yelps and growls, then taking a step forwards he swept the blade sideways using every ounce of his strength.

Bazaliel fell backwards away from the Hound, which was strangely silent as the bile-green luminescence in its eyes flickered, before its head parted company with its body and fell to the floor, the body following suit.

Mike was gasping with the exertion, covered in the

Hound's blood and gouts of flesh and fur, but the light in his eyes said he wasn't finished. Bazaliel rapidly reassessed Mike's capabilities. He would need to be careful and cunning to carry out his plan. He should deliver him to Malgron as soon as possible, there was no time to play it slowly, dragging the strength from him, torturing him with images of his wife at the hands of Malgron..

Mike was staring at him, trying to decipher his expressions which were as insubstantial as morning mist.

He raised his blade and pointed it at him. "We need to move. Which way?" he demanded.

CHAPTER FORTY-SEVEN: RULE EIGHT

Dai's spirit was weakening as Beth was regaining strength; she stood over him, tears welling in her eyes and falling like heavy raindrops. Hell's hunger was devouring his soul.

"Dai, what should I do? Tell me." She knelt at his side, perplexed at her sudden boost of energy but casting the thought aside, desperate to do something for the old man's spirit that was gradually losing its physical form.

She froze, suddenly aware of a presence behind her. It was true; the hairs on the back of a person's neck did stand up when fear took over. She kept her head facing forwards and, using every taut muscle, she stood up.

There was a familiar slithering sound, and she sensed the body coiling and uncoiling behind her. If she was going to die, she was going to see it coming; she turned in one slow movement. The Serpent of the Abyss towered over her, its slanted eyes black and shining; obviously the victor of the fight but not without battle scars. One of its front fangs was missing and there were gashes down the length of its body. None of it seemed to have any effect on the creature, however, as it fixed itself between Beth and freedom, watching, waiting, mirroring.

Beth was trapped and soon Malgron would come. And if he was pleased, he may let the Serpent have her after he had finished with her.

The lunge she expected didn't come. The Serpent remained static in front of her, watching her. She took a tentative step to the side, it mirrored her movement. She stepped back. It slithered in the same direction. Her mind was fast in its conclusion; the Serpent had its instructions; find her and hold her. She glanced back at Dai - could a spirit be killed? It looked that way. Dai had entered Hell by she didn't know what means, but he had done it for her. He couldn't save her, he said, but he wasn't going to let her die alone. Now it seemed as though he was the one that was dying. Again. It was too much. Too bloody much.

She sat beside him. "Thank you, Dai, and I'm so sorry."

He drew on the remnants of his strength and pushed his cap to the back of his head. "Not over yet, see." He closed his eyes and slumped against her.

"*Dai!* No, please. *Dai!*"

***

Bazaliel knew he could waste no time in delivering Mike to Malgron. Sight of the Hound and the Serpent meant that their master was not far away; they were his pets and his slaves. So Malgron must still be in the region of the lost souls. Perhaps he was going to pull this off after all and Malgron would show his gratitude and reward him. Yes, things were looking better than he had anticipated.

It had been easy to let Mike believe that he had closed the portal, he had made the incantation sound believable, but , - unless the portal could be closed by the recitation of gobbledygook - the way was still open for him to return to the world, free and clear.

Now to lead him straight to Malgron. "This way."

Mike stared at him for a long moment. There was something not right, but he didn't know what. So working on the basis of Lovecraft's Rule number one - the demon was lying. He looked in the direction that Bazaliel was heading. The darkness seemed less intense that way and he thought that if Beth was able to move, she would move in the direction of light. He nodded to Bazaliel and followed him; but he was watching him like a hawk, and with all of his senses alert and the blade in his hand, he was the embodiment of distrust.

The light was fading again, and he wasn't sure if it was the shadows thickening or the light diminishing. Either way, it was getting harder to see more than ten feet ahead. Bazaliel stopped ahead of him and bent down. Mike allowed his gaze to follow.

Lying in a mangled heap of muscle and sinew, blood and vertebrae, the three-headed snake lay massacred in a pool of its own blood at their feet. Mike bent down and picked up something covered in the red-black blood. He wiped it on his jeans and looked hard at it in the gloom. A fang.

"Looks like this one came off worse, but it put up one hell of a fight." He put the fang in his pocket.

"The Serpent," Bazaliel said. "We should go this way," he pointed in the opposite direction. Mike was looking tired. Bazaliel smiled; Hell's hunger was taking effect already. He had to get to Malgron quickly now, his instructions had been crystal clear; bring him here *alive*! "Come on, follow me. We don't have much time. I know where we're going."

Rule number three popped into his head: *If you think the demon isn't lying, you're wrong and probably about to die.* He gripped the hilt of the blade even tighter and faced up to Bazaliel. "You're lying! I told you I would gut you like a fish, and I will!" He shook him. "I think we should go the other way. In fact I'm going to. So you can come with me or you can die here. Choose. But choose quickly."

"I'm not lying!"

There went Rule number one.

"It *is* this way!"

Aaand Rule number two.

Mike toyed with the idea of putting Rule five to the test, *Demons don't die quiet,* but, as he brought the blade into the demon's chest, he heard something that stabbed through him like a knife.

It was faint at first, echoing in the half-light, but he heard it; *"Dai!"* Even distorted as it was, he knew her voice like he knew his own. His hesitation cost him dear, as Bazaliel slipped from his grasp and melted into the dark.

Mike didn't care; Beth was alive! That's all that made sense in his brain right then. He ran through the greyness towards her voice.

"Beth!"

The silence swallowed his echo and there was no answering shout. He called again. "*Beth!*"

Not far ahead the Serpent of the Abyss became agitated, coiling and uncoiling, slipping and slithering, all the while keeping track of Beth's movements. It was getting impatient; soon it would ignore Malgron's order and finish her off. The old man was almost finished anyway. It wanted her alive; her blood would taste better warm.

Running footsteps made it spin around as Mike almost fell on top of its coils. It moved its head out of the way just before he slashed at it, and with a loud hiss, it backed away. Mike slashed again, nicking it. It was rearing up for the attack but just before it struck, it turned away and with a heaving ripple of its coils, it sprang away.

Mike fell to his knees, hugging her, not speaking; just letting her cry, allowing himself the relief of his own tears. Her hair was caked in blood and sweat, her face dirty and her shirt torn. They both looked as if they'd been through a shredder.

He had one eye on Dai, what was he doing there? Was he … alive wasn't the word … but he knew what he meant. And how was he …? He let the thoughts go and gently pulled Beth away, leaning over Dai, not knowing what the life-signs of a spirit in manifestation were. He felt suddenly stupid and ill-prepared.

"He came to be with me. He didn't want me to die alone," she said in a broken voice.

"You're not going to die. None of us are. Oh God, I thought I'd be too late."

She still clung to him. "I thought I *was* going to die. He

said it was Hell's hunger, sucking my life-force away, and it was, and I couldn't fight it. Then I saw Addie."

He held her at arm's length, staring into her wet eyes. "*Addie?* No, she's in Avalon!"

Beth saw the panic in his eyes, "Yes, it's all right, she is. But I saw her, and it made me fight it. Then, when I thought I was going to die, I suddenly had strength and energy back. I don't think it had anything to do with Addie, though. It was more … I don't know … like I just recovered. I can't explain it."

"Neither can I and it doesn't matter right now. The important thing is to get us all out of here. And when I do, I swear to you, I swear, I'm done. Finished. I won't do this and put you all in danger again. We'll all go somewhere no demon will find us." He bent to Dai once more, without a clue how to help him. They needed to move, but there was no way he was leaving him behind.

Her reaction shocked him. "The hell you are! These … *things* … these … demons and monsters … they are real, and they live for inflicting pain and death, and you will track them down, wherever they are, because it's what you do! You can't just walk away, knowing that they are out there in the darkness. And, for your information, when we get out of here, I'm with you. I mean, *really* with you, I'm your goddamn partner. I can learn with you. You're a demon hunter now, Mike. And I'm coming with you."

He held her away, the better to look into her eyes and the fire that he saw in them brooked no argument. He smiled at her. "Let's get out of here." He would make her see sense later.

"But, Dai … ."

Mike prayed his instinct was right and he pulled her close to him, hearing a familiar sound and sensing again a powerful presence. Good instinct.

Azrael stepped from the shadows. He bent over Dai and touched him. For a second there was the smell of ozone in the air and Dai began to mumble something incoherent.

Azrael raised an eye-brow and put up a hand to halt Mike. The now familiar electric-blue light hit Mike with force, bringing him to an immediate stop.

"Azrael, you son-of-a-bitch, I don't know how to kill an angel … yet. But I will and when I do, I'm coming for you."

"Really? Because in my eyes, you're pinned to that point in space and won't be able to move until I release you. Listen to me, and listen well. Cast your mind back to Afghanistan, to your death, and to your agreement."

Mike frowned. "Agreement?"

"When you died in that helicopter crash and your soul was freed, you were given an opportunity: to come back into the world to fight against supernatural evil. You agreed and so the doctors were able to revive you. You have been allowed to do this slowly, but it's time now to do what you agreed to do. You are a demon hunter; it's what you are and what you will be. Are you not curious as to why you and Beth have not succumbed to Hell's hunger?"

"I'm sure you are going to enlighten me."

"You, Michael have angelic blood; angelic blood that protects you from the hunger. You are a descendant in a very long and distant line from a union of an archangel with a human woman. Archangel Michael himself. He would have become one of the Fallen for that sin, but apparently he was too adept with his sword. You have already answered your instinct and called on him, right back at the beginning in that church in Crowsmoor. In every generation of his lineage there is always one named Michael, and that Michael wields his sword for the light. It is why you were saved from the mangled wreck of a helicopter – bad landing by the way – you agreed to this and you were sent back."

Mike allowed the information to settle, the implications of it fuelling his fury. "And Beth? How is she protected?"

"Quite simply, she has borne your child. Your blood has coursed through her body. Not pure angelic blood, but enough to protect her spirit from being devoured by Hell."

"So all this, all this is engineered to set me up as a demon hunter? You bastards!"

"We have been called such, and worse."

Oh, I can think of worse." Mike growled.

Azrael appeared to ignore him, leaning instead, over Dai. He shook his head. "Foolish. He's fortunate that I am here to reclaim him. If his spirit fades down here, here is where he will have to stay. So if you will excuse me, I believe you should leave in a hurry."

Mike's voice was iced and bitter. "Keep looking over your shoulder, Azrael; one day I'll be there."

Azracl smiled, "I'll take him now," the archangel said softly.

Mike's eyes glinted dangerously. "Your game is over, Azrael, you'd better take bloody good care of him. And for your information, I quit," he said through gritted teeth.

Azrael appeared not to notice his hostility.

"This is no game, Michael - I'm sorry, you prefer Mike, although, that I still don't understand – no game at all. The evil that inhabits this place has found ways out into the world, your world, and I don't see you as one to walk away from that. Don't underestimate yourself. You did well, today."

"Thank you so much. Now if you've finished my appraisal ..."

Azrael smiled. "I'm not your enemy, Mike. Don't fight me, save that for the demons. The portal is still open; something I intend to rectify, so I'd be much relieved if you would hurry there, so that I can close it again. There has been enough damage caused by its opening already. I'd say you have less than five minutes to get back there. After that, it will be closed."

Electric-blue light blinded them momentarily and, when they could see again, Azrael and Dai were gone.

Mike gave a small sigh of relief on that score, but there were more pressing issues. They had to get back to the portal before Azrael shut it; the problem was, he had lost his bearings and it would have to be on instinct. He grabbed Beth's hand.

"Can you run," he asked?

She nodded, ready for flight. "I meant it, Mike: I'm part of this now, too."

"Then, I shall enjoy you all the more!" Malgron's voice in the dark. "Raziel!" This to the Serpent.

It sprang at Mike before he could move, coiling itself around his legs in an instant, winding its way up his body, taking Mike to his knees. Bazaliel slunk from behind Malgron, a satisfied smile on his face. It soon faded as Malgron turned his attention to him.

"Bazaliel, you think this will please me enough to not kill you? You betrayed us when you took the deal with the Angel of Death. Betrayal has consequences. You should know that."

Malgron muttered a spell and the demon, Bazaliel, exploded in a shower of red-black blood and slimy bits. Mike was fighting the coils of the Serpent, making just enough room to bring the crucifixion blade from his pocket in awkward, painful movements. He twisted it in his hand, feeling the blade cut into him. He pushed it forwards with the last of the strength in his arm.

The sound of sizzling flesh, and the foul smell of burning Serpent, made him gag. He thrust it forwards again. This time the Serpent screamed and he felt the coils relax. He pulled back and plunged again, twisting the blade this time in the increased space between it and his hands.

It fell to the floor and began to slither away, slowly now it was injured.

A roar echoed around them and Mike realised it had come from somewhere deep and dark within him. He lunged forwards and planted the crucifixion blade square between the Serpent's eyes. It fell, life extinct.

The sound that came from Malgron would live in his consciousness forever, never to be erased by anything good and wholesome. He spun to face the demon, which now had Beth in a choke-hold.

He had heard of the red mist; something that descended over conscious thought and reason, removing any barriers formed by years of compassion, fired by the intense emotion of hatred and the instinct for survival. It descended over him, taking control of his movements and his thoughts. In a succession of fast-firing synapses in his brain, he knew he had to move instantly, but Beth was in his line of attack. But Malgron knew that too, and banked on using her as a shield. Mike's eyes met hers and he flicked his gaze momentarily to the right and prayed that she had understood him. As he leaped towards Malgron, it was apparent that she had. She threw herself sideways out of his way, leaving Malgron open to Mike's attack.

The crucifixion blade first found a home in the scaly neck, causing a wide gash that poured out the black-red stickiness that made Mike want to throw up. He followed it with another hacking motion as Malgron began to regret his underestimation of this fledgling demon hunter.

The blade was all that stood between them and Malgron and he plunged it forwards and up, mentally hoping that a demon's heart, should they have one, would be located in the same pace as a human's. It entered Malgron's chest as if it had been plunged into butter, and he gave it another thrust and a twist.

He heard Beth's voice in the background but her words were lost in his rage.

He was on top of Malgron, thrusting the blade in and out of the demon's chest, each thrust accompanied by the smell of seared flesh.

He didn't realise that he was shouting as he cut the head off and kicked it as far away as his boot would take it. "Rule eight! It aint dead until it's really dead! And that probably means taking its goddamn head off!"

He wiped the blade on his jacket, his breath coming in heaves. He was shaking with the sudden release of adrenaline, and as the red mist began to clear he took stock of what was before him.

He fell to his knees, blood spattered and in shock, shaking from the release of adrenaline and the sheer enormity of what he had done. He looked down at what had been Malgron and then up into Beth's white face. She was trembling.

For an instant he had allowed his humanity to be over-ruled and had succeeded in hacking the demon to pieces. He was so far over the line he didn't know if he could even see it any more. He searched Beth' face for signs of horror or disgust. He couldn't read her.

She stood unmoving in front of him, and then took his hand in hers.

"Can you run," she asked him.

CHAPTER FORTY-EIGHT: THE DEMON HUNTER

Mike's heart felt as if it was being pierced by a thousand hot needles and then squeezed in a gorilla's fist. They were running for their lives and they knew it, but there was more. He knew that something had happened to him, something that he had no control over and something that would not be reversed. He had allowed his rage to govern him and had not been content to kill Malgron, he had hacked the demon to pieces, riding his own fury to its inevitable end. And Beth had witnessed it.

He could hardly bear to think what was going through her head and he didn't have the luxury of time to explore that. They were running blindly, or rather, he was dragging her blindly, towards the open portal. Or were they? His inner compass wouldn't register.

And then they were running into the remains of the three- headed serpent. He allowed himself a breath, they were running in the right direction.

He didn't know how long they had taken to arrive there but the swirling particles of air seemed to be weakening. He didn't know the spell that would take them out of there; instead he stopped and released Beth's hand, threw his head back and yelled.

"Michael! Archangel Michael, hear me! I bear the sword, I am Michael of angelic blood, your blood! Hear me!"

If he had expected thunder and lightning, a flash of electric-blue light, or a choir of angels, he was disappointed. Instead the swirling energy field of the portal weakened enough for him to see the roughened sides of the portal. This he could make sense of. He found a foothold and pulled Beth up after him. Hold by hold he hauled them to through the dizzying heights to the surface, where they collapsed in a heap onto the damp grass beside the crumbled remains of the tombstone in Llanthony Priory.

They lay there, breathing heavily from exertion and emotion. Mike's mind was a whirl of dark fears that had nothing to do with demons. It was all about him and what he had become. Eventually he trusted his voice.

"Beth, I'm sorry. I would have given anything for you not to have seen that. There's been something dark inside me ever since they took you and it's grown into something else. It's a part of me. My own darkness, maybe I'm not the same person you married, and I'm terrified that ... "

She looked at him, fixing her eyes on his, "You'll find a way to control it," she said in a clear, calm voice, that she had no right to own. "That darkness drove you, Mike, but it was a darkness born of love and I believe that sometimes evil like the demons, sometimes needs the same darkness to defeat it. Please take me home, now."

He pulled her to him then and allowed himself a tear. Just one.

They sat is shocked silence in his car, both afraid to move, afraid to look into each others eyes, afraid of what they might see.

He put his hand over hers briefly, then started the car, and slowly, very slowly drove away. Silence was the order of things as he drove home, both of them knowing that nothing would be the same again, both of them knowing that a war had been declared and that they would fight it. Together.

It didn't sit well with Mike and he sought to occupy his mind with ways to veto it. Beth's silence was filled with thoughts of Adain and how she had communicated with her telepathically. Their respective silences were pierced by Mike's phone. Beth grabbed it,

"Hello?"

A moment's quiet at the other end was broken by a deep sigh of relief.

"Beth? Thank God. Tell Mike to come to the hospital. Jack had a heart attack but he's going to be all right, it was small and he's being kept on the coronary care ward, mainly for observation and after care. ... Beth I'm so glad you're all right. And Mike?" The question was hesitant, as if he was afraid of the answer.

"He's fine, or will be. We both will be, may take a while, but we'll be fine." She looked across at him, and sensing it, he dared to look back at her. And from somewhere, God alone knows where, he found a smile. They would both be fine.

"Beth put me on loud speaker, I need to speak with Mike."

She frowned but did as she was bid.

"Mike, something has happened that I don't understand. Not yet, anyway. Am I to understand that Bazaliel is dead?"

"Yes." His monosyllabic reply seemed enough.

"Thought so, it would explain it. Maybe"

"Explain what, Ben? And how did you know Bazaliel was dead?"

"Because his seal is back on Jack's arm."

"We'll come straight there."

He looked at Beth again, something about her was different, something had been lost, something that would never come back. But he had lost something too, a part of himself that would have stopped short of hacking Malgron to mince. They would find their way around their losses together.

The phone rang again. Mike answered it and left it on speaker.

"Mike? Mike Travis?"

Mike knew the voice but before he could identify it, it said, "It's Josh. Josh Hammond. We've a big problem, Mike. The Dark Ark is rising, and the place is swarming with scientists that have thrown the archaeologists off the site. The Dark Ark, Mike."

"Er, Hi Josh. Care to explain?"

The impatience in the distant voice was immediately apparent. Mainly because he had no idea what Mike and Beth had just emerged from. "The Dark Ark! The evil counterpart to the Sacred Ark! It's the opposite of everything the Sacred Ark is. And its returning, Mike, coming to the surface."

"Where are you, Josh?" His voice was serious and aloof. No room for emotion, no room for anything.

"Megiddo. On the plain of Jezreel, Mike. Christ, I shouldn't have to explain that one!"

"No. No, you don't. The predicted site of the final battle between good and evil, according to the old sacred texts. What do you want from me, Josh?"

The silence was pregnant with high-octane anxiety. "Mike, if the Dark Ark is activated, it opens every gateway to Hell on the planet. Every one, Mike. The way open for every inhabitant of Hell to rise. We need your help again."

Mike didn't answer, he looked at Beth, who spoke for him.

"We need a minute or so here, Josh. Mike will call you back." She switched the phone off. "I want to see, Jack first," she said.

Not knowing what else to say, he settled for, "He looks like crap." Then catching a glance of his blood-caked face and clothe, black eye, and cut lip in the rear-view mirror he looked at Beth, really looked at her; her face was smudged with coal dust, her face had a cut along her cheekbone, a cut that, unlike his own scar, would heal nicely. Her clothes were torn and a huge bruise was turning a deep shade of purple on her chin.

"We do too," he said. "We all, look like crap."

THANK YOU!

To my Reader:

Many thanks for buying *Fallen Angels and Demons*, I hope you enjoyed reading it.

If you did enjoy it, please post a review at Amazon, Goodreads or your favourite social network site and let your friends know about *Fallen Angels and Demons*.

I hope that this has whetted your appetite to read the other novels in the Mike Travis paranormal investigation series. You can find details of these in the next page as well as the short stories collections.

And don't forget to sign up for my newsletter for details of my latest books and a FREE short story at:

janmcdonaldemailsign-up.gr8.com

Happy Reading!
All the best
Jan

ALSO BY JAN MCDONALD

Mike Travis Paranormal Investigations
The Crowsmoor Curse: getBook.at/Crowsmoorcurse

Long Shadows: getBook.at/longshadows

The Sacred Ark: getBook.at/sacredark

The Haunted Diary of Victoria Little:
getBook.at/haunteddiary

The Merlin Manuscript: getBook.at/merlin

The Sin Eater: getbook.at/sineater

Mike Travis short stories
Beginnings: getBook.at/Beginnings

Halloween: getBook.at/halloween

Christmas Spirits: getBook.at/christmasspirits

The Beckett Vampire Trilogy
Midnight Wine: getBook.at/midnightwine

Lycan: getBook.at/lycan

Part 3 coming 2016

ABOUT JAN MCDONALD

Jan lives close to the Welsh borders which have their own mystical quality and provide endless resources in the way of legends and folklore surrounding paranormal experiences. She loves all things paranormal and has read the best: Dennis Wheatley, Stephen King, Edgar Allan Poe, Bram Stoker and all those authors that excel in the creepy or downright scary world of paranormal events.

When she embarked on the Mike Travis series, she realised that the field of paranormal investigation is more than we see on the popular TV programmes. So in order to provide compelling ghost hunting tales but with the greatest accuracy, Jan trained as a Paranormal Investigator and has studied parapsychology.

ACKNOWLEDGEMENTS

Thanks to Ken Clarke, ex-miner, author and local historian, for spending an afternoon with me discussing possible locations of the coal mine. And to the staff of Big Pit, National Coal-mining Museum of Wales, for their info and tour, it was great.

CONTACT DETAILS

Visit the authors website:
    jan-mcdonald.co.uk

Follow on Twitter:
    www.twitter.com/janmcdonald1

Cover designed by: Raven Crest Books
Cover photography © rolffimages – fotolia.com

Published by: Raven Crest Books
    www.ravencrestbooks.com

Follow us on Twitter:
    www.twitter.com/lyons_dave

www.ingramcontent.com/pod-product-compliance
Lightning Source LLC
Chambersburg PA
CBHW060905250626
47159CB00008B/2873